The Maple Seed Helicopter
Marco Collina

MAC Press — Patterson, NY
ISBN: 978-0-578-65194-1
Library of Congress Control Number: 2020909729
Title: *The Maple Seed Helicopter*
Author: Marco Collina
Digital distribution | 2020
Paperback | 2020

This is a work of fiction. The characters, names, incidents, places, and dialogue are products of the author's imagination, and are not to be construed as real.

Dedication

I would like to devote this book to my dad George, my grandpa Dario, grandma Isabella and last, but not least, my mom, Giuliana. We all grew up together.

Prologue

They named me Marco, life began with a struggle for survival. After I had become blue in my mother's womb, I was granted a gift. A chance to see this world, to feel my parents love.

One day soon after, I remember the maple seedlings as they dropped like helicopters from the trees, I was amused and happy. I remember as I placed a seed casing on my nose and I pretended to fly with my arms open wide. My playmates soon followed, and I was so truly and simply happy as we flapped our wings around the maple tree. A child is given such a glorious gift. The gift of being innocent. Every parent should cherish the gift of their child's innocence and nurture it. As their child will carry that love and strength throughout their life. This shared love is truly the only piece of ourselves we can leave on this earth.

Our life voyages will differ in consideration of the cards we are dealt and the way we choose our specific paths. But in the end, we likely will all realize that our time as children has stayed with us throughout our life. We will carry that child within ourselves for the duration, as we seek what was lost. One must live their life to be able to truly absorb this fact.

After all the struggles, the selfish dreams, the promises, gluttonous greed, lies and deceptions. We will eventually conclude that life is meaningless. Unless you can grasp and love the maple seed helicopter.

Chapter 1

" Sister Mona," As I raised my hand at the dinner table.

"Yes, Marco?", she replied.

I hesitated and then showed her my piece of stale bread and said. "My bread has green spots on it."

The sister stood up holding her baton, "Marco, come up here and show me."

I walked over to her and looked at her in the eyes with hope she would have a better piece for me. In return, she looked at me with stern eyes.

"Well, Marco, that is what the Lord provided tonight, you should have some of the soup." , she said as she pointed her baton to the soup pot on the counter.

I looked at the soup with a scornful eye, it consisted of hot water, stale bread and some spices.

The sister replied firmly, "We are at war you know. It is difficult to have fresh food these days."

I lowered my eyes and went back to my seat in silence.

I looked to the other side of the table, Dario and Isabelle sat quietly as they had eaten most of their soup. I thought to go visit them and walked over with a grin on my face and asked. "How was the soup?"

Dario replied with a frown, "The same as last night."

Isabelle leaned over to me a bit and whispered.

"hey, Marco, can you and Dario get us some sausages later?"

I smiled at her and looked over to make sure Sister Mona wasn't close enough to hear us. Sister Mona was occupied and looked over all the tables to make sure that all the children had their soup. She would always walk up and down the aisle with her hands cusped together. This way she made sure to project to everyone her stern rule of silence at the Lord's table. She would always wear her coif, bandeaux and veil on her head in public as well as at dinner time. I never could figure out her hair color, but she had brown eyes and was kind of stocky. The cafeteria also served as the auditorium and gym. We spent a lot of time here, especially in the winter months.

Suddenly, there was a loud crash at one of the tables. We all looked over, two boys had gotten into a fight. Quickly two attendants ran over and took the boys outside. I think the boys were newcomers as I had never seen them before. I'm sure they went without any food that night. They would soon learn to follow the house discipline, or they would pay the price. We all followed the rules, except for those of us that would try and help ourselves. We had to survive somehow and we did what we had to do.

Bedtime was early as usual, my hunger pains throbbed and in turn I had a headache. Once all was quiet and everyone was asleep, I quietly woke Dario and we proceeded our way to the basement. There was a secret key hidden on top of a wooden book case that we discovered long ago from one of the older kids that are no longer here. Dario stood guard at the stairs and I proceeded to the pantry. I picked a few goodies and I always tried not to leave any evidence so I placed everything back in place neatly. Dario and I quietly ate our dinner and made sure to save some for Isabelle.

Once I filled my belly, I said to Dario as I licked my lips. "We better get back to the room, are you done eating?"

Dario finished to chew and replied. "Yes, Isabelle said she would meet us at the girl's dormitory entrance."

I replied, "Okay, I will be the lookout in the hallway."

We proceeded and Dario brought some proper dinner to Isabelle, one that all the children should experience.

The following morning, I quickly got washed up and went to the breakfast room. My friend Dario looked sad so I tried to make him laugh. I said to him, "Hey, Dario, do you know what the Eskimo gave to the penguin for his birthday?"

Dario looked at me with a smirk and said. "What?"

I replied with a big grin on my face. "Hehe, Ice in the winter!!" He smiled and chuckled. We were both the same age, and we seemed to get along. I was blond and blue eyed and he was dark haired and brown eyed. For some reason, we felt comfortable together, like brothers. I suppose one would explain it as good chemistry. I was told by the nuns that my mom had died six months after I was born and my father immediately thereafter left me in this orphanage. I didn't quite know Dario's story, but he was an orphan just as well. Although we both had experienced troublesome childhoods, we were both ten years old and we held on to our very good imaginations as it was all we had. Together we could fill our hearts with adventure.

I looked around the room and noticed Isabelle. I wanted to go wish her a good morning so I asked Dario to meet me outside when he finished eating. I went over and sat next to Isabelle. I said. "Good Morning, Isabelle." She was very pretty with shoulder length auburn hair and blue eyes. She never knew her father nor her mother, they died when she was 4 years old. She held a piece of bread and an unappetizing mish mash made from old potatoes in front of her. Her blouse was wrinkled and stained and her hair was uncombed. She didn't seem to belong in this place, she was always kind and never complained. We always said she would be the first one of us to be adopted, as we all dreamed and wished for to happen to us.

Isabelle replied. "Good Morning, Marco."

I whispered to her ear. "It's a good thing we found those sausages last night." She chuckled a smile. We both looked at the food. I said to Isabelle "Do you want to skip breakfast?"

She pushed her plate away and said, "Yes Marco, that's a good idea."

I asked her as I reached for her hand, "Would you like to go out in the morning sun before church?" And she agreed happily.

George was outside as he sat by the big maple tree in the yard. We called out to him, "George!" He looked over and gave us a smile. I said to him, "Why are you sitting there all alone?" He had to think a few seconds, shrugged his shoulders and

said, "I'm just waiting for Friday mass to start."

3

Isabelle jumped in and said, "Well now, that's exactly what we were doing."

George was a year or so younger than the rest of us, he was orphaned when his parents were killed by fascist rebels at a public demonstration in Rome. George's story was unusual, as was his American name in an Italian orphanage. George's father had emigrated overseas to America as a young boy of 15 and became a railroad laborer. At the time the war broke out George's father chose to serve in World War I on the American side and gained his citizenship. George told me his father lived in America many years after WWI had ended. However, eventually he came back to Italy to visit relatives. At that time, he met his Mom and fell in love and married. Some years later, George was born. His parents were anti-fascists and tragically met a dreadful fate. It seemed all of us were filled with stories of struggle and hardships. It was 1941, I don't think we understood all the inhumane and outrageous events that evolved around us. To us, we were abandoned kids and this orphanage was our home. Our school mates were our family, and we were hungry.

The church bell rang, Father Buckius stood at the church main entrance which is on the other side of the yard from the cafeteria. We all made our way from under the maple tree and headed in for mass. Sister Mona always sat in the rear of the church so she could keep an eye out for anyone who misbehaved. All of us were very respectful and remained on our best behavior at mass time. The father spoke of wars and the growing evil in society and how important it was for us to pray to the Lord to give him strength to remove evil from his blessed creation. Our world was created for the Lords children to live harmoniously and to help one another. We should not point blame on one another, instead, we should all try to be the best we can be using the gifts the Lord provided us. It was not something most children could comprehend. However, I could already see how although we are all different, we also all have the same needs. The greatest need being to keep the Love of God in our hearts.

After church, we went back out to the yard for recess. Present were Isabelle, George, Dario and myself. The wind blew nicely and we decided to pretend we could fly, we ran around with our arms open wide. I noticed the maple seeds that seemed to float as they spun around in the wind. They reminded me of tiny helicopters. I had read about helicopters in a magazine George had received in the mail from his American sponsor. But I had never seen one, and this was how I imagined they would fly. I picked one up and put it on my nose, it stuck on like a propeller in front of my face. Quickly Isabelle looked over and pointed at my silly creation.

Isabelle said, "Hey Marco, you look like Pinocchio!"

I didn't know who Pinocchio was, and I didn't care. Everyone started to laugh and placed maple seed helicopters on their noses. We all ran around in a circle in our dirty clothes and worn out shoes with our arms out wide as we envisioned to fly around like helicopters. All the hardships life had presented us with were forgotten, and we were so happy to be alive.

Sister Mona called out from the classroom, "Time for class children." As we gathered our belongings, Isabelle asked if we wanted to go to the playground again after reading class, and we all agreed. Sister Mona greeted us into class as we all made our way to our seats. Once we sat quietly, the sister announced that today we would read a book named 'La Formica e la Cicala' (The Ant and the Cricket). It was a fun story, there was a cricket that sang and danced all summer while the ant worked hard to build a shelter and gather food for the upcoming winter. The cricket would make fun and laugh at the ant. He mocked the ant for the hard work he endured all summer and claimed the ant did not know how to enjoy life. Winter arrived and the cricket started to feel cold. The ant found himself nice and warm and ate food that he stored from last summer. Now, the cricket found himself out in the cold and complained to the ant that it wasn't fair that he would not share the food.

The ant replied, "Well, what have you been doing all summer?"

The cricket shivered and replied. "Well, I sang and danced."

The ant replied. "Okay, that's nice. So now you can dance in the cold and keep yourself warm." Then slamming the door on the cricket's face.

It wasn't exactly what father Buckius had preached earlier today. However, Sister Mona said that it is important that we all contribute and work an equal share so we could all have a good life. It was a lot to take in for one day.

We all went out to the playground after class. Isabelle made fun of Dario because he started to play with a stick and pretended he was a pirate captain.

Dario shouted at her and said, "Hoist those sails mate, winds are chasing aft."

Isabelle replied, "I'm not the mate, I'm Tinkerbell!"

Dario frowned and said, "Crazy maiden."

George jumped into the set and shouted, "I'll hoist the sails captain!"

Then I grabbed an old wooden wheel and made believe I was steering the ship. I said, "What course shall we chart, Captain?"

Dario proudly shouted from behind us standing on a rock. "Head west south west, Quarter Master, we seek warmer waters."

Isabelle replied, "Are we looking for buried treasure?"

Dario's eyes opened wide "Yes, of course. Treasure we seek!"

We all smiled and played to our hearts content. It was a fun afternoon.

Later in the evening, all was quiet in the recreation room. Dario sat quietly and read a magazine and I sat nearby and thought how I would like to see something besides this orphanage tomorrow. We had strict rules that we could not leave the grounds as there were soldiers around. However, I missed going over to the river. I had the urge to go and play pirates and sailormen. I said to Dario, "Hey, Dario, what do you think if we go down to the river tomorrow?" Dario gave me a look and silent stare.

"Are you crazy?", he said.

We looked at each other. Then I replied with a serious face, "It can't be that dangerous. They just don't want us to do anything except stay here and die of boredom." Then George walked over and I said with a big smile on my face. "Hey George, do you want to go down to the river with us tomorrow?"

"Marco, how will we get out of the yard without being seen?", he replied with a discontented look.

Quickly I replied as I waved my hand off at them in frustration. "Ooh, you guys worry too much, It's not that far. And there is never anyone around there. We can just sneak out when everyone is busy and not able to see us."

Dario sighed, George nodded, and they both replied "Okay."

I smiled. Now I could go to bed and dream pirate thoughts.

In the morning at breakfast, I met Dario and George and we sat at our usual seats and played with our food. It just was not worth eating. Sister Mona walked up to the podium and Father Buckius stood next to her. This was not a usual event and the entire cafeteria became silent.

Sister Mona announced. "We have discovered that there are substantive victuals that have been removed from the food pantry. Those stores are the calculated rations that belong to all of us to be used throughout the year. Whomever is responsible is in violation of our campus rules and regulations."

She paused a moment in silence with her hands clasped at the podium. We all sat in complete silence without motion. What she didn't say was that those stores were used only by the nuns and priests. The children never received sausage and cheese and fresh bread.

Sister Mona continued, "Father Buckius and I have an idea of the responsible parties as we have received some information in confidence. Does anyone have anything to say?"

The room remained completely silent. Sister Mona walked off the podium and started to walk around the room as she observed each of us while she held her baton. She stopped in front of one of the boys that was involved in a fight the other day.

Sister Mona said, "As we are in a Christian facility, the Father and I have decided to forgive the culprits as long as they come to us voluntarily and admit their guilt. This would be the honorable thing to do. We will give any party that wishes to admit their guilt or contribute any information related to this offense until tonight. You may come to my office or Father Buckius residence as well. Your only punishment will be to have dish cleaning duty for 30 days. I suggest that anyone of you that know anything come to us before the night is over. If we verify the parties that are involved, and you have not voluntarily admitted your guilt. The punishment will be severe."

We all knew what that meant. She walked over to a wood cabinet by the gym and removed a wooden paddle. She carried it over to the podium and placed it on the top.

Sister Mona said, "Examine your conscience, I suggest if you know that you are guilty, you take advantage of our offer for forgiveness."

I met Dario and George after breakfast in the courtyard. We didn't say anything to each other as to not attract any attention. It was a lovely spring day and we were set for our plan. Once morning mass was called and everyone was inside, we made our way to the breach in the fence that we had used previously to make our excursions. And we slipped away unnoticed. Once outside the fence we ran quietly for a little while. It was a long hike on a country road, there was nobody around this time of day.

Dario said, "Marco, what do you think we should do?"

I replied, "we should go to the river and have some fun."

George said, "Did you see the paddle she carried?"

I replied, "Last time I saw them use that, the boy had black and blue marks on his butt for months."

George and Dario stared at me a bit. I said, "Let's move on, we'll talk it over on the way." There were almond orchards as well as fig tree orchards and we would always make our stop along the way and fill our bellies. There was a water fountain that flowed into a mossy basin where the farmers would let their animals drink, and we also took advantage. What a beautiful scenery my memory recalls with large green fields, trees and mountains of central Italy, you could see for miles and miles on a day like this one.

We arrived at the river around noon. We made good time as we tried not to make too many stops. The river roared its might today as there had been some recent spring rains. We had to speak up so we could hear each other. I shouted. "See, now wasn't this a great idea? I told you we would have fun!"

Dario smiled and said, "Okay, but let's not stay too long as we will need to get back before dinner, or they will notice we were gone.

I replied. "Fine." I looked around and I noticed George wasn't anywhere to be found. "Where's George?" I said.

I knew we had arrived all together. Maybe he went to pee in the bushes. Quickly, we went about and looked for him shouting.

We shouted, "George!" Pausing in between shouts to listen, "George!" We shouted. There was no reply. We got a bit worried and started to walk around the area as we called out for George. Suddenly from behind a bush, we heard George.

George said, "Hey guys!!, come over here and see what I found!"

We stared at George's hands with our mouths open. He held a Luger revolver.

At first I was in disbelief and I ran quickly over to George and asked. "George, where did you find that? Is that a pistol?" George seemed trancelike as he stared at this cold piece of steel in his hands. I don't think he ever held one before. Neither did I. All I knew is that it was dangerous.

Dario arrived quickly and asked, "George, do you know how it works?"

George looked at me and didn't say a word.

Dario asked, "George, Can I hold it?"

Quickly I interrupted and said, "George, let me see it." George handed it over to me. I guess he respected me. I made sure not to point it at anyone and kept the muzzle pointed to the ground. I started to study all the levers and buttons. I knew the trigger would make it shoot so I was careful with that.

Dario seemed worried and said, "I wonder who left it here."

Which made me think as well. This had to be left here by a soldier, like the ones we were warned about by the nuns. But why would they leave it here. George wanted to hold the pistol again. I pulled away and went into a stance. As I aimed, I attempted to look through the sights. I felt an urge to see what it would be like to shoot it.

9

George said, "Let me try." Dario looked up and his face froze in fear.

We heard a frightful voice. "Halt!!, Nimm das Gewehr nach unten."

We turned around and there appeared a German soldier. I didn't know what he said, but I knew to put the gun down.

Before I could think, a group of soldiers appeared out of the dense woods and brush, they circled us. One of them, who appeared to be a Captain, came over to us. He picked the gun up and looked at it carefully. He stared at a soldier that stood nearby.

The Captain said, "Das ist die Waffe, die Sie verloren?"

The soldier looked at the pistol and nodded yes.

My instincts told me he was angry with himself for the error he made. The error was he misplaced his weapon. There was another soldier by the river and he had a dog with him.

The Captain called out to him, "Horst, Was sollten wir mit diesen Kindern?"

Then the Captain spoke to us in our language. "Where are you boys from? What are you doing here?"

I was stunned. I stuttered. "We are orphans from the monastery of San Benedetto. We, uhm, we, we."

The officer interrupted sharply. "Are you here Alone?"

I looked at my friends and we all had the same fearful expression on our face, and then we all said "yes."

The officer and Horst turned away and started to talk amongst themselves. I looked at my friends as I spoke with my eyes as to what we should do. I noticed the dog was a German Shepherd and had glistening steel teeth. To run off would not be a good idea as we would not get far.

Horst quickly came over to us and expressed with a heavy accent. "You will come with me."

George erupted in fear, "Where are we going?"

Horst immediately replied, "Silenz, Stille."

Without much choice, we followed him along the river for about 5 minutes. Also, the soldier that had recovered his lost pistol followed us from behind. We came upon a truck with a few other soldiers around it. George started to look at the river. I could sense what he thought. For the first time in my life, I felt fear. We arrived close to the truck and inside there were other men. These were not soldiers, they looked like civilians. This military convoy likely was destined somewhere with these prisoners and they stopped for a break along the river. The soldier must have lost his pistol and then they came back to look for it, and then found us. Horst told us to get in the truck with the others. Hesitantly, we climbed aboard.

I'm not sure if it felt better to be in the truck with other civilians, or if we were on our own in the back of this truck. Everyone had a look of desperation on their faces. There was one guard in the back next to us, I noticed it was the soldier that had lost his pistol along the river that George had found. He looked at George, a skinny boy with brown hair and blue eyes, and then at us. I felt he had a guilty conscience. If he had not lost his pistol, we would not have found it. And we would not be here on this truck going, we don't know where. We drove for hours and it started to get dark. We came upon a hill and I could see a bridge coming up that crossed over the river. The soldier looked up front by the corner of his eye. He observed the others whom were occupied in a conversation.

Quickly he grabbed George and then Dario, and said to me "follow."

We quickly went to the back side of the truck. He looked out and pointed to the river. George hesitated, then he picked George up and threw him over the hill, then Dario.

Then he looked to me sternly and said, "My nam is Patrik."

And I just jumped afterwards with my eyes closed. We landed on grass as the truck moved slowly around a turn. And we continued to roll down a steep hill. As soon as we were all able to rise our heads from the ground. We looked up and waited patiently for the truck to be gone. We were alone.

I stood up, no broken bones, just some scratches and bruised a little. Dario and George were ok as well. I started to walk down hill to the river. We were tired and it was now late in the day, we would not be able to get back to the orphanage before dark. We needed to find a place for the night and then follow the river back to where we found the pistol in the morning. We found some pine tree branches and built a make shift tent, we camped away from the river and in the woods for the night. We decided one of us should stay awake as the others slept the night so to lookout for any possible danger, and we would take turns throughout the night.

We awoke at the first sign of light, none of us slept very well. And we were very hungry. I looked down river and pondered our journey, it was going to be a long walk back. I wasn't sure how far we were from the orphanage, nor was I sure I wanted to return to the orphanage. I asked my friends "What do we do now?"

Dario replied, "What will the sisters say when we finally make it back, will they have noticed we were gone?"

I shrugged my shoulders and said, "I'm not sure."

Dario sighed and then said, "I wonder if anyone has looked for us? I wish we never made this trip. We will be in a lot of trouble when we get back."

George answered, "Well, at least we are not at Sunday Mass today!"

I laughed. Then I said, "This is really not as bad as you think Dario. We can make our own rules now."

Dario looked at me and said, "Yea. But what will we eat? And where will we sleep?" George and I looked at each other.

And I replied, "Yes, I really miss that stale bread porridge from the orphanage."

Dario stopped in his tracks, pointed ahead and said, "Look up there!"

We saw a man as he walked with his dogs, he carried some tools over his shoulder. The dogs saw us and started to bark. We looked at each other for some insight as to what to do. The man stopped and looked over to us, then he turned away and started to walk his path again.

George yelled out, "Hey, mister!!"

Immediately George started to run up the hill. Dario and I looked at each other, and then followed. The man turned around and told his dogs to stay quiet. He petted them on the head. As we got closer, the dogs sat and panted with their tongues out.

The man said to us, "Pet the dogs on the heads boys, let them smell your scent, it's okay."

We petted them and the dogs were happy.

The man continued and said, "What are you boys doing out here? You must be far from home. There are not many people that live around these parts. Are you lost?"

Quickly, George replied, "Yes. We are lost. We wandered of our path while on a hike and we lost our tracks."

The man observed Dario and I as we stared at George, we didn't know what to say. I think the man knew there was more to our story, however, he didn't ask further. He looked at us in the eyes.

And he said, "My name is Domenico. I live just over a two hours hike from here together with my wife Elisetta. Please, come home with me, maybe we can help you find your parents."

We were tired and hungry. And probably lost as well. This seemed our only option, so we all agreed and followed Domenico and his dogs.

It was a nice day, but the sun was strong and the air had gotten quite arid. The path was packed dirt and very rocky so we needed to be careful not to trip. The old man was in very good shape as he outpaced us quickly and we were really felt tired in our attempt to follow. He turned around and saw us kind of winded, so he stopped under a tree.

Domenico said, "Here we take a break, have a seat boys."

He opened his sack and took out a bottle of water, handed it to George and said, "Have a drink, share with your friends."

He took out another flask and had a drink himself, only I think it was wine. He also had some hardboiled eggs, one for each of us. George looked so happy he almost forgot Dario and I were there. I think he also forgot that we were supposed to return to the orphanage.

George said "Mr. Domenico, what are your dog's names? They are very nice."

Domenico looked at his dog's and smiled as he rubbed them on their chests.

Domenico said, "Yes, Sandro and Enzo, these are my two favorite companions. I always take them with me when I hike up this way."

George smiled and joined Domenico as they both rubbed the dogs. Dario and I watched and smiled as well although we still had in the back of our heads that we would be in trouble once the orphanage found out what we did.

After we rested and ate and drank, Domenico stood up.

Domenico said, "Okay ragazzi, andiamo, it's time to move on. I'd like to get home early so we can help Elisetta with dinner."

We all got up and started to follow. Domenico led the trek with Sandro and Enzo by his side. George was right behind them and Dario and I were lagging a little behind. I turned my head to Dario as I whispered, "What will we tell him once we get there. Should we tell him about the orphanage?"

Dario looked at me. "Why don't we tell him the truth?"

I whispered. "Because I don't want to go back to the orphanage." We both looked at George. He seemed so happy since we met Domenico. We continued our hike in silence. Eventually, we reached a road. And in the distance one could see a few homesteads around in the hills.

Domenico broke the silence. "Hey, boys, we have made good time. We will be to my vineyard soon. From there it will be only a fifteen-minute walk past the town."

We arrived at a building, it looked like a general store and café bar. There were a couple of men that played a card game and sipped coffee. We continued our trek, and it started to be a steep uphill walk. Domenico stopped and pointed at this wooden fenced in land lot with all his grape vines, it was all uphill with walking paths in between the vines.

Proudly Domenico exclaimed, "This is my pride and joy, my brother and I planted these grapes many, many years ago."

George looked and said. "Do you make wine with all these grapes?"

Domenico grinned and said, "Of course!"

14

They started to walk again, we were so tired, we didn't say a thing and we just followed. There was a big stone archway for the entrance to the village, the road was all cobblestone and the homes were all attached and made of thick stone and mortar walls, they looked very, very old. We reached a piazza and there was a church and a couple of buildings for the village community. There was a large fountain in the middle of the piazza and then there was another building with a balcony. There were 5 different roads that entered this piazza.

Domenico walked over to the fountain and said, "When I was a boy, my younger brother and I used to play in this fountain."

It seemed to me Domenico must have lived here all his life. I wondered where his brother lived. I asked Domenico, "Does your brother live here too?"

Domenico lowered his face, pouted and said in a sad voice. "No. Unfortunately he is no longer alive."

He started to walk again. We took one of the roads that was again, going uphill.

Domenico continued to speak of his brother, and said, "My Brother, he died during World War one. As he crossed a bridge along with his brigade, the bridge was blown up. The entire brigade was killed. His name was Eliseo."

We all walked a bit in silence, not in the right mind as of what to say.

Domenico continued, "I returned from his grave this morning when I met you boys. I go there every so often to pray. And to clean up his grave site."

We reached another cross road. This one was smaller, with a general store. There were chickens loose around in front of a nearby stable. The road to the right of us went up hill, the road to the left went downhill. Domenico pointed straight ahead. It was level ground and it looked like it was surrounded by open fields. We reached a water basin with perpetual water that flowed from a nearby brook. It reminded me of the fountain we used on the country road when we left the orphanage. I was happy not to be there anymore and I did not intend to go back. I knew there was not a thing there for me and I wanted to start my own life. As we walked further down the road, there were some cows fenced in a yard, and then some sheep and pigs too near an animal stall. The road was bordered by stone walls that looked like they had been there for centuries. Finally, we reached a break in the stone wall and we walked into a field, we could see a home at the end of this field.

Domenico said. "We have arrived!"

It was a very old home made completely of large stone and mortar, just like the rest of the town. Only this was on its own land. The walls were almost 2 feet thick and the doors looked very solid of heavy wood. It was shaped like a cube with the entrance door on one side, and a porch on the right side. There was also a cellar entrance on the left side with some stairs leading down into it. The second floor had two windows on each side of the home. We stared at all the surroundings and noticed a couple outbuildings and some penned in areas. I thought to myself how I would love to live in a place like this. Suddenly, an elderly woman came out of one of the buildings, she had a chicken in one hand all cleaned up and ready to cook. She looked at us with a smile and did not flinch,

Domenico looked at her, smiled and said, "I've brought home some guests."

She walked over quickly. And as she came closer, we could see she had a lot of wrinkles on her face, but she was quite radiant and glowed with a tan on her face. The first words we heard from her,

The elderly woman said, "Well then, I will get an extra chicken for dinner."

Domenico replied with his hand held out open faced towards her, "Boys, this is my wife, Elisetta."

We smiled and said, "Nice to meet you Ma'am."

And then Domenico pointed at us and said to his wife, "Elisetta, this is George, Dario and Marco. Three young men I bumped into and they helped me find my way home."

Elisetta blushed a little and replied with a smile. "Well, it's a good thing they found you, otherwise you probably would have stopped at the café to play cards or work on your vineyard."

Then she looked at Domenico and pointed towards the house and said, "Domenico, please take the boys inside and show them the guest room, I will start dinner, you all must be very hungry after your journey."

Domenico looked to us as he smiled, "Boys, let's go."

And he guided us into his home. At first I felt a little awkward to accept their kind hospitality. I had never received such a kind gesture from anyone before. However, I was so tired, I quickly acclimated to their generosity.

A few hours later, we all lied down in the guest room with our eyes closed, we didn't even hear Elisetta as she called us for dinner.

Domenico knocked on our door and said, "Boys, we have some nice chicken and rice tonight, come and eat, you have walked a lot today."

George appeared to sleep on the bed, I walked over and tapped his arm. I said to him, "George, time for dinner."

His eyes popped open and he said, "Huh."

I replied, "Dinner time."

He exclaimed excitedly, "Oh, we have dinner? Okay!"

George, Dario and I humbly walked into the kitchen, we had not recalled ever being blessed with such kindness from anyone. There were some very delicious scents in this room and we didn't want to show how starved we were, but our instincts took over and we began to devour this wonderful loving meal of Chicken and rice which was prepared for us by loving people, and we did appreciate it. Domenico and Elisetta sat next to each other and looked at us, I could sense they were so happy to see us as we enjoyed this meal. It was the best meal I ever had and to this day Chicken and Rice is my favorite dish.

Once we finished to eat, George stood up with his plate.

George asked, "Excuse me, where do we return our plates?"

Elisetta replied, "George, don't worry. I will take care of that."

Domenico said, "Good Job boys, are you all feeling better?"

I looked at George, and then at Dario.

We all came out at once and said, "This was the best meal we have ever ate!"

Elisetta smiled and Domenico replied, "I am very happy to hear that. Elisetta is quite a cook and I have been blessed with her delicious meals. It's hard to believe, but we have been married 42 years now. It seems like yesterday. And the funny thing is, my mind hardly realizes it. However, my body points it out to me often as a reminder. Instead, Elisetta gets younger every year, I don't know how she does it."

Elisetta got up and laughed, "Domenico, thank you for your compliments. However, tomorrow I need you to go to the orchard and find us some produce from the garden, we need some fruit in this house, see if there are strawberries and maybe the asparagus have come up. It's been warm."

Domenico said in a humble voice, "Tomorrow I was going to the vineyard, I need to grow healthy grapes this year!"

Then he sighed and said, "Okay Elisetta, I will make sure I go to our garden first."

Then he looked at us boys, "Boys, I could sure use some help tomorrow."

We all looked at Domenico.

And then George with a big grin shouted out, "I would love to help you Sir!"

We all smiled at each other happily.

Elisetta replied as she looked at Domenico, "Well, you boys, young and old ones, better get yourselves to bed. Tomorrow morning will be here soon and you must all be tired from your journey today."

We all said thank you and good night and went right off to hit the sack. We all were asleep as soon as we found our bed. So much had happened in just a few days. We hardly had time to think about where we had been or what we did, it just felt good and we happily went with it.

Chapter 2

The rooster crowed and I noticed the aroma of fried eggs in the air.

Domenico knocked on our door and then opened it and said, "It's a new day boys, let's get breakfast."

I was not used to awaken to savory scents. And as I walked into the kitchen, I noticed we all had a plate with 3 fried eggs and potatoes placed on the table. I thought to be in heaven.

Domenico said, "Eggs must always be eaten in odd numbers, not counting 1. So, you can have 3 or 5 or 7."

Elisetta interrupted, "Domenico, that's not healthy! Don't teach these boys any bad habits. Today you can have three because you are going to work hard all day. Di tutto, il troppo nuoce!"

With a sigh Domenico replied, "Yes, she is right, of anything and everything, too much is not good. And that includes everything."

Domenico looked at us in the eyes and said, "Don't forget."

We all ate our breakfast and cleaned our plates.

Domenico stood up and said, "Boys, there are some empty baskets out by the tool shed which we will need to carry back what we will pick today, please go get them and meet me at the front door.

The tool shed was made of stone and mortar with some wood beams to hold up the tiled roof. There were all kinds of tools that were hung on the beams, also some on the wall. The floor was packed dirt. We found the bags hung up on some hooks. George and Dario quickly grabbed them and ran out to meet Domenico. I noticed a cross on the wall and next to it a medal with a picture of a young man. I thought it was a curious place for a cross. It seemed almost as a place to pray in silence. Then I heard a faint call.

Domenico shouted, "Hey, Marco, where are you? We need to arrive to the field before lunch time."

I was upset I held up the team, I ran out and they waved me over. They started to walk and I ran to catch up with them. Enzo and Sandro came with us too. It seemed like they were used to this trip as they led the way. I quickly caught up and Domenico turned his head.

Domenico said, "Well, we have some good news and some bad news. Which do you want first?"

We looked at each other and wondered what the bad news could be. I thought to myself as to how we could be in trouble already.

Domenico said, "Boys, always ask the bad news first. This way it can only get better. Bad news is first, we are going to the garden. The garden is uphill."

We sighed while we looked at the steep hill ahead.

Domenico continued, "Good news is that on the way back, we will drop our tools off at the root cellar, and from there the vineyard is downhill."

We just continued to walk. I don't think any of us cared, we were so happy to be on an adventure and out of that orphanage. We could walk all day if we had to.

It was a beautiful day, you could smell the sweet spring air as the birds called all kinds of chirps, it sounded like nature's announcement of spring concert. I enjoyed the quiet time and to absorb natures magic. For the first time, I really appreciated and loved the spring. We came upon a break in the stone wall and entered a large field, there was a pond at the end of the field and a wire fence. I think this is where the garden was.

Domenico broke the silence. "You boys are quiet today."

We smiled and made eye contact with Domenico, I pointed to the fence gate and said, "Is that the garden?"

Domenico replied, "Yes, Marco, that's the garden. My brother and I dug it out and fenced it in long time ago."

We soon got close enough to see inside. My estimate is that it measured about 150 feet by 150 feet. There were plowed rows of dirt and they were sectioned off with some wood planks. There were some asparagus in one of the sections and some strawberries in another. I noticed some channels that ran high to low using rounded bricks to carry the water as an irrigation system. I guess he somehow got the water from the pond to flow through the channels. Domenico looked concerned. I asked, "What do you see?"

Domenico responded, "Weeds! Have you boys ever pulled weeds before?"

We all looked at each other with a stupefied look.

Domenico blurted, "I guess not. Well, here is your first lesson. We need to pull the weeds out of this section first before I can plant tomatoes here today. Otherwise the weeds will kill the tomato plants. Take this hoe and try to rake and rip up as much as possible. Whatever is left over you will need to bend down and pull with your hands. Keep doing this until all you see is the black soil. Try your best to loosen the soil with the hoe. Then we can plant the tomato plants which I have in the greenhouse."

Without wasting time, we each grabbed a hoe and started to work.

Domenico said, "I am going to the greenhouse to bring back some plants."

He pointed and we could see a structure a few feet tall with some glass panels over it, I guess that was the greenhouse.

Domenico continued, "I started the seedlings several weeks ago using the seeds of last year's crop."

I said to Domenico, "Will you teach us how to do that too?"

Domenico started to walk to the greenhouse and said, "Sure, stay around here and you will learn lots of things."

We all smiled and continued working as a team. We worked the section from opposite corners and we made good progress in short time.

The sun was now high and I could feel it had gotten warmer, we took off our heavy sweaters and kept our tee-shirts on. To pull weeds was not an easy task. Domenico showed us how to shake the earth off the roots and pile up the weeds where they would dry up in the sun. He said we would burn them later in the spring.

Domenico brought back a few trays of plants in a hand cart.

Domenico looked at us, smiled and said, "Hey, kids, that is pretty good work you did there. Soil looks nice and dark, we should get some nice tomatoes this year."

We all smiled. I felt so good to learn how to work in the field. I watched Domenico as he got on his knees and he started to part the soil with his hands. He placed the plants a couple feet away from each other.

Domenico said, "Watch as I do, this is how to plant."

We all looked intensely.

Domenico parted the soil and said to us, "Part the soil with your hands, place the plants about 2 feet apart. Then cover the roots up with soil with your hands, very gently packed."

We got down and started doing the same. In no time, we had planted the whole section. As we proceeded, Domenico took the hoe and broke up the soil.

Domenico said, "The secret is you have to make sure the soil is nice and loose before you plant."

Domenico took his hat off and wiped off his brow.

Domenico said, "Whew, it's gotten warm fellas, I think we are done planting tomatoes for today. Now we need to put some water in the soil."

He went behind the fence and there was this large tank with a faucet valve on the bottom. He opened it up and out came the water into the channel. The water flowed the whole way through the channel into the tomato section. I was mesmerized as the water flowed. It was Mother Nature's miracle at work.

Domenico said, "These tanks collect the rainwater, and when they run out, we will need to siphon some out of the pond into the tank. I will show you how to do it another day. There is a tank for each of the sections. Works pretty good eh!"

We were all amazed with Domenico's garden.

Domenico smiled and said, "We will have nice tomatoes by Ferragosto. For me it is the best part of the entire crop season. With some of Elisetta's bread of course, a little olive oil and pepper, nice!"

After we finished watering the tomatoes, we all picked strawberries and asparagus and placed them in our bags. I tasted some

22

strawberries as I picked them, and they were so good. I had never tasted anything like it. As for the asparagus, those needed to be cut with a knife. Domenico did most of those, however, he showed us how to do it and we soon learned how to harvest asparagus as well. We had accomplished much, and I could sense Domenico wanted to leave.

Domenico got up and said, "We are finished here for today boys, let's gather our things and get going."

I had thought it was break time, however, Domenico had other plans. We all packed up and grabbed as much as we could. It's a good thing the root cellar was downhill. Once we were at the root cellar, we dropped off the bags and tools and went on our way. We still carried a couple small bags of crop. We continued downhill through the town, the same way we had entered the first day we arrived and soon found ourselves at the entrance of the vineyard. Domenico brought us to a table and put down his back sack.

Domenico said, "Time for lunch kids, let's see what Elisetta made for us."

He took out a nice loaf of bread and some sausages and cheese. He then started to cut and slice and handed out this lunch feast to us, we had never eaten so well in our lives. All kinds of goodies, olives and peppers and cheese and sausages so soft you could spread them on your bread like butter. We ate to our hearts content. Domenico had a treat for Sandro and Enzo too, a nice hambone for each. After our feast, Domenico stood up.

Domenico said, "Now it is time for the afternoon shift."

He looked to the vineyard and said, "We have more weeds to pull today, this is the number one priority. Bad weeds continuously grow around the grape vines and it is our job to stop them before they can kill our crop."

He walked us up to the first row of grape vines.

Domenico said, "We will continue this task throughout the summer, so make sure to bring hats next time as the sun will become hotter as we approach summer and you will really feel it out in this field."

23

George, Dario and I never worked so hard in our lives, but we were so happy to be doing so, it's like we had just started to live. Domenico and Elisetta suddenly became our family and we had a sense of purpose for the first time in our lives.

On the way home, we stopped at the general store. Domenico asked Dario and George to stay outside. He took one sack with him and asked me to pick up another one and go inside with him.

Domenico said, "Antonio, come stai?"

Antonio replied, "Domenico, what are you up to, who is this young man with you?"

Domenico replied, "This is cousin Eliseo's son Marco, he will stay with us for the summer. I have some nice asparagus and strawberries here, can we trade?"

Antonio replied, "Sure, will you take olive oil like last time?"

Domenico replied, "Exactly what I had in mind."

Antonio grabbed a case and put it on the table. Domenico put it in a sack and lifted it on his back.

Antonio helped him and said, "You are still strong Domenico."

Domenico replied, "Thank you Antonio. A presto!"

We all gathered up our things and started our trek back to the homestead. The olive oil was heavy and I could see Domenico as he started to struggle.

I asked him, "Domenico, can I help you with that, it looks too heavy."

He looked at me and smiled.

Domenico replied, "Thank you Marco, that's very considerate, but I will stop at the piazza and borrow a donkey from my friend. We can load this case on the donkeys back."

I still wanted to help him so I walked closely by his side. We arrived at the piazza. In the corner was a small stable with large wooden doors wide open. An old man slept in a chair with a glass of wine and cheese on a table beside him. The man was heavyset with a large belly. Domenico put the olive oil down and looked at the man.

Domenico cheerfully said, "Hey, Pietro, how are you? When you're not chasing the women, you are drinking wine."

The old man lifted his head and was almost startled by our presence.

Pietro replied, "Domenico, I don't see you around anymore, what are you doing with yourself? And who are these men with you?"

Domenico replied, "These are my nephews, they are staying with us this summer. Elisetta and I will put them to work."

Pietro replied, "Oh, that is very nice, we need some young people around here, too many of us old folks sleeping all day in this town."

He turned his head to us and said, "It's nice to meet you boys, let me know if I can help you with anything. Domenico and I are very old friends so we are like family here."

Dario smiled, while he pointed to us, he said, "I am Dario, and this is George and Marco."

Domenico interrupted, "Thank you Pietro for your gesture, I'm sure they will take advantage. In the meantime, I am going to borrow Ercole to carry our stuff up the hill. I will bring him back down in the morning."

Pietro replied, "That's fine, he will enjoy grazing your field tonight, he always loves the fresh grass up there."

Domenico replied, "Okay then, we'll see you in the morning. Grazie, e Buona Sera."

We packed most of our things on the donkeys back with some ropes and sacks, and off we were.

It was a steep cobblestone hill, and each time we climbed this road, it seemed to get steeper. Ercole did not mind, it looked like he was used to it as he knew exactly where to go and always guided our way. I was very happy Domenico brought him with us to assist to carry our things. I noticed an old woman as she walked down the road towards us. She smiled to Domenico.

She said, "Buona sera Domenico, how is Elisetta?"

Domenico took his hat off, and said, "Buona sera Vera, Elisetta is well. I hope she is making us some dinner because we worked all day weeding and planting."

Vera laughed and said, "You men are all the same, always food on your mind."

We all kept our pace and passed each other by. People seemed very friendly in this town, no one was considered rich or poor, they were all people that lived a simple life and worked to survive. They had no desire for greed or power, no need for expensive vacations or mansions. It seemed they all enjoyed the simplicity this world had to offer. Nothing more.

Once we arrived home, we were all quite tired. We sat down in the kitchen as Elisetta prepared a large omelette for us. She made it using tomatoes and onions she had canned from last fall. I had never seen anything like it but it looked delicious. Domenico went out to check on the chickens and Dario and George started to speak about the day's activities with much excitement. They spoke of how hard they worked with great pride and were smiling with gestures of happiness the likes I had never seen in them before.

Elisetta laughed and said, "Why don't you boys go wash up for dinner, it will be ready in ten minutes and I know you must be hungry. I have some fresh clothes for you on the bed, make yourselves nice."

We all happily agreed and did as she suggested. In the meantime, Elisetta walked out front to greet Domenico as he returned, she waved at him as walked over to meet him.

Elisetta said, "Domenico, I overheard at the market square today that Veneranda heard of 3 boys went astray from the Monastery of San Benedetto about a week ago. Seems they sneaked out for an excursion and never returned. The Carabinieri found some of their belongings near a river about 15 kilometers from the monastery. It was assumed that they were picked up by a German convoy that transported prisoners up North. The convoy passed over the bridge close to where you met the boys. Do you think it could have been our boys? Domenico's eyes opened wide, and then he looked down.

Domenico said, "I suspected they were runaways, perhaps orphans, but I didn't know they had come that close to danger."

He looked her in the eyes and said, "Poor boys, they must be very brave to have gone through that. Thank God they managed to escape. Let's not say a thing tonight, the boys seemed very happy today and I don't want to spoil their day."

After dinner, we all sat around the table and played cards. Domenico taught us to play his favorite card game, Tresette. It seemed quite complex, however, Domenico assured us he would make us champs in no time. We all had a lot of fun. Elisetta smiled as she knitted a blanket. And we all enjoyed the evening air which was cool and crisp. It was a nice evening after a long day at work. Soon after we all went to bed and slept solidly. I don't think I can recall having had a better day.

The days and weeks passed. The gentle spring air turned into a bold summer of hot days and thunderstorms. One morning, while we were all out in the field doing our chores. Domenico called us for lunch break together with Enzo and Sandro under a big oak tree. Domenico, as he cut a piece of bread, looked over and pointed at the garden.

Domenico said, "I want to say, you boys really did a nice job for this garden, I could never have done it without you."

We all kind of blushed and I said, "It's the best time we have ever had and we are so grateful for what you have done for us."

Domenico looked at each of us while he pouted his lips and nodded his head with gratitude.

Domenico said, "Well boys, all three of you have been very well behaved and I am proud to host your young lives and leave with you a part of me for your future journey in life."

Domenico shed a tear and wiped it.

Domenico continued, "Elisetta and I never were able to have a child of our own, so for us, your appearance in our lives is a benediction, you have filled an empty space in our hearts that I cannot express in words. I believe, 'Il Signore' has brought us together as we all need each other."

Then he pointed his finger up in the air.

Domenico said, "Il Signore Vede e Provede."

We all smiled and grinned. I interpreted what Domenico said as he believed our encounter that day was not by accident. God sees and provides and made our paths cross. It comforted us to have this bond as we all were made to feel secure to have received God's love. A security I would not let go of.

One morning after breakfast, Domenico asked me to guide Ercole back down to Pietro's stable as he was needed for some chores in town. I would afterwards meet them back at the fields. I eagerly took on the endeavor and grabbed Ercole's reigns as we walked carefully down the cobblestone road. On the way, I thought back to the orphanage, I had known no other home before this new life we had recently encountered by chance. I was happy of this new existence, however, I often wondered who my real parents were. Although I did not know them, I wondered who my Mom was and how she died, but I also wondered why my Dad left me in an orphanage. I guess he was too weak to handle being a parent on his own. It was as if I had no identity. I never knew anything of them, not even some photos or family members to visit me like some of the other children would receive from time to time. To have the realization that I was alone in the world was not something any child should have to experience. I always tried to be affectionate with others as a replacement for not to have had a mother or father. Although, even now that I found a new kind family, I still had the same emptiness, as having a lack of identity. I assumed I would carry that forever.

As I arrived at Pietro's stable a young man was standing at the entrance.

He said, "I see you have brought Ercole back home, I hope he behaved overnight."

I replied, " Oh yes, he is a very good friend. Domenico asked me to thank Signor Pietro."

The young man replied, "I am Carlo, I am Antonio's nephew but I am helping Signor Pietro this morning. What's your name?"

I quickly replied, "My name is Marco, my brothers and I are staying with Mr. Domenico as our parents have gone to America."

Carlo exclaimed excitedly, "America! Wow, I would love to go to America. Carlo asked, "Are you going to go to America too!"

Without hesitation I said, "Yes, Carlo, I will go to America as soon as my parents settle down and we will have a place to live in."

Carlo said, "That seems very exciting, maybe one day we can all go together to America. I love Rita Hayworth and Fred Astaire. Hey, are you coming to the festival tonight, it will be a lot of fun."

I replied, "I didn't know of any festival. Well, I will ask Domenico, perhaps we can all come."

Carlo said, "Good, see you tonight then, they will also have a cinema."

Excitedly, I waved off to Carlo and went on my way. I was so excited to tell George and Dario about the festival. I imagined the American movie they would play as I walked. This time, the uphill walk to the field vanished into my imagination. As I arrived, everyone was already hard at work. I joined George as he was the closest and started to pull weeds with him. Dario and Domenico worked together and watered the soil by releasing water into the channels. In no time, Lunchtime arrived and we all gathered under the large oak we seemed to always meet at on this field for lunch. As Domenico opened the lunch sack, I excitedly said, "I met Carlo at Pietro's cantina."

Domenico replied, "Oh, that's nice, he is a nice young man. Did you thank him for the use of Ercole?"

I replied, "Yes." I paused a moment and said excitedly, "He invited us to go to the festival tonight, can we go?" I was really hoping he would agree.

Domenico stopped for a second, then he sighed and said, "Well, I suppose you boys can go as long as Carlo is there, but first I need to talk with him."

We all tried to contain our excitement as we grinned at each other secretly."

Early afternoon arrived quickly and we had finished our chores at this field for the day. Domenico decided we would all now make our way down to the vineyard. On the way, we stopped at Antonio's. Both Carlo and Antonio were there.

Domenico said, "Buon Pomeriggio Antonio."

Antonio replied, "Domenico, may I offer you an espresso?"

Domenico cordially replied, "Thank you Antonio, I would love one."

Domenico sat down on a stool.

Domenico said to Antonio, "I understand Carlo is going to the festival tonight."

Antonio replied, "Yes, he is old enough now, so we let him go on his own now."

Domenico asked, "Is it okay if the boys go along with him?"

Antonio looked at the boys.

Antonio said, "Boys, you seem well behaved, but I can still remember when I was your age. Do we have your word you will stay out of trouble?"

Domenico interrupted and said as he looked to all of us, "Antonio and I are putting our faith in all of you, please don't disappoint us. The minute you see any sign of trouble for yourself or any one of you, you need to stick together and listen to Carlo as he is the oldest."

We all looked at each other seriously and replied, "Okay, we will, we understand."

Antonio blurted with a serious face, "Do we have your word?"

And we all cheered "Yes, we promise!"

We were so excited to go to a festival, we would have promised to just about anything.

That evening at the festival, we looked all about in awe. It was quite spectacular for us to see all the activity. There were many beautiful young women in costumes that paraded about with their boyfriends. We all were mesmerized. There were many vendors that sold everything from fried Baccala to Zeppole and cream puffs. The free movie to be shown tonight was going to be 'Dumbo', an elephant whose ears were big enough for him to fly. We enjoyed it so much we laughed and smiled throughout the entire film. It was a wonderful Disney masterpiece. Once the film ended, Carlo suggested we all go to have a gelato, and we all swiftly agreed. Carlo knew the vendor so they did not ask us to pay, we all said thank you and quickly commenced to enjoy our gelato. We all walked around and gawked at all the people and activities, there was music and even a puppet show. We had never had such a good time. That night I felt I discovered that the world had so much to be experienced. I felt enlightened and the world was mine to explore.

Carlo looked at his watch and said to us "Hey, guys, it has gotten little late, I promised Domenico you would all be home by eleven PM."

The night seemed to have ended for most of the people around, and we were also sleepy. We did not protest too much and agreed.

Carlo said, "It's time for us to go home now."

Carlo walked with us up the hill and made sure we got home on time. Domenico and Elisetta were already asleep and we quietly went to bed.

The following day Domenico let us sleep late, he went on his own to the vineyard and I awoke as the sun was already high in the sky. Elisetta was in the kitchen eating some fried eggs and toast.

Elisetta said, "Good Morning. It looks like you are the first to rise up today, did you have fun last evening?"

I smiled, "Yes, we all had such a great time, we saw a Disney movie named 'Dumbo'."

Elisetta smiled and said, "Oh, I've heard of that one, it must have been spectacular, Disney is a master artist."

Then she stood up and pulled a chair over.

Elisetta said, "Sit down Marco, what would you like for breakfast."

Quickly I replied, "oh no, please I do not want to make you work more, where is Domenico?"

Elisetta replied, "Well, he decided to let you boys sleep late today and went down to the vineyard, why don't you have a little breakfast and go meet him."

I quickly agreed. I went back to the room, Dario and George were still asleep, so I let them be. I went back to the kitchen and Elisetta had breakfast ready for me. I said, "Elisetta, may I call you Aunt Elisetta?"

She blushed and replied, "Well, Marco, Yes you may. I feel very close to you boys and I would be honored to be your aunt."

I smiled back at her gleefully.

Then she said, "You know, Marco, Domenico and I know you boys ran away from the convent. We never mentioned it to you. We know that your lives have been difficult and we are happy to have you in our home and in our lives. We intend to help you as we would our own children, if we had been able to have any."

Tears came to my eyes and I quickly embraced Elisetta. I had no words but I think she felt my same tears.

Chapter 3

T he seasons melded into each other as we watched the fields give birth to life. We ourselves progressed into young adults. I had awoken one morning after a hard day of work. I felt as if I had forgotten something. The sunrise brought on the new day as I slowly reflected on the day ahead. Suddenly I realized. Today is my birthday! Carlo came by that morning as we had planned for all of us to go to Carlo's aunt's town for a few days to celebrate my birthday. Carlo borrowed his uncle's truck and George, Dario and I joined him. George and Dario sat in the back and I was up front with Carlo. As we drove out of the village, Carlo looked at me and smiled.

Carlo said, "Hey, Marco, how does it feel to be 16?"

I thought about it and replied, "Carlo, I'm too old to be a child and too young to be an adult, it's not that great."

Carlo laughed. "Ha, yes, I remember. I was also 16 a couple of years ago. Now I am adult and I can go places on my own."

I looked at him and said, "That must be great fun, I can't wait to be able to drive too. But I want to drive in America!"

Carlo replied, "Yes, I know. I would like to go to America too, the big cars, movie stars and the rich and famous live in America."

I looked back to check on Dario and George as they talked. I looked to Carlo with a serious face and said, "I haven't spoken to you about it, but I really do not have parents living in America, but I have a dream of going there."

Carlo replied, "Well, Marco, I kind of suspected that, you have been here quite some time without contact from your parents."

I nodded and said, "Yes, but I still want to go to America. Dario does not want to go, but George said he would come with me. I think his father wanted him to become American. His father was an American Veteran."

Carlo replied "Really?"

I replied, "How about you? would you come with us? we would feel safer if you came with us because you are little older. We are still minors." Carlo seemed deep in thought.

Carlo replied, "Gee, this is a surprise for me today. I need to think about it."

We both smiled and continued our way. After a few hours, we could see Ascoli Piceno in the distance. I admired the view as we approached. There were lots of rolling green hills and trees. The colorful variations of green and blue sky made this a very beautiful place. We parked the truck and walked into the Piazza del Popolo, there were many of shops and passersby. Carlo seemed excited, he guided us into a bakery. The scent was breathtaking and we all started looking through the display cases. Carlo asked for a variety of pastries and we all walked outside and found a place to sit and eat. I don't think any of us ever tasted anything so good. My favorite was the Bigne and George liked the Napoleon. Dario was happy with his Sfogliatella and Carlo, I think he liked all of them.

Afterwards we went to visit the Cathedral of San Emidio. It was quite spectacular to see the building inside, and you could see how very ancient it was. I thought about how many people must have passed through this cathedral over the centuries and I wondered what they prayed for. Afterwards, we walked some more and we came upon the church of The Madonna delle Grazie, and I was mesmerized by her grace. I prayed to the Madonna, her figure was so beneficent. I felt she was the mother I had been missing all my life. Her figure remained in my mind the rest of that day as we visited the town.

That night we stayed with Carlo's aunt's farm. Carlo's Uncle had asked Carlo to attend and assist in a pig slaughter at his farm. They would butcher and make all kinds of meats to store in their cellar. It was our first night away from Domenico and Elisetta. It felt a little lonely, however, Carlo's aunt was very nice and made us a nice homemade pasta dinner. I thought to myself how lucky Carlo was to have a family, aunts and uncles. I wished I could have had the same. Perhaps one day I could make my own.

In the morning, we visited the farm and we went to see the hog. It was very large, I had not known pigs could get so large. There were several men there and I had no idea what I was about to witness. George and Dario decided to go back to the house and wait there. The men tied the pigs back legs and lifted him up off the ground with a hoist. Then one of them took a long knife and cut the hogs throat. The hog squealed wildly all-throughout. I folded my arms across my chest and observed with antipathy. There was blood dripping into a large metal bowl, it was truly a gruesome experience. I don't think I will ever forget that squealing sound. Afterwards, the pig was butchered and many families arrived to prepare the different meats and sausages. Well, I felt horrible as I watched the hog die, however, the meats they prepared for the families to share were truly delicious. Together with all the homemade breads and pastas, this certainly was a place I would like to visit again.

Once we arrived back home at our village, there was some unusual commotion. A military convoy was leaving the Piazza, it was the German military. Quickly Carlo drove to the store and Elisetta was outside and very upset with her hands over her mouth. She came over to us quickly as we got out of the truck.

"Marco, Carlo, the soldiers came and took the men to L'Aquila. I am so upset". Elisetta started to cry.

"Why did they take them.., where is Domenico?" I asked in despair.

"They took Domenico, I don't know why. They said they were looking for spies." Elisetta sat down on a bench and held her head as she cried.

Carlo asked, "Where is my uncle...and Pietro? Did they take Pietro?"

"No, luckily they were not here, Pietro had driven Antonio to L'Aquila for some business". Said Elisetta as she tried to control herself.

I looked to Carlo and asked. "What should we do?"

Carlo replied, "I think we should go to L'Aquila."

Elisetta interjected, "No, don't go there, they will take you too. You boys need to stay here with us, it's too dangerous right now."

Domenico found himself on a military truck together with other men that were taken for questioning.

Domenico said as he looked over the mountainside, "They are bringing us to the Castle."

One of the men answered with fear on his face, "What do they want from us, why do they bring us to 'il castello'."

Domenico looked to the castle entrance as the truck approached and also he wondered what was awaiting for them inside". The truck stopped at the front gate and a soldier opened the rear door of the truck.

The soldier waved his rifle as he ordered the men to exit the truck. There was a bridge to cross over that at one time used to be a moat. Upon orders from the German soldiers, the men marched their way to the castle entrance, the soldiers followed.

Once inside the fortress, the men were instructed to form a line and await for the commandant to call them into his office, one at a time.

Domenico thought of his brother whom was killed in WWI and wondered if today he would meet a similar fate.

One by one, the men were called in. Some of the men returned with tears in their eyes, others did not. They were all put into separate groups and all were kept quiet and reminded not to try any heroics as the soldiers stood pointing their rifles.

A soldier arrived and took Domenico by the arm and guided him to the Captains quarters. It was a beautifully decorated room and adorned with tapestries and paintings of men in uniform, it must have been used by elites of the military of times gone by. The Captain asked briskly, "What is your name?"

Domenico replied without any emotion on his face, "I am Domenico".

A soldier began to search him throughout and found a paper in his shirt pocket.

"Domenico complained, "What are you doing? I don't have anything, what are you looking for?"

The Captain interjected angrily while pointing at him, "Silence!"

The Soldier brought the paper over to the Captain, and the Captain opened it up. He looked it over, then looked to Domenico. "What does this say? Whom are you spying for?".

Domenico looked incredulously and thought to himself, what are they talking about. He did not even remember having the note in his pocket.

The Captain repeated sternly while he held his baton, "What is written on this note!" as he hit the baton against the desk.

Domenico jumped back from the loud sound, he replied. "I do not remember having that note in my pocket, let me see it please".

The soldier grabbed Domenico and brought him over to the Captain. The Captain opened the note and held it for Domenico to see while the soldier held his arms behind his back.

Domenico looked and squinted, and to his disbelief, he became angry of the way he was being treated over this stupidity. Domenico said. "This is my shopping list that my wife gave me yesterday. It says, half kilo of olives, quarter kilo of parmesan cheese, 1 kilo of flour, half kilo ground beef, 1 jar sun-dried tomatoes in oil and un fior di latte".

The Captain took back the note and looked closely, he instructed the soldier to find an interpreter. Domenico was told to sit while they waited and the Captain continued to interview more of the detained men. Eventually, one of the Captains colleagues arrived and read the note, and he confirmed that Domenico was telling the truth. The Captain reluctantly released Domenico that same night and he was guided back to the castle entrance and released, he walked over the moat alone and there was no truck waiting for him at the other side. Dumbfounded and tired, Domenico walked back home that night muttering to himself and complaining about the cold. Domenico's story spread throughout the town and people brought all kinds of gifts for weeks to come. We spent many lunches under trees and dinners by the fireside laughing and talking about his ordeal, and in the end, he would always say *'c'e sempre il rovescio della medaglia'* , or *'there is always the other side of the coin'*. He would always say it was better to walk home 9 miles in the cold through the mountains than to spend the night in a prison cell, or who knows...

A few years passed as Domenico and Elisetta guided us into being young men. My body had changed and I craved adventure. One November morning, I awoke and felt very cold. I got up and wrapped myself in my blanket, walked over and I looked out the window to a white snowy wonderland. Winter had arrived in the mountains of Abruzzi and it was time to sit by the fire. I went downstairs and Domenico already had the stove lit. He looked over to me as I walked into the kitchen.

Domenico said, "Good morning Marco, we have our first snow."

I replied, "Good Morning."

Domenico asked, "We need to light the fireplace in the cellar, please, may you get dressed warmly and go get some fire wood from the wood shed?"

I replied, "Yes uncle."

Domenico replied, "We will burn wood throughout the day."

I quickly agreed and proceeded to bring wood into the cellar. By mid-day the house started to become warm as Elisetta baked some bread, the aroma was divine.

Elisetta asked me, "Hey, Marco, may you get some corn husks from the cellar so we can put them on the coals."

I thought that was the best idea I heard all day. In a short time, the home had such an appetizing aroma and lunch called us altogether in the warm kitchen. We talked and joked and enjoyed the time together. After lunch, Domenico sent us boys down to the village to get some flour as Elisetta wanted to do more baking. This way the oven would not only keep us warm, but keep our bellies full. It was a very cold day, but very sunny. The air was very crisp and my lungs could breathe in deeply. Dario curled himself over rubbing his hands as he walked.

Dario said, "Oh my it's cold out here, my feet are freezing!"

George looked at me and rolled his eyes up.

George said to me. "I guess Dario is not one for the colder weather."

I took a deep breath, smiled and said, "I kind of like it, my lungs can breathe!" We reached the piazza and shook off our shoes as we arrived at the store. As we entered, I noticed It was a new clerk. I asked, "Where is Carlo today?"

The clerk replied, "He had to go to L'Aquila to get some supplies."

I was hoping to see Carlo today and I was a little disappointed he wasn't there. I asked the clerk, "We wanted to buy two bags of flour." Dario was looking at the magazines and then brought one over to the counter.

Dario asked, "Can we buy this too?"

I looked at it and it looked interesting. I asked the clerk, "How much is the magazine?"

The clerk replied, "It's free when you buy two bags of flour."

I smiled and said, "Thank you!"

We paid for the flour and then I said to the clerk "Please tell Carlo Marco was here and thank him also for the magazine." We waved off and left. George and I carried a bag of flour each. Dario followed and was absorbed in his magazine. He seemed to have forgotten about the cold.

George asked Dario, "You will need to share that with us later. I would like to read some too." Dario agreed and nodded.

I asked Dario, "What are you reading?"

Dario replied. "The soccer games."

Then he looked to me pointing to a soccer player in the magazine.

Dario said, "I would like to become a soccer player."

George and I looked at each other and kept walking. The flour bags were heavy and the snow was slippery, we didn't want to let the flour fall in the snow, so we saved our breath. Once we were closer to home and the worst part of the hill had past, I turned to Dario and said, "Hey, Dario, how does one become a soccer player for one of those teams?" Quickly he pointed to a picture of a University in Genoa in the magazine and showed me.

Dario said, "I want to go there."

George and I looked at the picture in the magazine."

George said, "Wow, that's a nice building."

I caught my breath and said, "Now we have an excuse to go to Genoa! I will ask Carlo if he can drive us there." Dario remained silent.

George asked, "How far is Genoa? anyone know?"

Dario said, "I've never been there but I know it's up north."

We walked and talked and that made the trip go quickly, we arrived home in no time. Domenico and Elisetta were in the kitchen.

Domenico said, "Here they are with the flour." Domenico got up and walked over, took the bag of flour from George and brought it to the kitchen table." Then he said, "Elisetta, let's make some bread for the butter." Elisetta smiled.

Elisetta said, "Okay boys, please go get me a few eggs from the cellar."

Elisetta noticed the magazine in Dario's hand.

Elisetta said, "Hey, Dario, you have a magazine? can I see it later when you are done?"

Dario excitedly replied, "Oh, of course, it has a picture of the University of Genoa."

Domenico said, "You are interested in the University?"

George blurted out and said, "He wants to be a soccer player for them."

Dario blushed. Domenico walked over to Dario and placed his hand on Dario's shoulder.

Domenico said to Dario, "Well, Dario, I've seen you play down at the piazza, and I have to say you are pretty good and have the body of a runner. Perhaps you have a good idea there."

Dario smiled. Domenico walked over to the stove and added some wood to the red coals. The fire quickly started crackling and Domenico placed his hands over the stove to warm up.

Domenico said, "You boys have grown so quickly. I remember when I first met you that day by the river, you were children yet. Now, you have become young men."

We all blushed.

Domenico said, "And now, I want to help you to become men. The kind that will pursue God's given destiny holding one's honor in their heart." He looked at Dario.

40

Domenico said, "Dario, In January when school starts we are going to go to Genoa and I will introduce you to an old friend of mine, he is a professor there. You are an orphan of war and we will go and get you on their soccer team."

Dario's eyes glowed and we were all excited.

Later that evening, Elisetta's bread was ready and the scent in the house comforted us as we sat by the stove. We all enjoyed the bread and the fire, it was so cold outside, but so warm in this household. I was in deep thought and wondered what it would be like without Dario at home, we have known him almost our whole life, and then it occurred to me, he was our brother. We were all brothers. Even if life will take us in different places, we will always be brothers. And then I picked up the magazine and started to look through it.

Dario said, "Enjoy the magazine, I'm off to bed, Good Night."

I replied, "Good night brother." Domenico stood up as Dario left the room.

Domenico said, "Good Night All, I'm also tired, time for my beautiful bed."

I started to read and found an article related to the end of the war. It reflected how America would soon enter a period of prosperity and opportunity. Elisetta walked over to the stove and sat down next to me. George played a card game and did not pay any attention to us.

Elisetta said, "Marco, what are you reading?"

I looked up and said, "It's an article about the end of the war, America will be prosperous now that they have eliminated tyranny and brought peace back to the world."

Elisetta said to George, "Hey, George, come here next to us."

George looked up and walked over to us.

George asked, "What is it?"

Elisetta looked at us as if in deep thought.

Elisetta said, "I have a nephew in America, he is in the shipping industry. I wrote him about you boys when you arrived. Well, he wrote me soon after the war ended. He wanted to know if you would like to go to America. There, I said it."

41

Then she stood up folding her arms and walked over to the kitchen table. Turning her head, she looked at us. George and I looked at each other, and then looked at her. We didn't know what to say, we had talked about this and I had dreamed about it, and now that the opportunity had arrived, I was without words. Elisetta sat down again.

Elisetta said, "I had to tell you as I could not take away your opportunity if you should choose to take it. You boys think about it, you have time. Let's all go to bed, it's been a long day." In consideration of all the excitement today and Elisetta's fresh bread, I slept like a log.

Not even the roosters crow nor morning sunlight caught my attention next day. Eventually, I opened my eyes and noticed the bedroom was empty. I thought to myself, George and Dario must have woken early today. I slowly pulled myself up and made my way downstairs. Domenico and Elisetta were in the kitchen. I said, "Good morning!" They smiled.

Domenico and Elisetta replied cheerfully, " Buon Giorno!"

Elisetta offered me some toasted bread and jam and I gladly accepted. Then I asked them, "Where are George and Dario?"

Domenico replied, "George went down to Antonio's cantina to help Carlo with a large order to go out by truck to Ascoli, Dario went to L'Aquila with Antonio. They went to the Soccer club to see if they will give Dario a good reference letter in consideration of the games he had participated in last fall. It will look good for his application."

Then Domenico stood up, walked over to me.

Domenico said, "Elisetta mentioned to me this morning that she told you about her nephew Luigi in Baltimore. I know both you and George have spoken a lot of going to America, well, we have listened and I think it is a good idea for you both. You will find lots of opportunity there now that the war is over. Elisetta and I will of course miss you dearly, however, we must let go of our selfish needs."

Domenico pulled a chair over and sat down next to me.

Domenico continued, "You will learn that life places each one of us on a path, and that path will teach us many things along the way.

42

Sometimes it is difficult to understand, sometimes it seems unfair, sometimes we make mistakes, and that is okay. The important thing is we learn from them. What I have learned on my path, is that the worst mistake you can make, is not to try. You boys have dreamed of America, and you should reach for your dreams. This is your opportunity, right now, at this moment. If you don't take this chance now that you are still young, you likely never will."

My eyes teared a bit while I listened to Uncle Domenico, I knew he was right in what he said. In this moment, I felt I did not want to go far away, and I knew I would miss this loving home. And for the first time in my life, I felt I belonged to a loving family, the kind I would never leave. I stood up, and then Domenico stood up and we embraced each other with open arms. I said, "Uncle Domenico, I Love you." Domenico was also emotional.

Domenico replied, "Thank you son, I love you too."

Elisetta wiped her tears with her handkerchief. I walked over to her and we embraced as well. Then I asked Elisetta, "May I help you with anything?" Elisetta looked around the kitchen and placed her fingers on her chin.

Elisetta replied, "Marco, all of this emotional talk has made me hungry. Would you mind to help me peel some potatoes? I would like to make frittata di patate."

I smiled and replied, "Yes My dear auntie, I would love to peel potatoes!" And we cooked and prepared a meal together.

George walked in around time for pranzo, we all sat down and had some of the frittata di patate we prepared along with some fried eggs.

Domenico asked, "Hey, George, how was work this morning?"

George replied, "We worked pretty hard and loaded up the truck, lots of canned fruit and vegetables, tomato sauce and flour and dried meats going out to market at L'Aquila. They really have quite a business going there."

Elisetta replied, "We know Antonio since we are children, he has worked hard all his life, and now it will be up to Carlo to take over."

43

With a surprised look on my face, I replied, "But Carlo will come to come to America with us, how will he take care of the business?" George looked up with an excited look on his face.

George said, "America! are we really going?"

Domenico brought his hand up to scratch his forehead.

Domenico said, "Marco, George, I have also spoken to Antonio. Carlo will not be able to go. He will need to stay here and keep the business going."

Quickly I replied, "But Carlo told me he wanted to go with us."

Domenico replied while he shook his head, "I'm afraid it won't be possible. Without Carlo, that business will die. Antonio kept it alive all these years in anticipation Carlo would take it over, the entire town will suffer if he abandons the cantina."

I didn't know what to think. I felt confident to know that Carlo would come with us as he was the oldest. Now it would be only me and George.

Domenico looked at me and said, "Hey, Marco, Luigi is a very good man, he will take care of you there." Then he looked at George and said, "Both of you."

Next day I went to visit Carlo at the cantina, he had just packed up an order and said goodbye to a customer. He turned to me and I said to him, "Hey, Carlo, what are you up to?" Carlo looked over to me with a serious face.

Carlo said, "Hey, Marco. Well, I need to pack an order of groceries as usual. What are you up to?"

I replied, "Not much this morning." Then I sat on a stool by the counter and said, "Domenico told me yesterday that you are not able to join us on our trip to America." Carlo sat next to me with a look of disappointment.

Carlo replied, "Yes, this is true."

Carlo shrugged his shoulders and pouted his lips in disappointment.

Carlo continued. "I just can't, that's it."

I opened my eyes wide and replied, "Why Not? Come with us Carlo." Carlo looked at me with a serious face.

Carlo said, "Marco, you just don't understand, my uncle has taken me under his care and we have worked hard for this place since I was a child. I can't let it all go, it would hurt him a lot. And it would hurt me too."

I nodded my head and raised my hand and sighed. "I understand Carlo, I won't make it harder for you." I walked over and gave him hug." Then I stood back and said, "But I will take this opportunity, a chance to see the world and create my destiny." He looked to me with a sad face. I said to him, "Well, wish me some luck then."

Carlo smiled and said "You guys will be fine, I will come and see you off when you leave. In a way I am jealous, but I know my place is here."

On the way back home, I found George as he sat under a maple tree, he looked up to the sky in a daze. I wondered why was he there under the tree all alone. Once I got closer, he noticed me as I approached and he smiled and waved me over. As I arrived I said, "What are you doing here? Didn't you get enough sleep last night?"

George smirked and said, "Well, I guess I'm just daydreaming here in the field. I'm going to miss this place."

I became stern and said, "Now don't start with this sentimental stuff George, this is our opportunity of a lifetime and we need to take it. What are you going to do here, grow vegetables? We are young, this is our time and the world awaits us."

George looked at me with a sad face. I continued. "America is the new world and the land of opportunity, we have hope to follow our dreams there."

George looked at me and said, "You're right, I know, but I will miss this place anyway."

I looked up and noticed the maple seedlings dangling from the tree, it reminded me of being back at the orphanage when we played altogether with our friends. However, now it was different, I didn't feel like playing with them anymore. Everything in this life seems to keep changing. I wondered how our old friends were doing. Suddenly I blurted out to George and said, "Well, one thing is for sure, you have to live life before you can love life." George looked at me with an incredulous look.

George said, "I guess you're right Marco."

I gave my hand to George and said, "Come on, we need to get home and see if we have any chores."

Back at home, Elisetta was in the kitchen as she prepared some food. I smiled and greeted her, "Ciao Zia."

Elisetta replied, "Hello boys! What have you been up to? Domenico had looked for you earlier."

George said, "Oh, I'm sorry, it was my fault, I lost time around town and Marco came to look for me, and so I made us both late."

Elisetta said, "Domenico wanted to go with you to L'Aquila to get your passports ready."

My heart was filled with excitement and fear at the same time, so many emotions flowed in my veins. I looked at George and I knew he was the same way. Elisetta noticed we were a bit shaken.

Elisetta said, "What's the matter boys, you should be excited."

Then she mumbled in Italian under her breath, "Chi a il pane non a i denti."

I thought to myself, 'who has bread doesn't have teeth'. What does she mean by that?

Neither George nor I slept that night, George read his magazine and I read a book named 'White Fang'. That night I dreamt of being marooned in the arctic with George. We had no choice but to survive on our own. We hunted and fished and had a lot of fun as we made camp fires. I awoke in the middle of the night and envisioned life in America could be similar as my dream. Then I wondered what kind of job I would have, where we would live. All I know of America is what I've seen in magazines and couple of movies. Could it really be all that different from the rest of the world? Only one way to find out. Go experience it for myself.

At daybreak, we were all asleep soundly when Domenico opened our bedroom door.

Domenico said, "Time to get up boys, today we go to L'Aquila with Pietro. He needs to get some supplies and he will drop us at the passport office, he has a friend there to help us."

Then he looked at Dario.

Domenico said, "Hey, Dario. Carlo asked if you could help him out at the store today."

Dario nodded his head and agreed. I did not sleep much so I was a little slow as I moved before breakfast. After Elisetta's fried eggs and coffee, we all walked down to the piazza to meet Pietro. When we arrived, he sipped his espresso and waved to us.

Pietro said, "Are you boys excited?"

We both smiled and replied, "Yes!"

Pietro stood up and said, "Good, well, you should be, if I were younger I would go along to America for the adventure."

Then he looked at Domenico and said, "But I will leave that up to the young ones."

Domenico smiled and replied, "Speak for yourself Pietro, I am still good, I stay here only to keep company for Elisetta, otherwise I would go with them."

Pietro laughed and said, "Okay Domenico, we know of how fit you are, must be all the wine you make and drink."

Domenico looked over and said, "Exactly, finally you understand my secret."

Pietro chuckled "Si, si, certo, don't fool yourself Domenico, like it or not, noi due abbiamo chiuso le messe a San Gregorio."

Domenico frowned.

Pietro got into the truck and said, "Come on, let's all get in, we have a long day ahead of us."

George looked at me when he got in the truck and said, "What does that mean, Gregorio what?"

Domenico overheard and replied to George, "Never mind George, Pietro tries to convince me that I am an old man like him."

Domenico looked over to Pietro and said, "Look, Pietro, I'm not old, I still can make the hike of 'Il passo delle Capanelle' all the way to Teramo when I go to visit my brother's grave."

Pietro replied with his forefinger pointed upwards, "Mai lodarsi Domenico."

Domenico looked over to us and said, "He is just jealous."

We drove the countryside like we had many times before, this time it seemed different. I observed the vista as we travelled the narrow road that spiraled along the mountain crest. It seemed an infinite view of green hills topped with evergreen trees that merged into the high mountain peaks, capped with snow. One could see for many, many miles. What a beautiful place this is I thought to myself, it really shows you the hand of God, only a divine creator could form such beautiful nature.

Once we arrived at the passport office, Pietro dropped us off outside.

Pietro said, "I will meet you all here at one o'clock."

Then he looked to Domenico as we stood by the car. Pietro said, "Domenico, you need to ask for Ernesto, he already expects your arrival."

Domenico replied humbly, "Grazie Pietro."

Pietro replied, "okay fellows, See you soon, ciao."

We entered the passport office and it was a little busy, we got on the line and waited.

Domenico asked, "Would you like to have a cornetto?"

George and I replied without hesitation, "Oh yes!"

Domenico told us to wait as he went over to the espresso bar. The line moved slowly, however, soon afterwards we found ourselves closer to the receptionist. There was no sign of Domenico and we were next in the line. I remembered Pietro saying to ask for Ernesto.

The receptionist called out, "Next in line!"

George and I approached the window.

The receptionist asked, "How may I help you."

I replied, "We would like to see Mr. Ernesto, we have an appointment."

She replied, "Ernesto! You mean Mr. De Nuntiis? What is the purpose of your appointment?"

Domenico arrived and tapped me on the shoulder.

Domenico said to the receptionist "Excuse me Miss, we have an appointment with Ernesto."

She rolled her eyes and then replied, "One minute please."

She called over an assistant and instructed him to escort us to Ernesto's office. On the way, Domenico handed us a nice cornetto each. I think we needed it. I always had one when I came to L'Aquila. We arrived and the assistant knocked on the door.

We heard someone say, "Come in please."

Domenico entered first.

Domenico said, "Buon Giorno, Signor Ernesto?"

Ernesto replied, "Yes."

Domenico said, "Pietro advised me to see you."

Ernesto abruptly interrupted and said, "No need to speak further Signore Domenico, Pietro explained to me your situation, you are the father of these two boys, Marco and George. And they wish to go to America as laborers. I have everything ready here for you, just sign here."

Domenico was without words, he didn't realize Pietro had such friends with authority. Domenico signed and once we received our papers, it was one o'clock. Mr. Domenico expressed his gratitude to Ernesto.

Ernesto said, "I am happy to assist these fine young boys."

Domenico walked out of the office and we both followed.

Domenico said, "let's go meet Pietro, we need to thank him."

We made our way to the place we left off with Pietro, and he was there waiting. He had just arrived and parked the car. He opened the window and looked to us cheerfully.

Pietro said, "Well, how did it go?"

Domenico cordially replied as he grabbed both of Pietro's hands, "Dear Pietro, I can't thank you enough."

Pietro raised his hand and replied, "Basta, Domenico, how long do we know each other, lascia perdere. You are my friend a very long time. let's go have a pizza."

Pietro exited the vehicle and we all walked down to the piazza. There was a trattoria and we followed the incredible aromas coming forward. I wanted to have my favorite which was the suppli, basically a rice ball with meat ragu and mozzarella cheese in the middle that stretches out into a string until you could manage to put it in your mouth. Oh my, what a treat. We all enjoyed lunch and it was now late in the day. Pietro needed to get back to the Cantina, so we all got into the truck and made our way home. It had been a productive day and we were all tired.

We arrived back at Pietro's Stable as the sun had just set over the hilltop. Ercole chewed on some hay by his stall and the chickens had already gone to roost in their coop.

Pietro parked and said, "We are home boys, it was a busy day. Would you like to bring home some eggs for breakfast?"

We looked at Domenico. Domenico nodded as if we should thank Mr Pietro personally.

Pietro continued, "Go get them from the hen house."

George and I walked over to Pietro. Humbly I said, "Signor Pietro, you have been so very good to us, we won't forget it. One day we will come back to thank you."

Pietro shed a tear and replied, "I wish you boys all good things, go to America, embrace her and give her all you have, the Lord will reward you. All I ask is for you to remember sometimes this town and the time you spent here with us."

Domenico took Pietro's hand, and shook it with both his hands.

Domenico said, "Pietro, forgive me for earlier today, you are right, 'Mai Lodarsi'. I am old and I am still need to learn my faults."

Domenico turned to us and said, "Did you hear that boys? never laud yourselves, we are all children of the Lord and we are here to learn from our faults."

We all said our goodnights and we proceeded home. It was a quiet and cold evening. The sky was a dark blue under the moonlight, we could hear our steps as we paced the cobblestones.

Domenico said, "Hey, Boys, there is one thing Pietro forgot to mention, America was blessed by the Lord, blessed to be a home for people to live their life in Liberty. America was placed here as a gift to the people of the world, to create a balance on earth so we can all live life in freedom. Never Forget it!"

We arrived home, Elisetta and Dario were in the kitchen near the fire. We all felt the chill from the time spent outside. We all walked over to get warm.

Dario looked over at us and said, "How was your day?"

Domenico looked at George and I with a serious look.

Elisetta blurted out and said, "Did you get your passports?"

George and I at the same time without much emotion replied, "Yes, we did."

Then I said, "I'm excited and at the same time sad."

George quickly followed with "Me too."

Domenico looked to us and then at Elisetta, and then back to us as if he was confused. He took his coat off and placed it on a chair.

Domenico said. "I shouldn't admit it, but I also feel the same way. However, I also know that your emigration to America will be what you dreamed of, and this is your opportunity to do so. If you don't take advantage of this opportunity, it will pass you by. And the next opportunity may not be what your dreams envisioned."

Domenico took a deep breath and pointed his finger up.

Domenico said, "America is the new world, a land where opportunity is for the individual who is enthusiastic to work hard and use their God given talents in the way they choose to do so. It is the only country where one can be proud of their own accomplishment, a concept which has been taken away throughout history over and over by bureaucratic governments."

Then he looked down, shed a tear and said, "My brother Eliseo wanted to go to America, he loved the idea of America. Unfortunately, the Italian government took him and brought him to his early grave. I was the lucky one as I was too young to be taken into the army. Eliseo wanted to take me to America with him. But we never made it."

Domenico took his coat and walked outside. We all looked at each other with a surprised look.

Elisetta went to the door and called "Domenico! Where are you going?"

Elisetta said, "Boys, he went out to the tool shed."

She continued to look out and wait for him. I walked over to her.

Elisetta said. "He has gotten old this man of mine."

She looked worried as she knew Domenico always became sad and would go to the tool shed when he thought of his brother and his tragic death.

Dario asked, "What is wrong Zia Elisetta, do you want me to go see what he is doing?"

51

Elisetta still looked outside and replied, "No, he is okay, let's all sit down. Give him a few minutes by himself. He always goes to the tool shed when he gets sad about his brother."

Shortly after, Domenico came back and opened the door, he had something in his hand wrapped in a burlap cloth. He walked over, looked to me and unraveled the cloth.

Domenico said with a humble voice, "Marco, this is my brother Eliseo's photo when he was a young man like you."

I looked attentively at the photo.

Domenico continued and said, "This is the blessed cross our mother gave to him when he left for war."

I passed the photo to George and took the cross in my hand.

Domenico continued, "I want you to bring these to America with you and keep them with you as a memory of him and us."

We all shed tears as we observed Domenico in this sad manner. Then he went on, he showed us a medal he held in his hand.

Domenico said, "This is the medal the Italian army gave to my mom after he was killed, I will keep this with me."

I suddenly remembered these objects in the tool shed when we had first arrived here to our beloved family home. I meant to ask Domenico about them but never did. I had not paid any attention to them since. I will treasure them always. I went over to Domenico and gave him a big hug. I said, "I love you Domenico, you are the father I never had."

Domenico replied, "Thank you Marco, I love you too."

I walked over to Elisetta and hugged her as well, I said, "I love you Elisetta, you are the mother I never had and I will love you always, you have given me what I lacked in my heart and I will keep you there forever."

Dario and George walked over and we all hugged each other and smiled. It was a beautiful moment and we were all happy.

We spent the next few days as we planned our trip. Dario would be going to University of Genoa and George and I would accompany him to the University and afterwards travel by ship from Genoa as well. Carlo had offered to drive us all to Genoa in his truck. We were all outside in the field one afternoon, Dario, George, Carlo and myself.

Dario was in good spirits and said, "Hey, guys, if you meet Rita Hayworth, make sure you tell her that your soccer player brother in Italy thinks she is beautiful."

I smiled, looked to Dario and replied, "Yes Dario, I'm sure she will come right over to Genoa to give you a big kiss." We all chuckled. Carlo needed to go back to the cantina, Dario and George decided to go to the piazza with him. I took a walk out in the field to take in the view, one could see for miles from that hilltop. It was a view which gave me a sense of peace and brought my soul out to enjoy the moment as one with nature. A place where one could lose their earthly existence and truly enjoy God's gifts. Suddenly, I observed Sandro and Enzo run and play in the field, I started to walk over to them. They came over to me and wanted to play. Sandro sat on my foot. I patted them both and gave them a big hug. I would miss these guys a lot. I wish I could take them with me. My only consolation was I knew Domenico and Elisetta would have good company. I really didn't know when I would be able to come back and visit this place. However, I knew this was not the time to think about it. It was time to move forward, and so I made my way back to the house.

Chapter 4

It was the 11th of February, Dario received his official acceptance into University at Genoa. We all congratulated Dario. Elisetta made us all some sweet treats in celebration. Domenico brought home a special veal belly roast and Elisetta knew exactly how to roll it up with herbs and spices, it was a lovely family dinner. Domenico was quiet throughout the meal, once we were finished he took an envelope out of his pocket and opened it removing some paperwork.

Domenico said, "Well, boys, here we have your train tickets to Genoa."

I looked to Domenico and said, "What about Carlo? He said he would drive us there."

Domenico took a deep breath and said, "Carlo won't be able to make the trip. Genoa is very far and I don't think the truck would be able to handle the long distance."

I was disappointed, however, at the same time I was excited to go on a train.

Domenico looked at George and I and said, "you two will leave September 4th on the M/S Vulcania from Genoa. She will stop in Naples to pick up some passengers and afterwards your destination is New York. Luigi will meet you when you debark the vessel and he said he has some sponsors that will give you a place to stay until you find permanent residence. I would suggest you two stay together and help one another as much as possible. You will meet new people, some will be friends, and some will not. Remember, you two are family, not only to yourselves, but to Dario, Elisetta and I."

George became emotional and let his emotions go.

George said, "I love you, Mom and Dad, you have healed us of the pain we suffered as children, you have filled the emptiness we had in our hearts. I will miss you and this place very much, but I know Marco and I need to move on so we may become adults. You have both taught us so much and I promise we will never forget what you taught us. And we will always hold your love in our hearts."

Domenico looked to Elisetta, they smiled. Domenico walked over to George and placed his hand on his shoulder.

Domenico said, "Thank you George, you have helped us very much as well, you all have been a blessing to us."

Domenico walked over to the cabinet and opened the drawer and removed his cards.

Domenico said, "let's play some Briscola, you want to?"

We all replied excitedly "Sure, good idea!" And we played the night way.

The weeks and months passed, spring arrived and we started working the fields with Domenico. The power of nature was so incessant. A short time ago the cold of winter embodied the countryside. The ground was frozen cold, the trees were barren. It appeared as an unconsciousness of nature. Suddenly Spring rainstorms brought many beautiful flowers to the landscape of green hills flowing into blue skies. From nothing, life is born, it is the miracle of mother nature. The fortitude of summer quickly embraces the landscape, from wheat fields to thirst quenching thunderstorms bringing the essential bountiful nourishment to life. Only a divine creator could form such a nature.

Our departure date drew close and we prepared our bags to make the trip to Genoa. We would spend a few days in Genoa so Dario could get settled in at the University and we could spend some time together before the vessel made its sailing. Carlo would be able to bring us to the L'Aquila train station to see us off. Elisetta helped pack our bags, she enclosed lots of clothes and blankets and photos of her and Domenico from when they were younger. We were happy to bring them with us along with some photos of us taken around the town in the past few years. There was one of Domenico standing in front of his vineyard holding some grapes in his hand and a big smile on his face, he looked so very happy there.

August arrived and moved quickly as we boys were all anxious about the upcoming change in our lives, George seemed to be more talkative around town. He told everyone he was going to America and would become rich. Dario seemed to talk only about soccer all day long. He followed all the game scores in the newspaper every day. As for myself, I was engulfed in my own thoughts, I did not have any specific endeavors. I seemed to think constantly about our voyage on a ship across the ocean. I found it fascinating that one could travel such a long way over water to a land so far away in such a short time. Seemed to me the world was so very enormous, and yet so small.

Morning of Aug 15th we found ourselves at the L'Aquila train station. I remember Elisetta giving us all a big hug and Domenico standing with her. They both were teary eyed, and so were we three. Carlo looked sad.

Carlo said, "I'll miss you guys so much, it won't be the same around here."

Domenico looked at Carlo and said, "you need to find a girl, svegliati!"

Carlo raised his eyes while looking at Domenico.

Domenico said raising his hand, "Chi a il pane non ha I denti."

That was the second time I heard that phrase, 'who has bread doesn't have teeth', what does it mean, I thought.

Domenico looked at us with a stern look and said, "we won't see each other for a long time boys. Elisetta and I will think of you every day, make sure to write us so we know what you are up to. I am sure we will see each other again one day. We love you all, and this blessed family the good Lord provided."

Domenico wiped some moisture from his eyes.

Then he pointed his finger up towards us.

Domenico said, "Ricordatevi sempre 'Il Signore, Vede e Provede. Capisci?"

'God Sees and Provides'. I will never forget it.

We mounted the train with our bags, it was truly an emotional moment for all of us. If it wasn't for the support from Elisetta and Domenico, I don't think we could have done it. But we had to let go, and we knew it.

It was our first train ride. The train rocked and bounced more than I had anticipated. To walk around was difficult so we remained seated most of the time.

The conductor came by and announced, "Tickets please!"

We brought our tickets out and he stamped them.

The conductor said, "there is a dining car up 3 cars where you can get some snacks and drink, dinner will be served at either 5 or 6: 30 or 8 PM, which do you prefer?"

We looked at each other and picked the one in the middle.

I said to the conductor, "6:30 PM please."

The conductor wrote it down and said, "Welcome aboard boys, I see you are heading to Genoa, we will arrive there tomorrow afternoon as we will be making few stops along the way."

The conductor observed closely and said, "I see you are well behaved gentlemen. If you like, you may attend the lounge car up front and you can get some cards and play a game or read a magazine if you prefer."

We all smiled excitedly and said, " Thank you Sir."

I looked over to George and Dario and said, "what do you say, shall we play a game of cards?" George and Dario agreed and we made our way to the lounge car. It was equipped with tables and chairs and a closet where they kept games and books, there was also a magazine rack. George grabbed a deck of cards, Dario grabbed a newspaper and we all sat down at one of the tables. Quickly Dario was looking at the sport section, George dealt some cards around. I noticed a coffee pot. I asked, "anyone want a cup of coffee?"

George replied, "I would."

Dario didn't look away from the paper so I went and made two cups of coffee. Once I went back to the table, Dario looked at me with a frown.

Dario said, "don't I get one?"

I gave him my cup and said, "well, you should say something, I'm not a mind reader you know." I went back and made myself a cup. I noticed an old man as he looked at me while I walked back to the coffee table.

The old man said, "Young man, would you mind bringing me some sugar?"

I nodded, yes and brought him some sugar on the way back.

The old man said, "that's very kind of you young man, I appreciate your gesture. It's a little difficult for me to walk on the rocking train. Where are you boys going?"

I replied, "Genoa."

The old man replied, "Ah, that's also where I am going, I live in Genoa. It's a beautiful city, is it your first time there?"

I replied, "Yes, actually my brother Dario is going to attend the University."

The old man replied, "Really, I have been a professor at the University and I have retired only a few years ago. He is very fortunate to have the ability to attend there, it's an experience he will always remember."

I replied, "He wants to become a soccer player."

The old man replied, "They have a strong program for Soccer, he is going to the right place. Ask him to come talk to me later, I can give him a few pointers."

I walked back to our table with my coffee."

George looked at me and said, "Who were you talking to?"

I replied, "The gentlemen asked me to get him some sugar."

Dario said, "you were talking for a long while."

I looked at him and said, "Well, actually he is going to Genoa and told me he used to be a professor there. He said you should go talk to him as he can give you some information about the school." Dario's eves opened wide.

Dario said, "Marco, do you think he knows anything about soccer?"

I shrugged my shoulders "I don't know, I guess you can go ask him." George and I played cards, Dario continued reading his magazine. The old man walked over to us.

The old man said, "Hello young men."

I got up and asked the old man, "Please, take my seat Sir."

The old man accepted and said, "Thank you."

The old man sat down and said, "My name is Felice, whom do I have the pleasure of sitting with."

I replied, "I am Marco, this is George and Dario, my two brothers."

The old man looked at each of us and then to Dario.

He said, "Hey, Dario, Marco told me you are going to attend the University of Genoa, I used to be a professor there, I taught history."

Dario replied, "I am going to be a soccer player."

Felice replied, "I'm sure you will be a great addition to the team, and to the University. You will have many opportunities there. Will you be living at the University or staying with relatives?"

Dario replied, "I will be living at the University."

Felice replied, "Excellent."

Felice looked over to George and myself.

He said, "And you two boys, are you only accompanying your brother, or will you stay in Genoa?"

George replied, "we are going to take a ship to America."

Felice jerked back with surprised look.

Felice said, "America! Wow, on your own?

I replied, "We have some relatives that will provide us hospice."

Felice replied, "That's very nice. Well, they say America is the land of opportunity. Especially now that the war was won. I think you both are making a good choice. In any case, you are all very young, you have everything you need to make a good life. The worst thing one can do in life is not to reach for what you want."

We all nodded in agreement as we had heard that before.

Felice continued and said, "While you are in Genoa, there are many places to visit. The Palace of Doges, Piazza Matteotti, Piazza Ferrari. And George, you must go visit Palazzo San Giorgio. (pausing with a smile) And don't forget to visit Corso Italia. There is a beautiful view there and you can walk and get some fresh air and look at all the girls go by."

We all looked at each other and smiled.

George replied, "We will!"

Felice stood up and said, "Well, I'm sure we will see each other on the train again, if you need anything, don't hesitate to ask me, I will be glad to help you all."

I shook Felice's hand and said "Thank you Sir. You are very kind." and Felice walked out of the lounge car.

The day went quickly, dinner time arrived and we all arrived on time to the dinner car as we were hungry. We showed our tickets to the waitress and she showed us our table. We were so used to Elisetta that had always made dinner for us. This new experience required some adjustment. We ordered dinner and the waitress brought us some water.

Dario smiled to the waitress and said, "Thank you."

She quickly replied, "Prego" and walked away.

Dario looked at us excitedly and said, "Wow, did you see her? She is beautiful."

I looked at Dario and said, "You better calm yourself down brother, you're going to wind up married before you are 21."

Dario looked at me and replied, "Listen brother, I don't know about you, but I'm young and women are attracted to my good looks, I can't help it."

I looked at George and we laughed.

Dario smirked at us and replied, "Ridi, ridi, che mamma ha fatto i gnocchi. Non capite niente."

Dario continued, " I didn't realize it, but women find me attractive. Wait, I'll show you."

The waitress came back with our dinners, Dario could not take his eyes off her.

She looked at him and asked, "Is something wrong? Can I get you anything else?"

Dario looked at her with a smile, "Where are you from?"

She looked at George and I, rolled her eyes, and walked away."

We both chuckled at Dario. Dario grabbed his fork and knife and ate his dinner without any more words. That night we all slept to the motion of the train as it rocked back and forth. It was a little difficult, but we managed.

In the morning, after being accustomed to being rocked and bounced about, we made our way to the lounge car. Felice was there already and waved us over. We waved back and walked to him.

Felice said, "Good morning, did you all sleep well last night?"

Dario replied while he rubbed his backside, "It was a little too bouncy for me."

I interrupted and said, "Yes, it was bouncy, but I kind of like the adventure and I looked out the window often. There is so much to take in during train travel."

George replied, "It was bouncy, but it didn't bother me. It reminds me of trying to sleep in the back of a truck."

Felice laughed and replied, "That's a good one. Well, I guess I've become used to it as I've travelled by train many years now. My daughter Giulia lives in Rome and I often go to visit her. My granddaughter actually attends the University of Genoa."

Dario replied, "I have never been to Rome, I've heard it is beautiful."

Felice answered, "Well, Dario, yes, it is. Rome is named perfectly as it is a very Romantic city, full of mystical presence. Every time I go there I can feel the ancient people living and dying on that earth."

With interest I said, "I have seen many pictures of the Roman Colosseum, have you seen it?"

Felice replied, "Why yes, of course. But there is so much more, my personal favorite is the Pantheon. It is very ancient, and so mesmerizing. You really need to go visit one day, when you have time."

I went to the coffee table and made some coffee. I returned and sat down and listened as George spoke with Domenico."

George asked, "Is it true that the Aqueduct the ancient Romans built is still functional today?"

Felice replied, "Yes, it is true. It's actually amazing to see all the things that were built 2000 years ago and still in function. However, now, you two will be going to the New World. You will see many modern buildings and bridges that have been built. The American cars are a wonder of the world in itself."

George said, "I want to open a business and become rich!"

Felice answered, "Well, you are going to the right place if that is what you want to do George."

Felice looked over to Dario and said, "Dario, where are you and your brothers staying when we arrive to Genoa?"

61

Dario replied, "We will all stay at the room I will take at the University."

Felice replied, "I guess that works, if you have any problems, let me know. My granddaughter can help you as she is one of the sponsors for new students. Her name is Isabelle."

Dario replied, "Thank you."

Back home, Elisetta and Domenico were sitting in the kitchen after lunch.

Domenico said, "The boys will be arriving to Genoa in few hours."

Elisetta replied, "I miss them so much already, it is too quiet around here. Why don't we go to the Ferragosto festival in town tonight."

Domenico thought that was a good idea and agreed.

Domenico said, "I'm going to walk to town and see what is going on. Do you need anything?"

Elisetta replied, "No, just come back in time to take me to the festival."

Domenico replied, "I will dear, I just need to stretch my legs a bit."

Later in the evening, Elisetta and Domenico were at the festival talking to friends. Elisetta visited a stand where a young woman was selling soaps and trinkets.

Elisetta asked the young woman, "Where are you from?"

The young woman replied, "I am from L'Aquila. My father makes soaps of all kinds and I am here promoting his product."

Elisetta smiled and replied, "How nice, and what is your name?"

The young woman replied. "I am AnnaMaria."

Elisetta replied, "That's a pretty name. It's very nice to meet you, I will walk around now and visit you later."

Elisetta waved goodbye and walked back to Domenico. She grabbed his arm.

Elisetta jovially said, "And what are you up to young man."

Domenico looked away from her and replied, "Oh, I am looking for my girlfriend.

Then Domenico turned to Elisetta and said, "Oh, here you are Elisetta!"

She laughed at him and said, "Domenico, you will never change. Where is Carlo, I have something to show him."

Domenico looked around and replied, "Last time I saw he was in front of the store as he prepared sausages for the festival."

Elisetta made her way to the store and found Carlo.

Elisetta said, "Hey, Carlo, what are you doing? still at work?"

Carlo frowned and replied, "Yes, I work too much, sometimes I am not sure why."

Elisetta smiled and replied, "Oh Carlo, my dear boy. Take a break and have a little fun, come with me. I will speak to Antonio if he has anything to complain about."

Carlo took off his apron and shrugged his shoulders.

Carlo replied, "You are right, I need a break."

Elisetta smiled and replied, "Let's go."

They started to walk and Carlo quickly commented, "There sure are a lot of people here this year. This town seems to be growing."

Elisetta replied, "Yes, our village has become famous."

Carlo, looked around and replied, "Yes, it does seem so, although I think I liked it better before."

Elisetta took Carlo by the elbow and said, "Carlo, in life, everything changes. You need to adapt to the change and enjoy the challenge."

Carlo asked, "Elisetta, where are you taking me, we seem to be wandering away from the road."

And then his eyes locked on to a young lady.

Elisetta smiled and greeted AnnaMaria, "Hello AnnaMaria, have you made any sales with this big crowd?"

AnnaMaria replied, "Well, a little, maybe I need to change the display arrangement."

Carlo stared at AnnaMaria in silence.

Elisetta looking at Carlo said, "Carlo, this is AnnaMaria from L'Aquila, why don't you help her arrange these soaps so people will notice them more."

AnnaMaria looked at Carlo with her big brown eyes and said, "Oh, would you mind, that would be so helpful."

Carlo bashfully replied, "hum, well, yes, I think I can try."
AnnaMaria quickly replied, "Oh, thank you so much, please come here with me so I can show you what I have for sale back here."

Elisetta quietly slipped away.

Before the night was over, Carlo had all kinds of soaps at his store on display for sale and people really enjoyed the different scents. A lot of sales were being made, and Carlo seemed very cheerful suddenly. At the end of the evening, Elisetta walked over to Carlo and AnnaMaria with Domenico.

Elisetta said, "Hello kids, looks like you had a good night."

AnnaMaria replied, "Actually yes, it was much better than I had anticipated, Carlo was so nice to help me and he agreed to sell some of our products in his store."

Domenico looked to Carlo and said, "Bravo Carlo, you have made a good decision. Why don't you accompany AnnaMaria home, it's late at night and a beautiful young woman should not be traveling alone."

Carlo looked seriously to Domenico and replied, "Yes, you are right Signor Domenico, I will get the truck and drive her to her home."

Domenico smiled to Elisetta and said, "Well my young lady, may I accompany you home as well."

Elisetta blushed and replied, "Andiamo Domenico, show me the way my handsome man."

Carlo locked up the store and opened the truck door for AnnaMaria. They drove out of the piazza slowly and waved goodbye. The festival night closed on a happy note.

Chapter 5

The conductor came around and announced, "Genoa Station, we will arrive in 20 minutes." I looked out the window and could see the beautiful city in the distance. I had never seen a large city like this one, we were high up on a hilltop and I could see the sea behind the city, the Ligurian sea. It was my first experience of boundless water. It appeared vast, and so blue, I was captivated by the view. I felt another world appeared before me, a mystical world that projected beauty and peacefulness, yet so intense and restless. I could see the blue expanse as it undulated gently, and then changed its form as its ripples crashed onto the rocky slopes of its boundaries. It appeared alive and eternal, I was allured by its enchantment.

As we made our approach to the station, I grabbed my bags and went to the lounge car. Dario was at the coffee bar as he chatted with the waitress from last night. I noticed George as he sat with Felice and I walked over to them.

Felice looked to me smiling and said, "Good Morning. You are late!"

I smiled back and replied, "Well, the train rocked me to sleep and I think I kind of enjoy train travel. I wish maybe we could ride a little longer."

Felice replied, "That is a good thing young man, you are going to cross the Atlantic Ocean and I'm sure you will enjoy being rocked as you travel on your ship."

I sat down and looked out the window. I pondered briefly about how large the Atlantic Ocean is, and I tried to imagine it in my thoughts. Then I said, "Mr. Felice, I was looking at Genoa this morning from the window earlier, what a beautiful city on the sea."

Felice nodded and replied, "Yes Marco, it is very beautiful, I have lived here most of my life and I will never leave her. It's a beautiful place where the land meets the sea, to me it's a door between two worlds and my imagination."

The train slowed down to a crawl, we pulled into the station.

Felice stood up and said, "Well fellows, this is it. I suppose you will take the bus to the University now?"

George and I also stood up. I replied, "Yes, that is the plan Sir."

Felice replied, "Well, it's very easy, and not very far. I will be taking a different bus as I need to go to the other side of town. Remember to ask for Isabelle once you get there if you need assistance, tell her you met me on the train."

We all shook hands, and I said, "It was very nice to meet you Mr. Felice, you are very kind."

Felice smiled to us and said, "Thank you for the company, your parents should be proud to have raised such gifted and educated young men."

George looked to me first, and then he replied, "Yes, Mr. Felice, we were very blessed to have wonderful parents."

Felice left the car. I looked over to Dario who still flirted with the coffee bar attendant. I shouted, "Dario, hello!! We are in Genoa and it's time to leave the train."

Dario gave us a quick look and raised his hand to acknowledge us and said, "Okay, just a minute." He said his goodbye to the girl and followed us off the train.

It was sunny with a chilly wind, although it was the middle of August. It was strange at first to be on firm ground after being rocked constantly on the train. It felt good to be out in the open air and I took a deep breath.

Dario came over smiling and said, "She gave me her phone number!"

I replied, "And so, what will you do with it Casanova, she probably gave you the wrong number to get you to leave."

Dario answered quickly, "Well, that's for me to know and you to dream about."

George pointed to the bus and said, "Okay guys, let's stop with this nonsense and get on the bus before it leaves."

We hurried over to the bus and asked the driver, "Will you take us to Genoa University on this bus."

The driver nodded and said, "Yes, please pay the fare and board the bus to the left, thank you."

We proceeded and sat down. George read a magazine he brought off the train.

George said, "Marco, before we leave, I want to visit the Palazzo San Giorgio."

And then he showed me a picture. It was a beautiful medieval building and it seemed interesting.

Dario looked over smirking and said, "I guess."

George replied quickly, "It's a beautiful building."

The bus started to move, and the driver announced, "We will travel to the port industrial zone for our first stop and then onto Genoa University. We will be at the first stop in few minutes."

Within a few minutes, we could already see the sea at a distance. I was very excited as I wanted to see it face to face.

George pointed again to his magazine and said, "We should go see the Porta Soprano and the house where Christopher Columbus grew up."

I looked over to his magazine and said, "Well, George, that does look interesting."

The driver announced, "We will arrive to the industrial zone shortly, whomever is getting off the bus, please make sure to take your belongings. Thank you."

Few people stood up and quickly got off, they all worked in the port industrial area. I wondered what their duties were. Did they unload ships, did they sail the vast ocean's. Seemed to be an interesting place to work with vessels from around the world that arrived and departed almost every day.

The bus started to move again and the driver announced, "Next stop will be Genoa University, if you look to your left you can see the famous Corso Italia."

It looked like a really nice place to take a long walk along the shore. We were all so busy as we looked in every direction, there was so much to see in this area. I looked to the sea, and I thought of what Columbus envisioned and his courage to make the voyage over the unchartered ocean. The world became a lot smaller once Columbus found America. Imagine to live in a world where you really weren't sure of how big or how small it was, or to know if it was round or flat. Columbus discovered a whole new world to be explored. Those must have been exciting adventurous times.

The driver pointed to the right and said, "If you look to the right, you will see the Palazzo San Giorgio, it was built around 1260 and has its roots going back to Constantinople. It was used as a prison at one time and its famous for the imprisonment of Marco Polo. He was held prisoner of war there during the war between Venice and Genoa at the time. He wrote his famous book while imprisoned, 'The Travels of Marco Polo'."

I was awestruck, my mind was invigorated like it had never been before. This city is truly magical, First Columbus, now Marco Polo. This is the reason I was mesmerized on the train this morning. This city is a crossroads of adventure and inspiration, and here our adventure was about to begin.

We arrived at the University, it was a city unto itself comprised of many buildings. I was fascinated by its proximity to the port and the beautiful view of the open sea. I could see a light house tower across the harbor, it seemed very tall. I wondered if we could go visit it and go to the top to see the view from there. Dario was looking at the University as he tried to understand which building we should go to. We all looked at each other.

Dario pointed at a courtyard with a gated archway and said, "Let's go in there."

So we picked up our things and made our way. Once we entered the building we were quite amazed. The interior was quite majestic. Nothing like we had ever seen, so much marble and statues and the highest ceilings I've ever seen with a grand staircase and tremendous windows. This was a royal palace. Quietly we made our way to an office, there was a young man behind a desk as receptionist.

Dario asked, "Hello, I am a new student and I wanted to report myself present and find my dormitory room."

The receptionist asked, "Do you know which faculty you were assigned to?"

Dario replied, "I am here to join the soccer team."

The receptionist replied, "I see. Well, you are in the wrong building."

Dario replied, "Do you know where I should go?"

The receptionist pointed out the door, "Go to the information center across the square near the entrance and I think they will help you better."

Dario replied, "Oh, okay, sorry to trouble you then, thanks for your help."

Quickly I interrupted, "He was told to see Isabelle, do you know her?"

The receptionist was surprised and replied, "You know Isabelle? So why didn't you go see her first, she is upstairs."

The receptionist stood up and pointed out to the grand hall, and said, "Go up the staircase, it is the second room to your right."

Dario looked relieved, we were all a little tired from our trip. We started to walk towards the stairs, then I turned around to the receptionist and said, "Is there a rest room I can use here?" The receptionist raised his eyebrows and pointed to a hallway behind a column. And we followed route to the rest room.

Once inside Dario asked, "Was he a little annoyed with us."

I replied, "Who knows, he seemed to get upset when I mentioned Felice's granddaughter. let's go see if we can find her. Hopefully she can help us out."

George looked over and said, "Yes, and hopefully we can get something to eat! I'm starved."

We headed for the grand staircase, didn't even look at the fellow in the office. There were two majestic lions at the entrance of the staircase railing. Going up I noticed all the columns, the craftsmen that built this place where in a league of their own. Considering how ancient this building was, these people were truly ahead of their time.

We walked over to the second room on the right, Dario knocked on the door. We heard a sweet voice "Come in." Dario walked in first and we followed, at first glimpse, we didn't see anyone. We looked around, and then the young woman walked in quickly from another attached room. My eyes met with the girl and I was bewildered, I couldn't quite put my finger on it. I felt I knew her.

Dario shouted, "Isabelle!!" She looked at us, one by one, we stared at each other for few seconds.

Isabelle pinched herself on the cheek and said, "Am I dreaming? Dario, Marco, George! How did you find me? Oh my, you have grown so much!"

We were all without words.

Isabelle said, "Last time we saw each other was…"

She paused and then said, "We were kids, in that awful orphanage."

She paused again and said, "You guys disappeared one day, they told us you were captured by the Nazi's and they took you away."

Some tears came to her eyes, and she continued, "We all thought you were killed."

Without speaking, we all stood up and made a group hug, we all shed tears of emotion together. Once we got ourselves somewhat under control, I walked over to a couch in the room and sat. George followed, and then Dario. Isabelle sat as well.

Isabelle put her hands on her lap, looked at us, and said,

"I still can't believe this is real, how did you find me?"

Dario looked at Isabelle and replied, "We met your uncle Felice on the train, he told us to ask for you when we were on the train, but we did not know it was you, until now."

Isabelle looked even more confused and said, "You know my Uncle? You didn't know it was me. why are you here?"

Dario said, "I will be attending the university."

Isabelle replied, "That is wonderful! What will you study?"

Dario proudly answered with a grin, "I will attend as a soccer player"

Isabelle replied excitedly, "Really! that's great."

Then Isabelle looked at George and I and said, "George, Marco, will you also attend the school?"

And we nodded no. Then George said, "We are going to America, I am going to work hard, and become rich."

Isabelle was surprised and said, "America? , it's so far away, why don't you stay here?"

Then she walked over to the closet and grabbed her coat

Isabelle said, "Well, I will end work early today. I will ask Daniel to take over for me, we have much to talk about and I have to show you your dormitory room."

We grabbed our belongings and walked down the stairs.

Isabelle walked over to the receptionist we first met and said, "Daniel, I am leaving early today, I met some old friends and we have a lot to catch up on, please handle my duties for the remainder of the day."

Daniel looked at us scornfully, and then nodded, "Yes Miss Isabelle, absolutely."

Isabelle guided us to the dormitory, it was a large complex of several ancient buildings. It looked like they had been built centuries ago on what had been used as docks for the trade ships of those ancient times and situated on a canal which led to the sea. Our room was on the top, or 4th floor, so we carried our bags all the way up. We were all extraordinarily astonished by the day's events and we all agreed to get some rest. We decided to meet up the next day and catch up on our several separated years of existence. We said our goodnights and shared some hugs. What a wonderful day it had been.

I watched the sunrise next morning as I peered through the window. I wondered how many sailors had crossed this place over the centuries. As my consciousness awoke, I recalled Isabelle had said she would meet us outside around 8 in the morning. She said she would take us to get breakfast at the cafeteria where she normally went before her duties. I woke the guys up and we did not waste any time to make our way to the University main building where we had met yesterday. As we approached the building, we saw her at the entrance outside of the gated columns. She smiled and waved to us, and we all did the same in return.

Isabelle said, "Did you all sleep well?"

I replied, "I think we were all so tired that we didn't even realize we were at the University of Genoa dormitory."

Dario continued and said, "The sound of the waves crashing on the rocks was a little hard to get used to, but I slept well."

I looked at him incredulously and said, "Sure beats the sound of the train whistle as we bounced and rocked over the rail bumps." Dario smiled.

George replied, "When I did fall asleep, I dreamed that I was in America and I owned my own shipyard."

We all laughed at that one.

Isabelle waved us on, pointed towards the cafeteria and said, "Well friends, let's go get some breakfast, I am hungry."

George quickly replied, "Now I'm awake, let's go."

We walked into the main entrance through the arched gates, Daniel was sitting in his office and Isabelle walked over to him.

Isabel said, "Daniel, I'm taking my friends to breakfast, please cover my duties while I'm out. I will be gone most of the day."

Daniel stood up and replied, "Certainly Miss Isabelle."

And then he sat down again. She walked away and he turned to us with a frown. I don't think he liked us much. The cafeteria was in another area behind the building. We all followed Isabelle and made our way over. I started to notice the scent of some cooking, and it seemed appetizing.

Isabelle walked straight to a table and said, "We will sit here, you may go over to the buffet table. There is some focaccia and some cheeses and hard-boiled eggs, oh, and we also have some really nice cappuccino."

We all went over and filled our plates and a cappuccino cup. This was nice!

At the table, Isabelle looked to me and said, "Hey, Marco, you have met my grandpa Felice?"

I answered, "Yes, he is a very nice man, he was so very nice to us on the train."

She replied, "I was adopted less than a year after," she paused a moment, "after you went missing."

And with a sad face she continued, "they told us you were killed."

Isabelle took a deep breath, and said, "I was kind of in shock for a long time, you guys were my family there. I had a difficult time without your company in that place. Until, one day when I was fortunate enough to have been blessed with being adopted. By my

Mom Giulia. You have not met her. She is so wonderful to me, such a kind heart. I thank God all the time for his blessing."

I replied, "Well, we also received a blessing. Perhaps with a little adventure along with the blessing. We did get captured by Germans. They took us onto their truck with other prisoners. We were lucky to have found a soldier with a soft heart."

Dario interrupted and said, "Perhaps a guilty heart, it was his gun that got us into that mess."

Isabelle took a deep breath and said, "A gun! oh no! where did the gun come from?"

George answered that one and said, "Well, I found it by a bush, when I went to go pee."

Isabelle with her eyes wide open replied. "So you found a soldier's lost gun, and then they went looking for the gun and found you."

We all nodded and I said, "Exactly."

She was almost scolding us and said, "You could have been killed, you should never have left the convent, you knew it was dangerous."

I replied. "Well, I'll take the blame for that one. I guess I owe my friends here a lot. I put us all in danger."

George looked to me and said, "No Marco, it was not your fault. You didn't know I would find a gun in the bushes."

Dario continued and said, "And I could have said no, I don't want to go with you to the river. But that day, I agreed to go. And besides, look how it turned out."

Isabelle looked to Dario and said, "So what happened after the soldiers took you away?"

Dario replied, "Well, like Marco was saying, they put us on a truck with prisoners. The soldier that had lost the gun was also in the back with us on guard duty."

Then I interrupted and said, "His name was Patrik."

Dario said in surprise, "It was?"

I replied. "Yes, he told me his name before he was going to throw me off the truck, but I just jumped after you guys rolled down that hill."

George said, "You never told us his name."

I replied, "Yes, at the time I didn't think of it much, I was more concerned with sour survival, and everything moved so quickly, It didn't seem important at the time."

Isabelle seemed stunned, then she said. "Patrik told you his name because he wanted you to remember him as the one that saved your life."

I replied, "Yes, and I still remember that moment and his face, because I know that now. If he hadn't been in the back of the truck with us, we most likely would not be here with you today."

We all let out a deep breath and sat in silence a minute. Then George started to eat.

George said while chewing, "Hey, this Focaccia, it's really good!"

We all smiled.

Isabelle said, "Yes, try to put some blue cheese on it, and some walnuts. It's really good."

We all listened to her suggestion. She was absolutely correct. With cappuccino, it all goes very well together.

Our time together in Genoa moved very quickly. Isabelle showed us around the city. We visited a lot of places, starting with the home of Columbus and his family. From there the prison of Marco Polo, and of course the Corso Italia where everyone goes to enjoy and socialize by the seaside. My personal favorite was the Faro di Genoa, or the Lighthouse of Genoa. It kind of sticks out on the Genoa skyline as it is the tallest structure around. It has a large cross half way up on the outside, and the building has seen a lot of historical events since it was built originally about 1000 years ago. It has been through invasions, reconstruction and imprisonments. I had decided to go to see the top, it was a long way up. What I was most impressed with was a carved marble stone along the way up, its been there for centuries. It says in Latin, 'Christus rex venit in pace et Deus Homo factus est', (Jesus Christ king came in peace, and God became Man). I think it says a lot.

The view from the top was quite spectacular. One can see the curvature of the earth along the horizon, where the sea meets the sky. The ancient people thought it marked the end of the world, although it turned out it's actually just the beginning. Today we take this knowledge for granted. Lesson for mankind, always question the unknown and never fear it.

Chapter 6

September had arrived and the cool crisp air had changed the colors of nature. The trees in the surrounding hills glistened in the sun with hues of orange, yellow and red. This time of the year had become my favorite. Isabelle, George and I were at the soccer field watching Dario kick soccer balls as he trained with some other members of the team. I have to admit, he was very good at this sport. He was built to be a soccer player. Thin and nimble, and most important, very agile.

Isabelle was enjoying looking at the guys play.

Isabelle said while watching, "Marco, when is the ship coming into port?"

I turned to her and said, "We are supposed to depart Sept 4th, so it should be soon."

Isabelle looked at me and said, "Normally they arrive in a day or two before they leave, what is the name of the vessel?"

I replied, "It is the Vulcania."

Excitedly she replied, "Oh, I remember that one, it was here for some time last year as it was being reconditioned here. Afterwards they travelled to South America I was told. But, you are not going to South America, correct?"

Quickly I replied, "No, we are going to New York."

She said, "That's funny, I guess they changed the transit route. Imagine how many places that vessel has seen. I was told that it once belonged to an American company and they transported American troops during the war with it."

I was surprised and replied, "Really? that is very interesting." I looked to George and said, "Hey, George, now we can say we have been on a ship that American soldiers travelled on." We both smiled, and then I said, "I will write a letter to Domenico and Elisetta tonight and mention that to them, I'm sure Domenico will find it interesting."

Isabelle replied, "I would like to meet your parents one day, they must be very special people."

George replied, "Yes, they are. Very much so. I do miss them already."

I looked to George and said, "They are still with you George, we will now travel on an adventure that we will remember and tell stories to our children one day about it. We will see our parents again, sooner than you think."

Isabelle replied with a serious look and said, "Marco, you are very mature for your age, you have a lot of insight on life at a very young age."

I replied, "I hope that's a good thing." We all laughed.

Then I said, "Isabelle, it's almost surreal to see you again, now as a woman. Although many years have passed, it's almost as if it were yesterday that we played together. Only, now we are all grown up." I paused and then I added "Almost as if the lost time did not exist."

That night I began to feel some anxiety as to the arrival of the Vulcania. Once the sun peeked over the horizon the following morning, I walked over to the balcony and looked out to sea. A large ship approached in the distance. She had one large smoke stack and two masts. The waves vanished under her bow as she glided into the harbor. Our ship had come in and I was eager to see her. I quickly got myself dressed.

George looked at me and said, "Where are you going? It's still dark out."

Excitedly I replied, "Our ship arrived to port, come and see with me."

George laid back to bed and said, "I will come later after the sun rises and the normal people are about. Please close the lights when you leave."

I continued out the door and walked briskly to the harbor. I walked over to the berth and waited. It seemed to take forever, and then suddenly I spotted the ship as it approached. I could read Vulcania on the forward side. As she pulled in, I was amazed by the size of this vessel. Out at sea it looked a lot different than when I stood by her side. It was amazing to me that she was made entirely from steel, and yet managed to float on water. I studied the ship and counted about 7 or 8 levels, it was like a floating city. As she approached the berth very slowly, the dock men came out to portside. The crew threw large ropes over the side and they quickly managed to tie her down. The mooring ropes were very large, it took several men to carry them and hook them onto the mooring cleats. I observed every step and I was very absorbed in their procedures. When they were done, the men walked back towards where I stood.

One of them looked at me and said, "What are you doing here at this hour of the morning young man. If you need a job, go see the dock master back at the terminal office."

I was kind of surprised, then I replied. "Oh, well, actually I will travel onboard the vessel when it sails."

The man replied, "Really, you're going to New York, that's a good idea. There will be plenty of jobs available at that side of the pond."

And he just kept on walking. The pond he said, he must have crossed it a few times to call it a pond. I didn't know what I would encounter on the other side of this pond. However, since I arrived at this city, I was intrigued by the sea. I wanted to explore the worlds horizons and see the places I could not even imagine should I have chosen to settle down in one place on land.

Later in the evening, all four of us took a walk to see the ship. We stopped at a bench and sat.

Isabelle looked to George and said, "Are you ready George?"

George replied, "Yes, I've dreamt about America a long time now, it's time to go and see for myself. Besides, what else is there to do."

Isabelle smiled, looked at me and said, "And you Marco, how are you feeling about it?"

I thought about it a bit and replied, "I have always read and heard from other people about America, Domenico spoke very highly about America and what America has to offer. I am certainly curious to go there. For the moment, I think I have more passion to board this ship and to cross this vast sea. To think this ship can travel all over the world as it floats over water allures me."

Dario looked at me and said, "Yes, but you are only traveling a short time and then you will be in New York."

I replied, "Yes, well, one step at a time. For the moment, I will experience to cross this sea into another world, a new world."

Isabelle replied almost blushing and said, "Marco, you are very romantic."

I replied with surprise, "I am?"

Dario pointed to me, looked at Isabelle and said, "Him?"

I think he was jealous. Isabelle and Dario seemed to get along quite nicely since they met, visibly more than friends. We said our goodbye's and promised to write once we arrived at New York. Dario and Isabelle needed to attend class tomorrow morning, so George and I would go to the ship on our own. I asked Dario to write Elisetta and Domenico and let them know everything was well.

Morning of September 4th arrived, George and I arrived with our belongings to be loaded onto the vessel. We were 3rd class passengers so we were placed on the lower deck. We did have a window in our cabin, although it was indeed quite a small space. The window was not very high off the water, so we could not see much. It didn't bother us, we were happy to be on this beautiful ship, and we did not plan to spend a lot of time in the cabin. Once we settled in we made our way to the main deck, we observed the large smokestack. It was painted red at the top, a white ring to follow and then a blue ring underneath. It looked quite regal. Suddenly we heard a loud horn.

And then a loudspeaker announced, "Good morning ladies and gentlemen, this is Captain Alessandro, welcome aboard the Vulcania. This vessel has recently been reconditioned and I hope you will enjoy her accommodations. The vessel is 633 feet long and weighs 24000 tons, in consideration of these factors, the vessel is capable of a maximum speed of 21 knots. This will be the first voyage of a new service route to New York. We will stop in Naples tomorrow morning to pick up some passengers, and then onward to the strait of Gibraltar where we will stop briefly to let off a few passengers for transfer by shuttle to Morocco. After that it is non-stop open ocean until New York, you will briefly see some islands soon after Gibraltar, they are the famous Canary Islands. For the time being, the weather forecast is fair and the winds are in our favor, we should reach New York on schedule September 12th early morning. I wish you all a wonderful voyage. If you have any questions, please ask an attendant for assistance. Thank you."

During the announcement, we noticed the ship started moving. It was interesting as we could not really hear the engines. However, we did indeed move, we could see we pulled out of the berth. George and I went forward and had a look, there were two tugboats that pulled and pushed and turned the vessel. They must have been pretty powerful tugboats to move a 24,000 ton vessel I thought. Once we were towed out toward the harbor exit, I could see the smoke and hear the engines. The tug boats let go of the ropes and slowly followed us out. The wind started to blow as we passed the lighthouse, I quickly recalled my visit. The view was much different from the sea to the harbor. In a short time, we were out in open sea. I noticed the waves were a little larger, however, the ship was quite steady. I had imagined it would rock more than this. It quickly became a little chilly.

George said, "Why don't we go inside, it's a little too windy here."

I agreed and replied, "Okay, let's go get some warmer clothes." On the way to our cabin, we found the 3rd class lounge and we stepped in to look it over. It seemed nice enough to sit for a while and get some coffee and cake. George walked over to a magazine rack and picked out a magazine, he walked back and sat next to me.

George said, "Wow, she is beautiful."

I looked over, he had a magazine named 'Movieland' with the face of a beautiful movie star on the cover. I said to him, "Who is it?"

He turned to me and said, "Her name is Lauren Bacall."

I got up and walked to the bookshelf while he admired his magazine. I looked through a few books and one stood out to me, 'Robinson Crusoe'. It had lots of illustrations of ships and sailor men. I brought it back with me and started to read. Right from the start I was absorbed.

I found myself contented by the gentle motion of the ship as it rocked, it was a gentle movement from forward to aft. Together with my newly found adventure book, I was absorbed in my own new world. I did not notice that the sun was about to set as I was so absorbed with my book. George came to me and nudged me on the shoulder.

George said, "Hey, are you still with me? You haven't gotten up in few hours now."

I gazed at him briefly and then placed my book down. I said, "Sorry, I didn't realize the time, this is a good book."

George pointed to the door and said, "Come on, let's go take a walk up on the main deck, I need some air."

At first I hesitated, then I said, "Okay, but it will be windy, the sun is about to set down now."

Excitedly George replied, "Let's go watch the sunset."

It seemed like a good idea, so I replied, "That's a good idea George, our first sunset at sea, let's make our way starboard." George looked at me funny as we walked out.

George said, "Huh, make our way where?"

I shook my head in frustration and said, "Never mind George, just follow me."

Once we made our way out to the main deck, we could see a lot of people around as they enjoyed the sea air. It was not so windy on the starboard side as the winds blew in from the east. We found a clear spot where we could see the sun making its final peak at our section of the world for this day. Our first day at sea as we began a new life. I noticed the sun's gleam on the open sea pointing out as if leading a path, a path the ship did not follow. I wondered what may lie in the lighted path. As the sun lowered, its color became more orange and you could feel the warmth of the sun diminish as it slowly vanished over the horizon. George embraced himself with his arms together.

George said, "Let's go in now, I'm cold."

I agreed and we went inside, it was dinner time.

That night back at the room, I was lying in my bunk, my book in hand. The ship gently rocked me into my comfort zone and I was absorbed with *Robinson Crusoe* on his island of survival. I tried to imagine what it would be like to find myself alone on a deserted island. I was fascinated at the power of his ability to think and his perseverance to survive and make his life comfortable, although he was all alone. He was a determined man, ready to face any of life's challenges. I decided I wanted to be like him. There was a knock at the door, it was George.

George said, "Hey, Marco, what are you up to here all alone?"

With a destitute stare I replied, "I am going to go to sleep."

George replied in an energetic fashion, "Sleep? Our first night at sea and you want to sleep? Come on, there is a party at the third-class lounge."

At first I was hesitant, then I said, "I don't know George, I was already half asleep, you go on without me. I don't mind."

George insisted and said, "Come on, there are a lot of interesting people there and we are all destined to the same place. We may as well make some friends."

He talked me into it, so I put on some clothes and went with him to third class lounge. It was very crowded compared to what it was like earlier in the day. I guess people all come out at night around here. George walked over to a table with a few people and waved me on, I followed.

George put his hand on my shoulder and said, "This is my brother Marco."

I smiled and said, "Nice to meet all of you."

One man raised his hand and said, "I am Giulio."

Another man at the table replied, "Marco, Nice to meet you, I am Armando, are you two young men on this voyage alone?"

I replied, "Yes, we are on the way to New York to meet some family members."

Giulio replied, "Will you stay in New York or will you travel further?"

I thought about it a little and replied, "For the moment we will stay in New York, we have our accommodations in place."

Giulio replied, "That's good, just thought I would let you know that if you seek employment, there are plenty in Cleveland. That is where we are destined, we will be welders for the railroad company."

George replied, "That sounds kind of dangerous."

Armando replied, "Well, you do need to have some skill, or you can blow yourself and your friends up into pieces."

We all laughed.

George replied, "For the time being, we are going to work at the New York harbor terminal, most likely we will unload ships."

Giulio replied, "That's a good job, you can move on from there quickly."

Armando interrupted and said, "Let's go get a snack, I see lots of goodies there."

We all followed and enjoyed the feast. There was American music that played from the loudspeakers and people shared some of their homemade wine they brought from their homes. I thought to myself that Domenico would have liked to try some, and I wondered how he and Elisetta were back home. I had not seen them in quite a while now. I thought I should write them a letter during the trip so I can mail it off as soon as we arrive to New York. I felt a little guilty that I did not miss being back home. Every day was like a new adventure since we left and I enjoyed it. I finally realized that the world has lots to offer, and I was eager to see more.

I slept soundly that night until the sunlight peered through our porthole window and I noticed the ship was motionless. I got up and looked outside and noticed we already had docked. George had already left and I wondered how long I was asleep. I quickly put myself together and made my way out. I stopped at the 3rd class lounge, and I noticed Giulio was there. I went over to him and said, "Giulio, good morning, have you seen George?"

Giulio replied, "Good morning, Marco. Yes, I did, he had breakfast earlier and said he was going up to main deck. We are at Naples!"

I replied, "Yes, I see that, I slept all throughout the morning as we docked."

Giulio pointed to the food table and said, "That's too bad, you must have been tired. Well, go get some breakfast before they take it away."

I went over and grabbed some eggs and potatoes while Giulio read his newspaper. I went back over and sat down with him.

Giulio asked, "How do you like travel by vessel?"

With my fork and knife in hand I replied, "Well, yesterday was my first day, and I have to say I really like it."

Giulio looked at me with a dubious look and said, "Well, this is my fourth trip across the Atlantic. When the weather is nice like this, yes, it is nice. However, if you find a storm squall, things can change rapidly. One time, we found 20-foot waves. Believe me, the ship rocked intensely, some people can handle it, and some cannot."

I looked at him, took in a mouthful and thought about that a bit. It didn't seem to scare me. This ship was so big and strong, I don't think some 20-foot wave could do much to it.

Giulio continued and said, "We are in early September, we still have time before the rough weather season arrives."

I finished my breakfast and I said, "Recently I have considered to enroll as a ship worker, I like the idea of travel and to experience different places around the world."

Giulio smiled and replied, "You are an adventurer! Good for you. You should have your adventures now that you are young. Once you are older, we all settle down into similar situations."

I asked him, "Mr. Giulio, are you married?"

With a disenchanted face as he looked in my eyes and he replied, "Am I man? Are men all fools? Yes, I am married. I took a wife, I brought forth children and bought us all a home. The whole calamity!"

I looked at him and could not come up with anything to reply.

Giulio continued, "This is the reason I go to Cleveland. I have come back and forth to America. This is my fourth trip. Each time I go home, I ask my wife to come to America with me. She always refuses."

Then I replied, "That must be difficult to be away from your family."

He looked at me with stern eyes and said, "Listen to me, marriage, you won't understand until it's too late. Make sure you pick the right woman. One that understands you and thinks like you, and most importantly, respects you."

I looked at him and pretended to comprehend, although I really had no thoughts about marriage at this time of my life. Otherwise, I would have stayed back in L'Aquila and settled down selling produce or something. I felt a yearning to seek out and find that which would enlighten my life. I don't know what it was I sought, but I knew it was not back in L'Aquila. So I changed the subject and said, "Giulio, have you ever been to Naples?"

Giulio replied, "Yes, it's very beautiful. Well, we are here today, you should go outside and have a look around. You won't see too much around here, but there are many beautiful old buildings and castles and churches. This is an ancient city with lots of history."

I replied, "Yes, it does look very interesting from here, I will come back one day. Perhaps once I have a position as a crewmember on board a shipping vessel.

The ships horn blew, I got up and walked to the window. I could see we had started off as the ship glided off the berth. I waved off to Giulio and made my way to main deck. There were many people that looked over the railing and waved to onlookers on shore. People always seem to be warm and emotional when a ship leaves port, it's both a good feeling, and sometimes sad at the same time. I was at sea only a short time and already I sense that once you are at sea, you seem to be in a world all its own. A place where one can lose their burden and enjoy the moment one creates. We drifted away from Naples, and I knew I would not see her again for long time. I waved and smiled. I felt a tap on my shoulder, it was George.

George said, "What are you waving at?"

I smiled at him and said, "Well, as far as I know it's Naples. Thought I'd wave, it's only the polite thing to do when one leaves a friend."

George looked at me with his eyebrows raised and said, "Okay. What do you say we go and play some chess?"

I looked at George with my eyebrows raised this time and I said, "Chess? Since when do you play chess?"

George replied, "Since this morning, they have some board games at the lounge. I made couple friends. Come on."

He waved me on and we went to the lounge. I never really played chess in my life but I knew the basics. George beat me three times in a row and I gave my seat to another victim. I Wasn't sure where George learned his chess skills, but he had a good technique. The new contender asked George if he would like to place a bet and offered to play for 25 cents. They both placed the 25 cents on the table and played the game. This guy was better than I and gave George a good contest. I learned more of the game as I watched them. You need to pay attention to every move and what possibilities arise. In the end, George won and claimed the winnings.

The young man smirked and said, "Where did you learn to play so well?"

George hesitated a moment and replied, "Actually I never played the game before today."

The young man replied, " that's impossible."

The young man placed his hand in his pocket and said, "I want to play you again for a chance to get my money back, here is 50 cents."

I did not like this picture. This guy was few years older than us and I sensed a scam. I spoke out to George "Hey, George, we are late for our appointment."

The young man interrupted, "Appointment? what appointment. We are on a ship. There are no appointments here. You need to be fair and give me a chance, it's the rules."

George nodded yes and put his 50 cents back in the pot. A few new people started to come over to watch, one of them was Giulio. Soon after, Giulio tapped my shoulder and pulled me aside as he whispered in my ear, "Come outside with me."

I followed him out of the room.

Giulio said in a low voice, "You need to tell your brother to stop this game when he is done."

I asked "why?"

Giulio replied, "That guy is an excellent chess player, your brother is being played like a piano. He will let him win again this time, and maybe the next time too. But eventually he will take the pot and maybe all your money."

I frowned and said, "I had a feeling that was happening." Quickly we went back inside and sure enough.

George shouted, "Check Mate!"

I quickly said to George, "George, it's time to go, the captain is waiting for us."

George looked at me puzzled "Huh?"

The young man stood up and said arrogantly, "Oh no you don't, you are not leaving this room without one more game."

I grabbed George by the wrist and I pulled him with me, the young man grabbed George and a scuffle broke out. I pushed as he shoved, Giulio grabbed a chair and so did the young man, next thing you know there was some broken furniture and a few bruises. Some of the ship staff came in quickly and broke it up. We were all brought to the security room. Each one of us was questioned individually and we each explained our version, then we waited. Eventually a ship officer came in and asked to see me first, I followed him to another room. He told me to sit down.

The officer asked, "Are you the brother of George?"

I replied "Yes."

The officer asked, "Do you know the young man he was gambling with?"

I replied, "No."

Waving his finger at me he said, "You should know better than to get involved in gambling practices abroad a passenger vessel."

I replied, "It started as an innocent game, first George and I played and he beat me several times, then this person asked to take my place. We did not intend to play for money."

The officer looked at me, "I believe you, I can see you and your brother are not trouble makers. But now you have a problem."

With a worried look I said to him, "What do you mean?"

The officer replied, "You are on board a ship for the whole of next week with a trouble maker that has a sour taste in his mouth as he was not able to scam you and your brother."

I sat and thought about it a little.

The officer continued, "He will seek revenge. I'm not sure what to do with you and your brother, I know these types of hoodlums and there is no predicting how he will react."

I sat in silence and pondered the situation.

The officer said, "I will need to speak with the captain. For the time being I suggest you and your brother go to your cabin and stay there until I call for you."

I agreed and the officer asked me to follow him. He opened the door and George was there with another officer. We were told to stay quiet as they escorted us to our cabin. Once we entered the cabin, George placed his hands on his head with a worried look on his face.

George said, "What did they tell you?"

I replied, "They said they know we are not the trouble makers, but I think they feel we are in danger from the other guy as he may seek revenge."

At first George looked worried. then he became angry.

George said, "I'm not afraid of that guy, he's not so big."

I replied, "George, we need to be careful and listen to the officers, we don't need to get a record before we even make it to New York."

He looked at my eyes and replied, "I guess you are right. But I won him fair and square."

Chapter 7

Knock, knock. Someone was at the door, I walked over and opened the door. There were two officers, one of them was the man that had escorted George earlier, the other I had not met before. He walked into the room and told the other officer to wait at the door. I noticed that this officer wore a different hat. Before I could think, he spoke.

The officer said, "I am Captain Alessandro."

My eyes opened wide and I was a little shaken by his presence.

The Captain continued, "My first mate informed me of the trouble last night you two were involved in. I don't like these instances on my ship as I am responsible for the safety of everyone aboard and I am aware of the possibilities when such troubles arise. If I leave you here in 3rd class, you will be subject to vindication by your recent acquaintance, and then if you should get hurt, I am responsible and would have all kinds of paperwork and hearings to attend making my already demanding schedule overbearing."

George and I looked at each other and neither one of us said a word.

The Captain continued, "Do you have anything at all to say?"

I did not really know what to say, then politely, I said."Perhaps my brother and I can apologize to the young man?"

The Captain interrupted, "Apologize! You don't even know his name. I don't think he will accept an apology. It's a good idea for you not to see him again."

I replied, "Hmm, perhaps that's a good idea."

George nodded and replied, "Me too."

The Captain placed his hand on his chin and said, "I see only one solution here, you will leave this cabin and come join the crew in first class. You will need to perform duties like to cleaning dishes and perform room services and whatever they find suitable for you."

He then took his hand off his chin and looked directly at us and asked, "Agreed?"

George and I were stunned, but at the same time I was kind of liking this idea. I said, "Agreed!" thereafter, so did George.

The Captain said, "Good. The officer at the door will escort you to your quarters. Please gather your belongings and I will instruct him to direct you. You must report to me tomorrow morning and I will assign you for duties. Any questions?

George and I replied, "Yes, Sir!, No questions Sir."

We gathered our things and the officer escorted us. The officer directed us via the 1st class area to avoid the young man we had our issue with in third class lounge. The 1st class area was adorned with all kinds of artwork and tapestries, decorative columns and majestic stairways. It was a very different ship on this side. People were all nicely dressed, some walked casually, some sat as they were waited upon. We quickly made our way into a hidden doorway where only staff were allowed access. We quietly exited the area reserved for the elites. Once in the staff area, it felt a little more like where we came from, except cleaner. I could see that this ship was constantly being maintained, painted and cleaned spotless. We were assigned to a small cabin with 2 bunks. The officer said dinner would be at 6 O'clock at the staff lounge and we were to report to the captain at 6:30 AM for our assignment the following morning. Further, we were only allowed access to the Staff designated zones and not to venture anywhere near to the 3rd class section for the remainder of the journey. We agreed and understood. After all the adventures we had experienced for the day, we decided to stay in the cabin. We took dinner back to our bunk when the time came. I closed my evening with my friend '*Robinson Crusoe*'.

Following morning our alarm clock rang at 5:30 AM. We were ready for the day as we had been cooped up in this cabin for what seemed a long time. Washed and dressed in a staff uniform we made our way up to the Captains office. We knocked.

The Captain, said "Enter."

The Captain was at his desk with a cup of coffee and some large maps on his desk. He seemed to have a lot on his mind and at first, he did not pay attention to us as we walked in.

The Captain looked to us and said, "Good morning young men."

We both replied, "Good Morning Captain."

The Captain said, "I'm happy to see you are punctual, I dislike when people don't follow instructions and waste my time. Time is a gift and one should not waste it."

We nodded and said, "Yes, Sir."

The Captain looked at me and said, "You are Marco?"

I nodded yes.

The Captain pointed to George and asked, "And you are George, correct."

We both said, "Yes Sir," and I added "Correct."

The Captain sat at his desk, folded his arms together and said, "Well, it seems you ran into a little bad luck yesterday, I see you are not troublemakers. But sometimes bad luck can bring good things. I've looked up your documents and the manifest shows you are destined to New York for work. Well, this is a good way to start to train for good work skills."

Excitedly I replied, "Really!"

The Captain replied, "You seem to like the idea Marco. And what about you George?"

George replied, "Oh, yes Sir, I did not mean to cause any trouble yesterday, I just wanted to play some chess."

The Captain replied, "Yes, I am aware of this."

The Captain stood up and said, "How would you two like to come up with me to the bridge and see how we operate this vessel?"

We both replied excitedly, "Yes Sir, absolutely Sir."

The Captain walked over to his closet, put on his jacket and said, "Follow me mates, we are off to the bridge."

The Captain walked briskly and we had to struggle a bit to keep up with his pace as he was tall with long legs. We followed up a few flights of stairs and everyone we encountered saluted the captain with a Good Morning Captain. Once we made it to the bridge, the Captain introduced us as crewmates and asked one of the officers to show us around the room. I was fascinated by the big open view of the sea and all the systems and controls.

One of the officers announced, "Captain, we are on schedule and on present course will arrive to Gibraltar at 10:18 hours."

The Captain replied. "Very well Officer Phillips, stay on course."

Then the captain turned to the intercom and sent a call to the radio room.

The Captain said, "Officer Jansen, initiate a message to Gibraltar harbor master that we will arrive this morning at 10:18 hours and to have the tender vessel ready for us when we arrive. We have twenty-eight passengers that will disembark via the portside aft doorway at level 2."

Then the Captain turned to the First Officer and said, "Mr. Scott, what weather forecast do we have ahead."

Officer Scott looking at his weather chart replied, "We have strong headwinds past the Canaries, I suggest charting on a northern course."

The Captain replied, "Request is granted, chart a course for northern crossing."

The Captain now turned to us and said, "Have you enjoyed your tour of the bridge?"

We both replied, "Yes, Sir. Thank you."

The Captain replied, "Any questions?"

I thought a little, then I said. "I would like to learn how I can work on your ship Sir."

The Captain chuckled and smiled, "Already you've made up your mind to work on a ship? Well, you must really like being at sea and to obey orders."

I replied, "I don't mind orders Sir."

The Captain walked over to a ledger and ran his finger to a point and said, "Marco, okay, I have a position for your duty today, motorman assistant!"

I didn't know what I was getting in to but I agreed. George wound up as assistant in the kitchen, he didn't seem to mind. My first duty was to carry some mechanical room supplies from the storage room to the engine compartment. It was interesting to see all the equipment and I even got a close look at the engine shaft as it cranked the propeller up and down. I could only imagine the amount of force it required to turn that propeller and move this massive vessel. I was truly fascinated.

The Crew master shouted to me from outside the engine compartment and said, "Marco, Hey, you better come back up here, we are at Gibraltar and we are shifting propellers off. We will need your help assisting passengers onto the tender vessel.

Quickly I climbed up the ladder located off the engine compartment and followed the crew members to the portside aft door on level 2. The door was open already and I could see the water not very far from the door level. The tender vessel maneuvered its way to the door entrance against the current and a crew member stood at the doorway as he held a rope. As the vessel got closer, he threw the rope to the tender vessel crew and they tied it to their cleat. Both crews worked swiftly to secure the tender vessel to Vulcania's side, and we then placed a gangway in between the vessels. Then they asked me to go open the door to the passenger entrance and let the transfer passengers in. Customs came aboard first and checked the passenger's documents one by one. They asked a couple passengers to open their bags. As they were released they were sent to the gangway. The tender vessel bobbed up and down as the gangway moved along with the movement of the two vessels. We were asked to assist the passengers in the transfer the moment when the two vessels were evenly positioned and could make a safe disembarkation. At first I was a bit nervous about it. But once I saw there was a rhythm to the movement, it became a matter to hold the passengers hand and pull them through on the bounce back up. It worked out well, and I began to feel like a seaman.

The shift ended at 5 o'clock and I went back to the cabin to find George. He was laying on the bunk with his hands behind his head, and I asked, "How was your day George?"

George replied, "I spent the day as dish cleaner and floor mopper, but all in all, it was a good day."

I smiled and replied. "Sounds like work."

George replied, "It's a good thing Domenico trained us well. This work was easy compared to work in the fields."

We both chuckled. Then I said, "I assisted to unload the passengers at Gibraltar, it was interesting."

George opened his eyes and said, "Wow, that must have been exciting. Did you get to see the rock of Gibraltar?"

I replied, "Yes. For a short time."

George replied, "I got to see it as I carried trays from the dining room, it is a big rock. Well, today we saw two countries, Spain on one side and Morocco on the other."

I replied, "It's pretty interesting, it is the doorway to the Atlantic Ocean."

George replied, "I met some guys of the crew, they were pretty nice. They said that Captain Alessandro made the right decision to bring us up front. In the past, there were similar situations where the trouble escalated and then the police got involved at destination."

I replied, "We certainly don't need that. I'm glad to perform some chores and learn a few things. I wonder what duty we will have tomorrow?"

George got up off the bunk and said, "I don't know, but what do you say we go over to the crews lounge and see what is going on."

I agreed and we made our way there. We met a crew member that George worked with today, His name was Nazzareno. He wore a key around his neck and I wondered what it was for.

Nazzareno said, "Hi George."

George replied, "Hi Nazzareno, this is my brother Marco."

We shook hands and smiled to each other.

Nazzareno said, "I heard how you guys wound up as part of the crew."

I replied, "Yes, Nazzareno, I always wanted to learn how a ship's crew functions, so I guess this is one way to do it."

Nazzareno chuckled and replied, "Yes, become part of the crew!"

And then I asked, "Hey, Nazzareno, what other duties have you performed on board."

Nazzareno replied, "This is my first voyage on this vessel, although I have been on many others. On my last tour, I was at sea for 9 months. Afterwards I stayed in Genoa for a month and now I am on Vulcania."

With interest I replied, "Interesting!"

Nazzareno replied, "I have done all kinds of maintenance and even worked as a table server."

I asked Nazzareno, "What is your favorite duty?"

Nazzareno replied, "I like to paint and be outside on a sunny day. You can kind of get into your own thoughts and enjoy the quiet time by the sea."

I replied, "Hmm, I can see that being enjoyable."

Nazzareno replied, "well, I am on duty to paint the railings tomorrow, if you like I can request to have you join as my assistant."

With surprise I replied, "Really! That would be great, yes, I would like to join you if you can arrange that."

Nazzareno replied, "Wonderful, I will ask the crew master when he comes in for dinner."

And then Nazzareno asked George, "Hey, George, what about you?"

George thought about it and said, "Hmm, I think I will stay in the kitchen if the captain allows, I kind of like being around food."

We all laughed.

I made my way to the crews lounge the following morning as I observed the sunrise on starboard aft. It was quite mesmerizing to watch the sea turn brightly orange as the sun made its first glimpse over the horizon. Nazzareno, George and I were with our morning coffee in hand.

Nazzareno said, "So, you guys ready for the day?"

I replied, "I'm getting there with the help of my coffee."

George raised his cup and said, "Cheers!"

We all smiled.

Nazzareno replied, "Good, it's important to enjoy what you do."

The crew master heard us as we spoke and came over.

The crew master said, "Hey, guys, better go have your breakfast, your shift starts in about 10 minutes."

We all got up and followed him to the breakfast table.

The crew master said, "We will pass by the Canaries today, it will be calm and sunny. However, most likely the head winds will pick up tonight as we go into open ocean, may get eight to ten footers. Ship may bounce a bit tonight."

Nazzareno replied, "Good, this way I will sleep as a baby."
We all chuckled. I began to really like Nazzareno.

It was a great day to paint. Sunny and dry, in the open air the paint would dry almost as soon as I brushed it on. Nazzareno and I took charge of the forward portside railing. Nazzareno placed me on one section as he handled another. I was careful not to spill paint as there were guests that walked by often. I noticed one young family with two young children. The mom held hands with her young son and the dad did the same with their daughter. They all seemed to be happy as they enjoyed the view of the ocean. With the sound of the wind as it rushed by, I did my job subconsciously while I was lost in my thoughts. As the day progressed, I started to drift back to the days of the orphanage. I remembered nothing of my parents. At that time in my life I thought of Sister Mona and Father Buckius as being my parents, since they were in charge of me. But there was no bond or love. I remember my dreams to escape from that orphanage. Although I had no place to go. I just wanted to get out and find, I don't know what. But I knew a part of me was lost. It was a time in my life where I became aware. Once I realized that I once had a mother, I felt abandoned. As I learned about the outside world, I knew being a child was not supposed to be about being left in an orphanage. So, eventually, I talked my brothers into escaping with me that day. And I had no intention to return. Somehow God watched over us and crossed our paths with as kind of a man as Domenico. He and Elisetta were the first glimpse of warmth in this world we had ever known.

Chapter 8

To cross the Atlantic became reality and it was all that I had imagined and more. I now experienced being part of the crew. Nazzareno and I painted during the entire voyage and George learned a lot of kitchen skills as well as being assistant waiter. During the voyage, we did experience couple days of big swells. Captain Alessandro said they were 10 to 12 feet and the ship did bob up and down forward to aft quite intensively. Some of the passengers became seasick and remained in their rooms. As for myself, I was captivated by the power of the ocean. The force of the crashing waves and the scent of its mist in the air. All this force arising in short time without notice. I was convinced the ocean was alive and had a mind of its own.

It was now our last night on the ship and the crew arranged a party in the crew lounge. Captain Alessandro arrived to thank all of us for our participation on board the maiden voyage of this new transatlantic route for the Vulcania.

The Captain said, "My friends and crew of Vulcania, thank you for your participation on this maiden voyage to New York. Your work has made it possible for Vulcania to provide our passengers to have a safe voyage. It is the Captains responsibility to accomplish his duty to his ship and passengers, and only his crew can make it happen. Without all of you, this would not be possible. Thank you and God bless you."

Then he turned to the first officer and asked him to take over. The first officer thanked us as well and quickly announced that there was a buffet table and we should all serve ourselves and enjoy the party. And without hesitation, we did. I sat next to Nazzareno. George sat with another crew member he met on his shift.

Nazzareno looked to me and said, "Marco, how does it feel to have crossed the Atlantic Ocean?"

I looked to him and replied, "Actually we have not quite made it to the other side. When I see the Statue of Liberty, then I will let you know."

Nazzareno leaned back and said, "Yes, Marco, you are correct. Lady Liberty is very special. She stands boldly as she guards the gates of the land of Liberty, and at the same time she welcomes newcomers with a beacon of light. When I saw her the first time, I knew I had arrived in a special land. America is a land that protects a person's freedom to live their life by their own choices. And with the gift of freedom, it brings out the very best in people. America is blessed by God. It is a country where you can become who you want to be of your own will, by the will of your God given gifts."

Listening to Nazzareno reminded me of Domenico. He also told me similar ideas. I found it interesting, but I don't think I understood fully. Then I looked at the key around his neck that he carried all the time. And I asked, "Nazzareno, I noticed that you wear that key around your neck all the time, what is it?"

Nazzareno grasped the key with his hand and replied, "I have travelled much since I became a seaman. I've seen many ports around the world. From South America to Africa, Asia and even Australia. At first I felt alone and so I spent my free time as I listened to others and entertained myself when I would meet new people at the different ports. I enjoyed to observe different cultures and their unique creations. I made friends and I became close with some. I learned quickly that we all need to follow our destinies and that unfortunately, friends often come and go. I realized the only thing that really belongs to a person are the memories they create, so I decided to write. Every day I try to write what I encountered, or sometimes I will write a poem. I do it mainly for my own satisfaction, I often go back and read something from the past and enjoy it as it will help me get through a tough time. Anyway, the key is for the box of poems I keep, they are my prized possession. I carry the key with me to remind me of who I am, and most important that I hold the key to my own thoughts."

I listened very attentively as I was enchanted by his concept. Then I asked, "May I read one of your poems?"

Nazzareno chuckled. "I am flattered that you would want to read my poem. Normally I don't tell people that I like to write, as I said, it's all personal thoughts. But for you Marco, I feel comfortable enough. Sometimes you may need to read them a few times before you feel what it means to you. I try to write my poems so they mean different things to different people. As we all perceive things differently. He stood up and said, let's go back to the cabin."

Back at Nazzareno's quarters, he walked over to his closet and pulled out a metal box and placed it on the table. It was green and big enough to hold several notebooks. He pulled his key off his neck and opened the box. By the way Marco, my friends that know of my poems call me 'Chiavetta'. He took out a few books and then one marked Poem's. Carefully he removed one of them and then put everything back in the box. He handed it to me and said, "Here, this was one of my first poems. Take it back to your room and read it, let me know what you think in the morning if you like."

I put it in a folder he had on the side table and said "Thank you Nazzareno, well, Chiavetta that is. (Chiavetta meant special key). I will return it to you in the morning." I said goodnight and returned to my cabin. George had not yet returned, so I sat down and pulled out the paper, and read.

Passing clouds left behind,
new horizons soon to be.
Sounds of crashing sea,
bring my soul to me.

Every course will be churned away,
lest clouds behind choose my way.
Love in my heart guides my passage,
strength of my soul conquering challenge.

Clear sky with bright sea lie starboard,
rain squalls chasing aft.

Force of my soul thrust me away,
sound of calm seas carry me today.

This poem inspired me, it provided me with both a sense of inner peace and at the same time provided strength to endure life's challenges. I liked it. I could see how being out at sea could inspire one to write, and I thought that perhaps I could give it a try as well one day. I placed the poem back in the folder and fell on my bed, it was a long day and I was duly tired. In my last conscious thoughts of the day, I envisioned the Statue of Liberty. I had never seen her except for in magazine pictures, to me she symbolized strength and freedom. Thinking further, she is welcoming newcomers and at the same time holds a book. In essence, she is there to teach as well as protect. What a beautiful symbol I thought. It reminded me of what it must be like to have a mother as a child, which I never had. I was now ready to see Lady Liberty and receive her welcome in my heart.

I woke early next morning, I went to the crew lounge and was told we would arrive to New York around 1 o'clock. I was very excited to finally arrive. I went back to the cabin and found George packing his things.

George looked at me and said, "Are you packed?"

I looked at him and replied, "Yes, pretty much."

George replied, "I hope we find uncle Luigi at the terminal."

I replied, "I'm pretty sure he will be there, otherwise, we can always ask Nazzareno to help us find a place."

George shrugged his shoulders and said, "I guess that is an option too. But I really want to get the job uncle Luigi had wrote about. I think I am done with this ship for now."

I replied, "I kind of liked it George, actually, I think I want to get a job with a vessel operator and apply to be a crew member."

George looked at me seriously and said, " Come on Marco, we have not even arrived to New York yet. Give it a chance."

I replied, "It's not that I don't want to stay in New York, I just like the idea to explore the seas and see the world. America I am sure is great, and like uncle Domenico said, America is here to keep the world a safe place. But I want to see what else is out there too."

George looked to me seriously and said "You will leave me! I can't believe you."

I looked at George and said, "Don't worry, you will be fine. First let's meet Luigi and then we will see. I didn't even get the job yet. You will be fine, relax."

After lunch, we noticed a heavy mist in the air. There were a lot of gulls that approached the ship and flew all around us, sometimes diving for food. I guess we found new friends and they welcomed us to their land. The horn blew. Passengers started making their way to top deck. The mist was quite heavy and we could not see very far. Suddenly, I could see a tall shadow appear over the sea, and then I saw her face and crown, and then the torch. Just like I envisioned her, holding her book in one arm representing education and discipline. And in the other, the torch raised high to guide us a path. Uncle Domenico was right, this was truly a special land, and I could see now it was blessed by God. America's ambassador Lady Liberty greeted us. And simultaneously she expressed her duty to protect the rights God intended for humanity. An enlightenment to the world, as in the way our Lord intends.

New York harbor appeared soon after our reception by Lady Liberty, I was in awe of the skyline. This was almost a dream. I had never seen buildings so tall nor ever dreamed of them. It was like stepping into the future. The harbor had so many enormous berths with all kinds of machinery to handle the cargo ships. I believe that this day I was in a trance as I absorbed my new surroundings. It felt like I had lived a fantasy up until this moment and I had only now awoken to the world, the New World. It was clear that the world I had lived in all my life was ancient and that a new world had been born and grown on this other side of the ocean, leaving the ancient world to rest. I wondered how was it able to grow to these enormous proportions, everything was big and modern, I was in awe.

The tug boats pushed us into our berth, George and I stared at the docking operation. I was fascinated to see the coordinated work being performed. The crew made it look easy, however, I was sure it took them a lot of practice to make it happen safely. George put his arm around my shoulder with a big smile on his face.

George said, "We are here Marco, New York!"

I looked at him in silence with a smile.

George said, "Well, don't you have anything to say?"

I grabbed the railing and leaned myself back, shook my head back and forth and took a deep breath, then let it out " It's hard to explain George, I have so many emotions going on in my head. This city is more than I had ever imagined, I almost feel I am born again."

George looked out and up and all around and said, "Yes Marco, I have to admit I am also very excited. This is my new home and I am going to work hard and follow my dreams and pledge my life to America. The first thing I am going to do is apply to become a citizen. Then I will work and go to school and learn a trade and eventually have my own business and be my own boss."

I looked at him, and then I looked out to the city and all its energy, and then I looked back and said, "Hey, George, looks like you are in the right place for that George, I'm sure you will reach your goal, no doubt."

We heard a ships horn, it was not Vulcania's. We looked out to the harbor and another ship approached, this one was a cargo ship. There was so much movement here, so much energy being emitted. Suddenly I felt the need to get off the ship and go experience the city. I looked to George and said, "Come on, let's go find Luigi." We bolted off to get our things and make our way off the ship. We met the Captain in the crew area.

The Captain walked over to us and said, "Hello young men."

We replied, "Hello Captain."

The Captain said, "What do you think of the city?"

We both replied, "Amazing Sir."

He chuckled and said, "Yes, it is. Even for me after being here many, many times."

The Captain put his hand on my shoulder and said, "Since you guys became part of the crew during this voyage, I have a courtesy suggestion for you, meet me at the crew gangway portside aft and we will get you off the ship without thorough Customs exam, okay?"

We both looked at each other, and then turned to the Captain with a salute "Thank you Sir!"

Once we arrived at the crew gangway, we met Nazzareno.
He waved us to come over and said, "You guys got smart, yes, this is the faster way off the ship. Otherwise the clearance process can take a lot of time. So, you are going to meet your uncle now?"

I replied, "Yes, he came from Baltimore to meet us." Nazzareno then opened his bag and took out an envelope.

Nazzareno said, "Hey, Marco, I want you to have this poem, the one I gave you to read. This way you can remember me."

I was taken by surprise, and I replied. "Nazzareno, that is so nice of you. I'm sorry, I do not have a gift for you, I was not prepared."

Nazzareno smiled and replied, "That's okay Marco, for me, the experience we shared is what counts, and I won't forget you. It was very nice sailing with you guys. I hope you both find your dreams and they are in a happy place."

George and I replied. "Thank you."

Then I noticed Captain Alessandro as he arrived, he waved us to come over. He handed us a paper.

Captain Alessandro said, "Guys, once they open the door, you will get on the line to meet the Customs officer, he will ask you for your documents. Hand him this paper together with your passport documents, he will give you his blessing quickly. Marco, remember, if you wish to become a crew member you should contact the New York office of Zim Lines. They are a new company and growing very quickly. You can work your way up the ladder quickly there and they will treat you well. I have a friend there. His name is Sidney and he can get you a job quickly, mention my name."

The captain shook my hand and I graciously thanked him. George thanked him as well and we both parted away from the Captain with a salute.

George and I found ourselves in a large terminal station, the crowd of people was a little overwhelming. There were all kinds of lines for

Customs and baggage and transportation. I was now very grateful for the Captains assistance in clearing the vessel, otherwise we would have been here a long, long time.

George asked, "Hey, Marco. Do you see any sign of Luigi?"

I replied, "Well, I really don't know what he looks like, so that will be difficult."

George replied, "He must be holding a sign or something with our names."

I looked around and then I said, "Let's try and find a clear spot where we can actually be seen." I noticed a staircase next to an information desk and decided to go there. I asked the girl behind the desk, "We are trying to find a Mr. Luigi from Baltimore."

The attendant replied with a sour face, "What does he look like?"

With a flustered face I replied, "Actually, I don't know."

She smirked and replied, "Then how do you intend to find him?"

Then I turned to George and said, "Do you see anything?"

George looked in the crowd and replied. "Nope."

Then I asked George to stay next to the information desk and I would go up the stairs to have a look. At the top of the stairs I looked around and saw hundreds of people going in all directions. With this scenario, it will be difficult to find each other. I asked myself, where would I go if I was to meet someone that just came off the Vulcania? Ah! the baggage claim! I ran downstairs and quickly went to the information desk. I asked the same girl, "Where is the baggage claim for Vulcania?"

The attendant replied, "Let me see your baggage tickets."

I replied, "We don't have any we were part of the crew."

The attendant replied, "Then you cannot go in the baggage area, not allowed, sorry."

Frustrated, I replied, "So how do we meet our uncle?" She just shrugged her shoulders and looked back to her paperwork.

George tapped me on the shoulder and we walked away.

George said, "I have an idea, why don't we go to the main entrance to this place, maybe he is there."

It seemed like a good idea, and I agreed.

We walked and followed signs for exit to street, through a large tunnel and then more crowds. Eventually I could see some large doorway openings to the street. First thing I noticed were the large luxurious automobiles. Once outside there were automobiles everywhere, horns were honking, engines hummed. The amount of steel used in construction here was extraordinary. I could see now how America won the war, there was nothing like this I had ever seen anywhere. I noticed a man with a black coat and a round top hat that stood in the corner next to a paper stand holding a piece of paperboard. The hat reminded me of the hat Luigi was wearing in the picture Elisetta had shown us before we left. We walked over to read the paperboard, and it said. "I am Luigi from Baltimore."

We cheered, "Luigi!"

Luigi smiled, laughed and replied, "Are you George and Marco?"

George and I replied, "Yes!"

He gave us both a big hug and said, "I was getting a little worried, I thought maybe you had some problems with Customs so I had gone to look for you at the office, but they said you were cleared already as part of the crew, I didn't know what to think."

I kind of rolled my eyes and said, "It's kind of a long story, ahem, the Captain of the vessel took a liking to us and we..."

Luigi interrupted, "The Captain! He took a liking to you?"

George said, "Hey, Marco, I will tell the story. Well, the first night of the voyage, Marco and I went to the lounge and played checkers. One fellow talked me into a bet with him against our checker game."

Luigi sighed and said, "Ahh, I think I can see where this is going, okay fellas, well, the main thing is you made it to New York. Let's grab the bags and head to my car. It's kind of hectic around here and we can talk better once we can relax in the car."

We picked up our bags and started to follow Luigi. There were people that moved about everywhere. Luigi walked quickly and it was kind of difficult to keep up. I could see that in New York you need to move quickly, otherwise you will become an object that gets in the way of the waves of people that moved on the walkway.

Luigi pointed his finger ahead and said, "We are almost there, I'm parked at the end of this street."

We arrived and he opened the trunk and said, "Put your bags in guys, you should have plenty of room."

I was in awe of this automobile, it was huge and built solid. I walked all around and admired the beauty of the shape and color of this dark blue automobile. I asked Luigi, "What kind of car is this?"

Luigi replied with a grin, "This my friend is a 1941 Packard 120."

Pausing, he looked to the car and said, "Beautiful machine."

George and I both agreed. Luigi opened the passenger door and said, "Come on, let's get in. I will bring you to my business manager's home here in Brooklyn, his name is William."

We got in the car and Luigi started the engine. The engine had a sound like I had not heard before. Very powerful deep sound and smooth as we drove through the streets. It was a surreal experience riding in that car as I observed the streets of New York. I had seen it in magazines, however, pictures could not explain how I was captivated on this first drive around New York. Luigi drove confidently, we came to a tremendous bridge.

Luigi pointed and said, "Here we are, the Brooklyn Bridge!"

I had never seen anything like it. Everything seemed so big here in America. I looked to the arches of the bridge as we drove under them, I wondered how people managed to build things so high off the ground.

Luigi said, "I will stay here in New York for few days, after that I will need to return to Baltimore. William has a room where you can stay until you are settled in your jobs. William can drive you to work as you will work with him at the warehouse cargo terminal in Brooklyn, it's actually very close to where he lives."

I replied, "Thank you Sir for helping us."

Luigi replied, "Nonsense, first, Elisetta and I are very close, that makes you family. However, putting family aside. Here is how Americans look at it, this is a country with capitalistic work ethics. You give your employee an honest hard day's work, and your employer gives you an honest hard day's pay. This way, you both go home with your heads held high. And that is the best one can ask for in this life. So, you see, there is no need to thank me."

I dared not mention to him that I planned to go back out to sea. I didn't want to hurt any feelings. So, I thought I would save that for a later date.

That night, after we met William and got settled in our room, I thought of Nazzareno, and I decided to write a poem. I thought about what I had seen on this first day in New York, and this is what came out.

City streets, bright lights,
working folks and entertainers.
Fire trucks and horse drawn carriages,
homeless folks and five star savages.

Motor cars and limousines,
jaywalkers and pedestrians.
Their paths are disordered,
yet they all find their quarters.

Every time I cross this way,
my troubles seem to fade away.
Moving briskly, no time to speak,
all these people, what do they seek.

A place like this, is like no other,
for here we have become a number.
No names spoken, no hometown,
only meandering and looking around.

I try to come here from time to time,
for this reminds me, this time is mine.
And like no other, perhaps unordinary,
this time is only momentary.

Chapter 9

We learned a lot in the weeks that followed, New York is a place where life is constantly on the move. We met new people every day, each of them with their own mission. The one thing people around here seemed to have in common is they were quite open minded and willing to talk openly about their lives. But then, I'm not sure if what they spoke and what they thought were the same thing. People did work hard every day and were proud of their work. People primarily were concerned with work and money, and this would often be the most common topic in any conversation. George quickly made his way into a position in the office as a documents clerk for exports and imports. While I preferred to work outside. I loaded and unloaded cargo, prepared manifests and controlled inventory for the goods being received and shipped. It was good work, but every time a vessel arrived from overseas my mind started to wander. I felt if I stayed here I would fall into this materialistic realm that seemed to dominate ambition.

That night at dinner, I asked William for a day off. He looked at me with a surprised look.

William said, "Why do you need a day off Marco."

I replied, "I want to go visit Zim Lines and see if I can get a job on board a vessel." George had a look of disbelief on his face. William leaned back in his chair with his hands on the table

William said, "Have you mentioned this to Luigi?"

I nodded my head back and forth, let out a sigh and said,

"No, I did not have the courage."

William stood up and started to pace a little.

William said, "I kind of feel you are not giving this job a chance, you are only here a short time. Luigi will certainly be disappointed."

I clasped my hands together and put them on the table and said, "I appreciate what both you and Luigi have done for me, and I will never forget the opportunity you have provided, to both George and I. It's difficult to explain but I feel at this moment of my life, I want to go out to sea and learn more about this world we live in."

William put his hand on his chin and said, "You know Marco, I do understand, and you are a courageous young man. You may have your day off. Also, if you will be able to make it to work later in the day, we won't dock your pay for the day off."

I nodded my head and said. "Thank You."

William dropped me off at the train station early in the morning, George waved goodbye with a disappointed face. I didn't blame him for his discontentment with my choice, but it was just something stronger than I. And I needed to follow through. I followed my directions and made my way to downtown Manhattan, near what they call the 'Battery'." I took a couple of buses and walked around a little. There was a strong impression of wealth in this area. I passed by a building that looked like it was a copy of an ancient Greek temple, only larger and bolder. I read the inscription and it said, 'New York Stock Exchange'." I didn't know what it was about, but something told me that there was a lot of money involved. Then I walked upon another building. It looked like a modern castle, or better yet, a fortress. I stood on the corner and observed the building studiously.

A passerby stopped and said, "Are you lost?"

I replied, "No."

The passerby answered with a smile as he walked away, " Well, if your desire is to rob a bank, you found the right place. That's the Federal Reserve, they got plenty gold in there."

I stared at him as he walked away, why did he think I wanted to rob a bank. Then I looked back at the building, I just thought it was an interesting architecture, but now that I looked at it again, I suppose it could look like a large bank or fortress. Wow, it held a lot of gold. I had no idea. Anyway, enough being a tourist, I had to get where I was going.

I arrived at the Zim Lines office, it was a lot smaller than I had anticipated. Sidney was not available, so they gave me an application to fill out and they said if I wanted they could assign me to a job as soon as within 2 weeks going back to the Mediterranean. I wasn't sure that I wanted to go back to the Mediterranean, however, I handed it in and they said they would contact me in couple days. I was a little disappointed not to be able to find Sidney, all in all, at least I handed in my paperwork. It was a beautiful day so I decided to walk. I enjoyed the scenery and I had in mind to go see the Hudson river. I wanted to find the point where we entered the river and perhaps see if I could see Lady Liberty again, from another angle this time. On the way, I passed by a cemetery, it was very interesting as it seemed to stand out from the other surroundings. It was the Trinity cemetery. I stopped for a moment out of curiosity and entered to look at the graves. I read some historical signs and I realized there were some famous people that rested here. People that were founders of this country such as Alexander Hamilton and many signers of the U.S. Declaration of Independence and the U.S. Constitution as well. I felt I was in a special place and I was honored to have this opportunity. I sat in prayer for a few moments. And I thought to myself, what an experience it must have been for these people to be a part of founding this nation. And here they rest among all these great buildings, I wondered how proud they would have been to see what they created. Then I heard a car horn blast and I came out of my thoughts, it was time to move on. I walked a little further and I made my way to a park on the Hudson. I noticed an observation point and walked over. From there I could see in a distance Lady Liberty. It was different to see her this time, when we entered, I felt she was showing us the way into her shelter. Now that I arrived, it felt comforting to know she was there to remind us of what this land is about. We have all been gifted with a nation founded for and by its people to live Life in Liberty. She stood out in the harbor reminding us that with Liberty we must have unity, and very importantly, she was there to remind us to respect one another, and the laws of this land. Like a good mother would do for her children. Without respect for the laws of the nation and God's given rights for its people, Liberty will no longer exist. She is a symbol of integrity, an attribute all people endowed with the gift of life should learn and live by and teach others.

I felt my day was fulfilled, I was grateful for being able to make time for myself to follow my dreams and reflect on my life. Now the time arrived for me to return to my duties. I made it back to work in the late afternoon. I told William there was a long line at the terminal office and he didn't seem to mind. I finished up my day at work and assisted to load a truck with coffee from Brazil. I wondered what kind of place Brazil might be, seemed exotic from my understanding. I spoke to a crew member of the vessel that brought in the coffee, he said there were job openings if I was interested. I told him I would inquire about it. That night as I relaxed on my bed going over the day, I was excited and eager towards going back out to sea, but then I also craved something else. I realized I wanted to become a citizen of this land of liberty. I had only been here a short while and I already felt the sensation that emanated from this land. I felt I was in command of my life. In the short time I had been here, I felt a spirit of freedom in this country. People treated each other as equals, not according to what family you came from or what you did for a living or how you chose to live your life. People were respected by their God given rights and the fates they followed. I believe this is the reason this place was named Land of Liberty, and I wanted to become a member.

One day soon after before work we prepared for some breakfast as usual. George fried some eggs and I prepared toasted bread slices. William was at the table with a newspaper. We brought the food to the table and I sat down. I asked William "What is the process to become a citizen here in America?" William looked at me with a smirk and raised his eyebrows.

George looked at us with a concerned look and said, "I would also be interested in becoming a citizen."

William said, "Hey, Marco, I thought you were anxious to go out to sea. Now you want to become citizen."

I replied, "Mr. William, just because I will work out at sea doesn't mean I can't have a home, I want to make this country my home."

William replied pouting his lips as he moved his head up and down, "You are a smart young man, very smart for your age. I wish I had your insight when I was your age."

I replied, "Thank You."

William said with a smile, "Marco, to answer your first question, the easiest way to become citizen is to marry an American girl."

George looked over with interest.

I chuckled and replied, "I don't think I am ready for that at this time."

George said, "My father was a US Veteran of WWI."

William smiled and replied, "George, that certainly will help you. There is a lot of talk about. For Marco's case the Displaced Person Act will be his best choice of action. Being he is an orphan and from Italy, it may work for him. For George as well, and the Veteran father will make things faster. It will take some time, but will work out."

Excitedly I replied, "I want to apply, do you know what I need to do?"

William replied, "Let me speak to Luigi, he knows a little more than I do about this subject. As far as I know it's a new Act by Congress and I'm not sure of the details yet, but I'm confident by next year you both can be well on your way to citizenship."

I stood up and got myself ready to make the trip to work and replied. "Thank You William, I really appreciate your kind help." And with that off my chest, we made our way to work. It felt great just to know that I too could become a citizen of this country, and I would not give up until I officially pledged my allegiance.

The aroma of Brazilian coffee beans overwhelmed the warehouse today. The day was spent as I loaded trucks with coffee destined to cities across America. I pondered about how many people it would take to drink all this coffee and I concluded this was really a large nation. I decided to take a break and went in to see George in the office, he sat behind the telex machine typing a message. I walked over to him and said, "Hi George, who are you writing to?" He always looked like he was serious when at the telex.

George said without turning his head, "I need to send a message to our agent in Brazil to confirm the coffee arrived and is being broken down prior to being shipped out to the various wholesalers or consignees on the manifest."

I looked at him as I smiled and said, "Oh, you mean you need to inform them of the work that I have accomplished out there all day in the coffee warehouse."

This time he looked at me and replied, "Haha Marco. You are the one that didn't want to work behind the desk. Believe me, it's not as easy as it looks in here either, there is lots to keep track of and if you don't pay attention, you will send someone else goods to the wrong place. And that would cost lots of money. Not a good thing."

I then realized George really enjoyed this work and seemed to have a natural ability, to be a merchant let's say. I replied. "George, I think this shipping stuff fits you well, I think one day you will own your own shipping company, an American shipping company."

George looked to me and replied, "Yes, that sounds nice. Maybe we can do it together?"

I turned around to go back to work and said, "We shall see George. In the meantime, I want to become a seaman and visit ports around the world."

George went back to his telex deep in his thoughts.

Luigi arrived from Baltimore next day to visit and attend some business meetings. He stayed with William, George and I over the weekend. We all went to visit Newark New Jersey as Luigi was interested in buying some land there. He said that the port where we now operated will soon become obsolete. The Newark area would be built up and made into a busy port with modern facilities. The shipping technology was about to change as the demand for international shipping now that the war was over had increased. A new era of expansion in international trade had begun. We met a man at a diner and he took us out to a field where there were lots of heavy construction machines. It appeared they had recently cleared and prepped the land to build buildings. I looked to the open grass fields nearby that were left untouched and I was amazed at all the open space. I could see why Luigi wanted to buy land here adjacent to the ocean, with all this space they could build a port terminal free of the congestion of New York City.

On the way home, Luigi was talkative. He spoke of how when he first came to America he felt like a pioneer in a new land. He said that now it was already so built up, the ports are old and congested and need to be modernized.

Luigi looked to George and I and said, "You guys came here at the right time, there will be lots of growth here. By the way, both of your citizenship applications have been submitted by my attorney and are now under review. My attorney said he is confident you will have your citizenship granted within the year. I am very happy to help you guys out with that, it is something you won't regret."

Then he looked to me and said, "Hey, Marco, I have given thought to your desire to work on shipping vessels as a crew member. I think it will be a good experience for you. If this is what you feel is your passion, then you should do it now that you are young. I do recommend that you work for an American company, it will be good for your citizenship path. Perhaps I will be able to assist in finding you a position."

Then Luigi looked to George and said, "George, you have done a really good job since you arrived, the cargo agents overseas speak very highly of you and your work. The information they receive from you is much more responsive and detailed. I like to hear that when a young man has good work ethics, Domenico taught both of you well, and I am going to tell him that in my letter which I will send to Elisetta."

George said, "Thank you."

Luigi replied, "Hey, George, I think it would be a good idea if you took up some classes at a local University, you can attend part-time in the evenings"

George opened his wide eyes and said, "Hmm, yes, I could do that, but I am not sure I can afford the tuition."

Luigi took a deep breath and said, "Well, I suppose the company can afford part-time tuition at a community college. But you will need to keep good grades!"

George was a little surprised and overwhelmed.

George said, "Oh my, thank you Mr. Luigi. I don't know what to say."

Luigi smiled and replied, "no worries, this is my pleasure. I like to give back my good fortune, especially to good people, such as yourselves."

Several weeks passed, Luigi closed the land deal, George signed up for a couple classes in international trade and William had to go on a business trip to visit a client in California. Luigi came to New York to cover William's place while William was away. Luigi asked George and I to pick him up at Penn Station terminal. It was a busy evening with steady rain so we made sure to leave a little early. George was a good driver and knew the roads well. He got us there in time and we parked the car and we made our way inside. The train was little delayed so we got some coffee at a shop, I took a sip and said, "I wonder where this coffee came from?"

George said, "Who knows, maybe it's part of the coffee you off loaded on the last shipment from Brazil."

I put my nose over the cup and took a sniff, then a taste. I replied, "Nope, that Brazilian coffee was much stronger."

The announcer came on over the speaker and said, "Amtrak 505 from Washington and Baltimore will arrive gate 3."

That was our call, we left our coffee and made our way to gate 3. We stood behind the crowd so we would be able to spot Luigi as he walked his way through the terminal. He was one of the first people to come out and we spotted him and waved. He didn't see us at first but George walked closer up and then he waved back.

George said, "How are you Luigi, how was the ride?"

Luigi replied, "Oh, not bad. We were delayed due to an issue with the engine, but they fixed it pretty quickly."

I found my way through the crowd, met them and said, "Hello Luigi."

Luigi replied, "Hi Marco."

We started to walk out of the terminal quickly to get out of the crowd. Luigi, spoke and walked swiftly as usual.

Luigi said, "I have some news, some good, some not so good."

I had heard this before, so I replied, "What is the not so good news?"

Luigi stopped walking and put his hands on both of our shoulders, it was raining hard.

Luigi said with a serious face, "I received a letter from Elisetta, Domenico has suffered a stroke."

George and I were silent.

Luigi said, "He is okay and stable. The doctor told him it was a warning sign and that he needs to slow down a little."

George said, "Do we need to go back and help them?"

I looked to George as I knew that was not going to happen.

Luigi replied, " George, Elisetta said that Domenico does not want anyone going there to try and help him. Your brother Dario and his girlfriend Isabelle have been there to help Elisetta in this time of trouble. For the moment, Domenico has stabilized. He will have to adjust his lifestyle, as you know he has always been very active. He will need to adjust his lifestyle."

George looked to me and we both knew Domenico would have a hard time adjusting his lifestyle. He is a man that enjoyed being active.

Luigi started walking and said, "Come on, let's get out of this rain."

George started the car and we looked forward to some heat in the car as it was kind of chilly in the rain. Luigi made himself comfortable and I sat in the back.

Luigi said, "We have some more coffee that will arrive at the terminal in a few days, so we will be busy. It's good business, and I will ask you two to work overtime, as we need to impress the client."

We both agreed.

Luigi said, "Marco, I have talked to the captain of the vessel that will deliver the coffee beans. He has reserved a position for you in the crew. You will need to go to their office and fill out the forms. You can join the crew and set sail in as little as 3 or 4 weeks."

I was taken by surprise. And I replied, "Really? Is it the same vessel that will carry these coffee beans?"

Luigi replied, "They own a few vessels, it will be a similar vessel. Your first stop will be at Savannah and then onward to pick up the cargo in Brazil at Rio de Janeiro, then Buenos Aires and then Santos on the way back. Afterwards you will come back to New York and start all over again."

Somehow it didn't seem very romantic as I had imagined, but I was in too deep to back out at this point. It was a long rainy ride back to the apartment.

Chapter 10

The sea was rough as we left New York Harbor, winter had set in and the days were already short. We had to take advantage of daylight as the shorter days left us with little time for outdoor ship maintenance. I had some painting duty on the aft railings and it was very cold and windy out on deck. I tried not to think of the harsh environment and painted away while admiring the sun and the ships water trail. The gulls were flying low as they followed us and dove into the sea for their breakfast. I was on my own with no people around and absorbed in my thoughts. I thought of Elisetta and Domenico and wondered how they were. I hoped Dario and Isabelle would be able to comfort them. And then I felt guilty I was not there to help. I learned that the choices we make in life always have a price. And you can never make everyone happy. I felt the need to search the world, although I was not sure what for. Then I thought of Dario and Isabelle, now that they became a couple. In a way, I was envious of Dario because Isabelle was a very special girl, a woman that is. But then, that was their destiny of choice. They would make a good couple. Dario was very needy and Isabelle was very capable and compassionate. I on the other hand aspired for something different, and so I travel the sea with my gull friends as they follow.

That night at dinner, the crew master approached me and sat down next to me.

The crew master said, "Hello Marco, how was your day?"

I replied, "It was a good day's work, I made good progress on the aft railing. Tomorrow I hope to continue, as long as weather permits."

The crew master replied, "The forecast calls for no precipitation, it may be little windy but looks like a sunny day for tomorrow. Your uncle Luigi asked me to contact you. He has some business in Rio de Janeiro he would like to you attend to. He wants to know if you would stay there for few weeks once we arrive on the final leg of this trip. We would pick you up on the next voyage on our return back from New York."

I was kind of surprised, "Really! well, what will I be required to do there?"

The crew master said, "I don't know exact details, but I know that your uncle is involved in a sugar transaction and he wants someone there to supervise the loading and make sure the supplier delivers the correct amount as per the contract."

I was kind of inspired by the idea. A few weeks in a new land, Rio de Janeiro sounded like a nice place to visit. I replied, "Sir, I think I can handle that, I was doing similar work in New York."

The crew captain smiled and replied, "You won't be sorry, Rio is a beautiful city with lots of pretty girls. I will let your uncle know by telex, he will be happy to hear your decision."

Next day was fair weather as the crew captain predicted. I suppose after being at sea one becomes able to feel the weather pattern before it arrives. I spent the day on my rail and painted together with the gulls that seemed to follow and watch me as I brushed the white paint. Perhaps they liked the color, or perhaps they liked my companionship, or perhaps they wanted someone to throw them some food from another deck. In any case, we kept each other company. As I delved within my thoughts, I wondered about Rio de Janeiro. I was told of it's beautiful beaches and landscapes, but I really could not picture it in my mind. That night I visited the ships Library and found a geographical encyclopedia and found a Chapter on Brazil. I did not realize how large this country was. No wonder they can produce so much coffee and sugar. The country holds the largest tropical rain forest in the world, the Amazon. This river carries more water and feeds more fresh water into the oceans than any other river in the world. It sounded like the Amazon was a very important part of the worlds ecology, especially to the oceans which I found of great interest. I looked forward to call upon this land.

That night, I pondered my past. From the days at the orphanage, to the love we were blessed and shared with Domenico and Elisetta. I thought about them a lot and I hoped they were okay. I knew of no other family or parents. I felt as if my time stood still as I wondered if I would ever see Domenico and Elisetta again. I left the love of my family back in the hills of the Italian Abruzzi. However, my destiny brought me to make this choice to explore and search. I knew I owed it to myself to follow my urge, I wanted to see what other experiences the world held for me to absorb in my senses, whatever it might be. That night I decided to write my thoughts.

I carve the sea,
standing on two feet.
The sun lights a path,
A course I must take.

I look toward the horizon,
The suns path follows.
White caps crashing,
becoming blue sea.

Steadily the wind takes me,
My horizon unchanged.
The Suns path guides me,
in course seeking change.

The sea carved has no name,
horizons all look the same.
White caps crashing,
becoming blue sea.

In course my soul inquires,
horizons will I connect.
Winds providing guidance,
My heart providing strength.

We arrived to our first stop at Savannah to pick up some cargo going to South America, mostly cotton and peanuts. There were also some aircraft parts being loaded on board, crated propellers. It was interesting to see the goods and products being shipped around the globe. I got off the ship for a few hours to have a look around. There was lots of construction going on. The port was being updated from being a cotton barge wharf to becoming a large container terminal, just like in Newark. I could see America was becoming prosperous after the war. Domenico was right. I recognized one of our vessels crew, I said, "Hello."

The crewman replied, "Hi, I've seen you onboard, my name is Joe."

I put my hand out to shake and said, "I'm Marco, nice to meet you." Joe looked out to a ship that was docked next to us.

Joe pointed to the ship and said, "They are heading to Asia, and then India, through the Panama Canal."

I replied, "That sounds exciting. Have you been to Brazil before?"

Joe nodded and smiled, "Yes."

I asked, "So, Joe, how did you like it?"

He replied, "I am Portuguese by descent, my father was born in Portugal, so, in Brazil they speak the same language, Portuguese. I am familiar with the language and culture somewhat. It is a beautiful place, especially Rio is nice."

I replied, "I am glad to hear that because I will spend some time there once we dock."

Joe replied, "Good for you, this is a good time of year, the days are long and the weather is warm. You will enjoy Rio, it is a fun city with lots of tourism. What will you be doing there?"

I replied, "I've been assigned at the terminal for loading a project cargo."

He replied, "That sounds like a nice opportunity. If you need any help when you are there, let me know. I have some contacts and friends there."

I replied, " Thanks." He gave me a note with his contact info and I placed it in my pocket. The vessel going to the Pacific was now getting ready to leave, the crew was removing the ropes from the tie downs. We walked over and waved them off, in a still moments glance, they were on their way. We watched them drift out for a while. They would be out at open sea shortly, in their own little world.

Our ships horn sounded, it was the call for us to return. The crew master waited at the ramp doing a head count.

The crew master said, "Hi Joe, I see you've made a friend."

Joe smiled and replied, "Yes Sir, Marco Polo and I seem to have found each other on this vessel."

The crew master chuckled and said, "Well, next stop is Rio. Better get ready boys."

I smiled and wondered what he meant by 'better get ready'.

That night at the crews lounge, I heard lots of stories about Rio de Janeiro. It seems Rio is a place where they like to dance and sing and drink and gawk at women. I just wanted to see the city for myself and learn the culture a little.

Joe tapped my shoulder and said, "Hey Marco, what are you up to."

I replied, "Oh, I listened to all the sailor stories, I've had enough hot air for now."

Joe laughed and replied, "Yea, you will hear all kinds of things from a bunch of lonely guys at sea. They are all storytellers once they stay on this ship for a while. Just wait and see the stories they tell after they spend a couple of days at the local Rio port taverns as they drink Caipirinhas."

I smiled and replied, "I can only imagine. What is Caipirinha?"

Joe smiled and replied, "You'll find out when you get there my friend."

The crew master came over and said, "Hey, Joe, what are you trying to do to my new friend Marco, are you trying to corrupt him."

Joe laughed and said. "Me? No Sir, I would never steer a good friend into the wrong wind."

The crew master raised his eyebrows with a smile and said,

"That's a good one, steer a friend into the wrong wind. You sound a little like the Captain. How long have you been a crewman Joe?"

Joe raised his brow and replied, "Well, let's see, I think about 8 years now."

The crew master replied, "That's a pretty long time, did you ever think of going back to land life?"

Joe lost his smile and replied, "Actually Sir, I do think about it lately. Settling down and start a family and all that. But this life at sea kind of grows on you."

The crew master replied, "You should take a break Joe, eight years is a good number. We all should make a change in our lives every eight years."

Joe nodded, "Okay Sir, I appreciate that. Maybe you are right."

Joe got up and said. "Have a good night fellas, I'm going to hit the sack, I got to get up early."

The crew master and I both wished him a good night.

The crew master looked at me and said, "And you Marco, how do you like being at sea?"

I replied, "I like it a lot Sir, I have a lot of time to get to know myself out here."

The crew master replied, "I understand Marco, it does put you in touch with your soul. But you need to be careful. Sometimes when you spend a lot of time at sea, you forget there is another world out there. It's good to spend time out here and have the sea touch your soul. But life is meant to be lived and to conquer our challenges. Most of us come out here to run away from our realities. We are on this earth to live our life and create our destiny."

I listened to the crew master, nodded and said, "I understand Sir."

The crew master replied, "I don't believe you do Marco, but we all are here to learn something. As for me, I spent my entire adult life at sea, I married once. Life at sea does not mix with marriage and family. She finally left me and I never tried to find another."

I didn't know what to say.

The crew master said, "Marco, I am 56 years old. When you get to this age you can see through young people, you develop an insight. Because you have been where the young people now are, and you can envision what they desire and think. As you get older you start to appreciate different things, you will see. As for me, youth was wasted on the young. I thought I knew everything, I lived only for today. I Didn't want to make commitments to anyone or anything. I changed my course as the wind blew. I sought to find new things that were really all the same.

The crew master took a sip of his drink.

The crew master said, "I can see through you Marco, you have the same look in your eye that I carried in my youth. You want to see the world, and all it has to offer. You are on a search. You don't know what for. Perhaps, perfection."

I was listening as if he really knew who I was, he told me things about myself that perhaps I did not even know myself.

The crew master continued, "There is no perfection Marco, there is only the destiny you follow. It is not meant to be perfect, it's about being true to yourself, be true to your heart. True to your word, Marco. That is all we have."

I was in awe of how the crew master was so candid with me.

The crew master continued, "Marco, listen to me. Find yourself a good woman with a loving heart. Love her, respect her, make a family with her. And give them the love they deserve. Give them your life and guide them to live their lives in the way the Lord intends. You will have no greater satisfaction in the end greater than the satisfaction of having been true to your word."

I looked at him while in deep thought and said, "Thank you Sir."

The crew master replied. "You won't find that out here Marco, you won't find anything. The sea without land is like a woman without a man, they are both very different, but they need each other to exist."

I nodded my head as if I understood.

The crew master got himself ready to leave and said, "Well, don't take this old man too seriously. You are young yet. But don't forget what I said."

With his index finger pointed upward, he walked off.

I thought a lot about the crew master the next day as I continued the paint duty. I looked to the sea, her waves undulated and crashed into the blue. A beautiful deep blue color I observed, this was the Caribbean Sea. I had heard others speak of this sea and its beauty. I could see there was some truth to it. I wondered what other secrets it held. From a corner of my eye I glimpsed and I could see land. I put

124

my brush down for a minute and looked out, I could see some buildings and a city. Then I looked out to the forward deck and saw some other crewmen looking out to sea as well, I pointed at the land, they waved to me. I walked over to them and asked, "Do you know what that is?"

They crew members replied, "It is San Juan."

I looked out and said, "Puerto Rico! Wow, I did not know we would come so close."

One crewman said, "Tomorrow we should be able to see St. John."

I replied, "Sounds like a nice place."

The crewman replied, "The water there is beautiful."

I waved goodbye and went back to work. The water was indeed very beautiful, together with the sky and puffy clouds, it was almost paradise. Or perhaps this could be paradise if one wished it to be. Although the reality was that beneath all its beauty lurked also the dangers such as sharks and barracuda. I was starting to learn, Life is what you make of it.

The captain slowed us down as we passed St. John, I must admit this island had me particularly captivated. Everyone took some time to gaze around at all the little islands. The water was a light crystal clear blue and turquoise, against the rolling green hills and rocks jutting out of the sea. I found this place to be an inspiration to my soul. As we passed by some smaller islands, I could see far down throughout the clear water. There were sea turtles and starfish and stingrays and schools of bright colored fish. The captain was careful not to get too close as there were some coral reefs around the islands as well. It appeared the Lord truly gifted this place when the earth was created. The day passed serenely and at sunset most of the crew went on break. The day was so peaceful, it just took away the mood to work. That night at the lounge, everyone was rather quiet. The crew master stopped by.

"I hope everyone enjoyed the day." , he said.

Most of us replied "Yes, Sir."

The crew master continued, "Well, I have passed through this blessed place many, many years. And still to this day every time I come here I feel refreshed, it just seems to take away all my troubles."

I had to admit I also did feel relaxed after being here today.

The crew master continued, "From here on we will be at open sea for a of couple weeks until we reach the east coast of Brazil, Rio de Janeiro that is. Rio is also a special place, we will spend a few days there to unload and load cargo."

Then he looked at me and said, "Marco, you will stay longer as you will be on assignment."

I nodded yes.

The crew master continued, "Gentlemen, tomorrow the day starts early, and the Captain has a full list of duties for all of you. Please check your assigned schedules at 06:00 posted on the bulletin board as usual. I will turn in early this evening, and I suggest you do the same. I wish you all good night."

We all replied, "Good Night Sir."

The next days at sea were exhilarant for me, I got to know much of the crew and I learned all kinds of new duties such as being lookout, engine room maintenance, rope mending, and I even learned to navigate by the stars. I was enamored with my new life. I learned that while one is out at sea we become solely dependent on our knowledge and skills, and there is not much room for errors. One had to think and make well planned decisions, as not only your own life is at stake. We were all responsible for each other, as a team. As for the captain, well, most of the time he had a serious look on his face. And understandably so, a lot of responsibilities came with that job. And always respected honorably, the Captain was required to sacrifice his needs for the benefit of the crew and vessel. Without a healthy happy crew, the voyage could easily become perilous. Every Captain needs a crew that respects him and knows that their assignment comes first, and vice versa, the crew needs to know they have a Captain that looks out for his crew first and the vessel as well.

I was on lookout the following morning. The captain decided to take a route which kept us close to land, off the islands of the southern Caribbean due to a storm in the south Atlantic which was whipping up some turbulent wave activity. We could feel it even as we were positioned a few hundred miles away. The visibility was clear and I could even see an island from time to time. Being a lookout can become tedious after a while and was not my favorite duty, but it was my job so I did my best to stay alert and keep an eye on my sector. I tried to count waves and estimated wave heights, I would get excited when I would see a dolphin or a gull diving for fish. Often, I would look at the paint work I had done and how much more needed attention to break the monotony. I learned quickly that a vessel required lots of paint maintenance to prevent sea salt corrosion of the metal. I noticed some corroded spots on a lifeboat lift and I thought about asking the crew master if I could repair it, and then I saw something out of the corner of my eye. At first I could not determine exactly what it was, but it was not a wave or a dolphin, I tried to focus closer as I walked towards mid-deck. I tried to focus and get a better look with my binoculars. It was difficult to position it into the binocular's view sight. Eventually, I focused the object into my view. There was a small boat with a few people on it. My first thought was, what are they doing out here? A couple hundred miles from land. Then I thought there must be an island around here and maybe they are local fisherman. Quickly I got on the speaker phone and called the navigation room and reported the boat with some people on board located maybe a mile away off the starboard bow. There did not appear to be a distress signal, however, they were too far away to make any judgment as to why a small boat would be way out at sea. The Captain decided to change course and try to get closer to make an assessment. As we drew closer to the small vessel, we could see the people wave at us. They were in distress. An alert siren blasted a call and most crewmen reported to the crew master's office. Orders were given to proceed to deck one door opening and to prepare to lower a lifeboat into the water. I was assigned to the deck one door aperture and I waited for confirmation to open the door. I arrived at the deck one door and there were already several members of the crew there, including the crew master. We got our call to open the door. We placed some safety ropes across the door opening and I pulled a ramp out with a rope ladder. The door opening was very close to sea level and if the waves had been higher, it would be very dangerous to attempt this rescue. I could see the small boat. There were 5 people on board and the boat appeared very low in the water, it was about to sink. We were all concentrated on the rescue effort and did not speak unless necessary. The crew master asked me to tie down the rope ladder and throw it over the side. The ships motorized life boat cautiously approached the vessel and the driver attempted to communicate. I noticed Joe was on the life boat and ready to throw a rope onto the distressed boat. Joe managed to tie up and he managed to push the afflicted boat and passengers close to the door opening. We secured some lines to the troubled boat and threw the men some ropes. The crew master asked me to get some blankets ready. The men came aboard while they held the ropes with all their last might. One of the men had a sack he held tightly and could not manage to climb aboard with it. We repeatedly instructed him to drop the bag and come aboard, it appeared he did not understand. The wave activity made it difficult to keep the vessels from crashing into each other, the situation was perilous. Joe decided to take-action. He went on board the ill-fated boat. He grabbed the bag from the man and tied it to our rope. We pulled it aboard. The man followed. Joe got back on his lifeboat, and then we untied from the faltered boat. Once the rescued passengers were on board, I quickly gave them some blankets. The crew master asked me to bring them to the infirmary where the ships medical officer awaited. The 5 men shivered in distress and a couple of them seemed in shock. Joe did a great job and I could see he used his skills effectively. We closed the door and secured it.

The crew master said, "Good job men, you make a nice team."

He paused as he threw a rope to the side.

The crew master continued. "Please put all ropes and accessories back where they were and clean this room up, once you are finished please report to my office for further detail."

We all replied, "Yes, Sir."

The crew master continued, "Marco, these men need attendance by the medic, bring them over to the infirmary and report to the office afterwards.

I replied, "Yes, Sir."

As I guided the 5 men to the infirmary, the man with the sack came up to me with his hand open.

The man said, "For you."

He held what looked like a shiny ring. I didn't pay much attention and I said, "No, thank you, this is my job."

He insisted and as we arrived at the infirmary he placed the ring in my pocket. I didn't think anything of it at the time as there was a lot going on. The medics assistant quickly intervened and took the men into the infirmary. I was now relieved of this duty. I continued my orders and reported to the crew master's office. The first mate was there as well. He questioned me regarding what I had seen. Where I was when I spotted it, what did I see, what time did I first see the object. He needed to make a log of the event for the record book. From Joe's account, one of the rescued men told him they were refugees from Venezuela. They had been at sea for many days and the currents took them way off course. They were trying to get to the northern coast of Brazil. The current took them a few hundred miles out to sea. Their boat began to sink and they were very tired trying to keep it afloat. I had saved their lives when I spotted them as they were very distant from our vessel, and no one else had noticed them. The first mate commended me and logged this event in my file for future references. I kind of felt good about being able to help save the lives of a few men. If we did not rescue them, they probably would not have survived another night at sea.

Sometimes life's path brings us places where just by chance, unusual things happen, and sometimes they are very special. This was one of those moments. Kind of like the time Domenico crossed our paths along that river bank.

I became kind of popular on this voyage since my keen vision brought about some excitement. Well, the truth is that we were now behind schedule due to the time it took to rescue the refugees. My crew mates started to call me 'The Hawk'. I had become used to my friends call me, 'Hey, Hawk!'. Some of the crew did not speak English clearly and it would sound like 'Hey, Ak!' It was a little awkward, but they meant well. The first mate liked me so much, he decided to train me in the navigation room, I learned some basic navigation skills. Together, we plotted a course to try and save some of the time we had lost due to the rescue. The new course would take us a little further out to sea at first, directly towards the northeast coast of Brazil. We would pass close by to Natal and Recife, and then straight south to Rio de Janeiro. We assumed the winds would remain favorable as per the latest weather report charts. We calculated 9 days, which would save us a day.

Chapter 11

I remember clearly as we navigated the coastal waters of northeastern Brazil, it made an impression in my mind as if I entered a world of pre-historic times. The closer we moved towards Rio de Janeiro, the more I felt I arrived into another realm. The giant rocks that stood erect by the seashore as if someone or some creature placed them there, firmly in the sand. The giant rocks gave me an impression that they were conscious creatures, as if they had a story to tell. I can only imagine the things they had seen, if they could only tell.

Once we docked the vessel and tied down all the ropes, I was told to deliver the ship's cargo documents to the terminal office so they can start to prepare the Customs clearance process. In the meantime, the crew started to offload the cargo destined for this port. I walked into the office and I asked for the ship-owners office. They told me to go upstairs and it was third door on the right. I proceeded and made my way, it wasn't a very busy place and rather quiet. I counted 3 doors, the door was open and I entered. There was a young lady and I interrupted her as she looked out of the office window towards the ship. I said, "Hello."

The young lady turned around and said, "Bom Dia. Are you from the ship?"

At first I was a little taken, my impression was that the woman was not only beautiful, but so very feminine. I felt as if time had stopped for a moment and I became dazed.

The young lady looked at me with a concerned look and said, "Fala Portuguese?"

Then I regained my composure and said, "Oh, no, I'm sorry, it has been a long day, yes, I am from the ship."

She smiled and replied, "Long day! You mean long night. It is morning!"

I smiled as well and replied, "Well, yes, I suppose you are correct."

And then she took the paperwork from me and gave me her hand to shake.

The young lady said, "My name is Rose Marie."

Her hand was so lovely, it left an imprint in my mind. I had forgotten my duties for the moment. The fact that the ship needed to be offloaded and the crew needed me to supervise as I knew which cargo needed offloading disappeared from my mind. She took the papers to her desk.

"And your name?", Rose Marie asked.

Awkwardly I replied, "Oh, Sorry, I am Marco, we just arrived from New York."

Rose Marie placed her fingers on her lips, "Marco, Marco, ... sounds familiar."

Then she sat down and looked at some papers, she placed her hands on the desk.

Rose Marie asked, "Aah, are you the Marco that is going to remain here to oversee the incoming cargo for the next vessel?"

A little hesitantly I replied "Actually, yes, that is me."

Then she stood up and walked to the window again, she turned around and said, "You must be excited, do you have any friends here?"

I thought about it and replied, "Well, I met a crew mate on the ship,"

Rose Marie interrupted and said, "Don't worry Marco, I will find you some friends. However, for the moment, you better get back to the ship now. I see a bunch of men with their arms crossed and they seem disturbed, I think they need help offloaing the ship?"

I looked out of the window and realized I had forgotten my duties completely. I said. "Oh, I better hurry," I ran to the door."

"Nice to meet you Marco." Rose Marie waved as I was exiting,

I turned around with a bashful smile and replied, "Nice to meet you Rose Marie, I hope to see you soon."

Rose Marie replied smiling, "Ah Marco, you will, I will be here waiting for you."

As I made my way back to the ship, I could not get her out of my mind. She was tall with long brown hair and brown eyes, a thin and curvy hourglass figure with delicate features and smile. I had never met a woman with such a sweet feminine loving personality, I think I was in love. As soon as I approached the loading ramp, the guys were calling me.

A Crewman said, "Hey Hawk, which one of these crates are coming off? We can't figure it out."

I walked over and pointed to the marking and said, "If you look and read, you will find it. What does this say?" They all looked somewhere else and made believe not to hear me.

Another crewman said, "Oh, looks like Rio de Janeiro."

I shook my head and said, "That's the one." Then I pointed to a whole row of freight and said "Guys, this entire section must come out, put it on the dock and I will check the markings."

We proceeded to offload the cargo. And in the back of my mind, I only thought of Rose Marie the whole time. What a pretty name I realized.

We worked until the afternoon, around 3 PM we called it a day. We all went back to the ship to wash up and get ready for dinner. Afterwards, I had an urge to spend some time on dry land, so I decided to take a walk. I walked over towards the office, I noticed Rose Marie looked at me from the window and waved to me with a smile on her face. I walked to the entrance door, and there she was as she walked down the stairs to meet me.

Rose Marie said, "Hi, Marco, come in."

Some of the people in the office looked at me with a grin on their face, I did not care. I only stared at Rose Marie. She held a letter in her hand

Rose Marie said, "This is for you, it's from your uncle in New York, he has arranged a room for you to stay while you are here in Rio. It is in Santa Teresa, I will bring you there."

I took the letter and opened it, it had some receipts and some written instructions."

Rose Marie continued and said, "It is only about 10 minutes from here, and if you like I can pick you up in the morning on my way to work."

I looked at her with a glow on my face, "Oh Rose, you would do that for me?"

She smiled and replied, "Marco, of course, Cariocas are always good hosts to visitors."

I replied, "Thank you Rose, how can I repay you, can I buy you dinner tonight."

She pouted her lips and raised her eyebrows and replied,

"Marco, yes I can have dinner with you since you are my new friend and we will be working together."

I replied, "Great!"

Rose Marie continued, "But I will need to get home early as my mother will wait for me at home."

I replied with a serious face, "Oh, absolutely. I hope you don't live far away."

Rose Marie replied, "I live in Niteroi, it's not far, just a short ferry ride across Guanabara bay."

I waited for her to finish up her work.

After work, we took the bus to Santa Teresa. The town was built on rolling hills, there were lots of green trees. It was a short walk from the bus stop to the hostel I would stay at, although it was all up hill. The building had many steps to climb as it was built on a steep hill close to the top of the road. We walked into the lobby and I presented my papers to the clerk.

The clerk looked at Rose and said, "Ciao Rose, como vai?"

Rose Marie replied, "Boa tarde Paulo."

Rose Marie placed her hand on my shoulder and said, "Paulo, this is Marco, he will be staying here for a few weeks as he will be working with us at the port."

Paulo looked to me and said, "Hello Marco, welcome, it is nice to meet you."

I replied, "Thank you Paulo."

I was kind of surprised that Rose knew the clerk, he was a young man, maybe little older than I. He seemed to smile a lot at Rose, in my opinion with a kind of a phony attitude. He handed me a paper to sign and gave me the room key.

Paulo said, "Marco, your room is number 931, it is ready for you now."

I looked at Rose and said, "would you like to come up?"

"Oh, No Marco, it is not proper." She replied.

Paulo kept that smile with that same phony smirk on his face.

Paulo said, "Señor Marco, Rose has been here to bring guests before, she knows what the rooms look like."

Rose Marie looked at Paulo with a scornful look and said, "Paulo, I have only been upstairs once or twice to assist our guests with their bags when you were not around."

Paulo apologetically replied, "Desculpame Rose Marie, mea culpa."

Then Paulo looked at me and said, "Excuse me Sir, I need to attend a call."

And he walked off into another room.

Rose and I left the hostel and into the street. I did not have any bags with me so we decided to go for dinner. I would sleep in the ship tonight and go back to the room and settle in tomorrow. It seemed a nice part of the city, on some hill tops I could see the Corcovado mountain. It is famous for the statue of Christ the redeemer with open arms embracing the people of the entire city. I think it gave people a good feeling, a feeling of community and kindness. You could also see the

Sugarloaf Mountain from a distance. Rose started to walk swiftly as a tram arrived behind us.

"Come on Marco, let's get on the tram." She said as she chased the Tram.

We hopped on as it moved slowly enough for us to board. It was a little tricky to get on board, but much better than to have walked up those hills. We arrived to Rua Paschoal Carlos Magno, the name of the street stuck in my head as Charlemagne was the great king that began the restoration of Europe after the fall of the Roman Empire. We learned that in school when I was a young boy, and I was surprised to see it mentioned here in Rio. I could see the world was very large, yet small and its people held similar values.

We arrived at a big church and there was a bar restaurant next door with open doors. We hopped off the tram as it slowed down and we walked in.

A gentleman waved to Rose and said, "Rose, como vai, tudo bom?"

Rose cheerfully replied, "Tudo bem Anselmo, meu amigo e eu gostaria de jantar."

Anselmo replied, "Certo."

And he walked us to a table and handed us menus.

I looked at Rose and said, "What a nice place, I take it you come here often?"

Rose Marie replied, "This is my favorite place to have Feijoada."

That rang a bell, and I replied, "Oh, I have heard of that, what is it again?"

"I will order it for you, I'm sure you will like it.", Rose Marie replied while looking at the menu,

"Thank you, sounds delicious.", I replied,

"I hope you did not take what Paulo mentioned earlier seriously. He can be a, well, I think in English it is male chauvinist." Rose replied while placing her menu on the table.

I pressed my lips pouting a bit and said, "Hmm, yes, he did give off that kind of attitude. No, don't worry about me, means nothing to me whatever he said. I just didn't want to be rude and leave you there in the hall."

Anselmo came over and asked, "Well, what may I offer you two. Rose, will you have your usual?"

Rose Marie looked at Anselmo, "Si, dois Feijoadas por favor."

Anselmo replied, " Certo."

Anselmo walked away.

Rose Marie said, "Well, Marco, so you know, Paolo has a girlfriend. But he always tries to get fresh with me, and I don't like it. But the company makes me go there from time to time to bring guests."

I replied, "Oh, I'm sorry Rose, you should have told me, I would have gone in on my own."

She waved her hand at me and replied, "Oh Marco, don't worry, I can handle him. There are much worst men in Rio."

I asked, "Rose, were you born in Rio?"

Without emotion on her face she replied. "Yes, my mother is Brazilian, my father Portuguese. My parents married very young and I was born soon after. My father was too young to handle a family and he left us. My mother has had to struggle as a worker in a factory sewing to support us."

I didn't know how to respond, and then I said. "I think I understand Rose, I also have had a painful childhood."

She interrupted and replied, "Painful! No Marco, not Painful. I was too young to remember my father and I have never known him. My mother has been a very loving woman. I think it has made me stronger."

I replied. "Yes, I can see you are a strong woman." The waiter arrived with our dinner, and it looked very yummy.

Feijoada was as good as it was described to me, but a little on the heavy side.

Anselmo came over and asked, "How is your Feijoada? May I get you something else?"

Then he looked to Rose and said, "Can I offer you two a Caipirinha?"

I looked to Rose and said, "I've heard of the Caipirinha."
And then I said to Anselmo, "Yes, I think I would like one."
Anselmo and Rose Marie both smiled.
Rose said, "okay, why not, I will have one as well."
Anselmo replied, "Right away."
And then he took off to see the bar man.
Rose asked, "Marco, tell me about your childhood."
I sat back in the chair, took a deep breath and said, "Well, it's not all that complicated, I never knew my parents and I was left in an orphanage." The bar man arrived with Caipirinhas.
Rose said "Obrigada Anselmo."
Anselmo replied, "De nada."
Rose Marie looked at me and said, "An orphanage, oh my, that must have been so lonely for you."
I took a sip of the drink and said, "Oh wow, that is good!"
Rose Marie replied, "Don't drink it too fast, it has a strong punch afterwards."
I replied, "Well, yes, I suppose it was lonely sometimes. I made my friends and we survived and made the best of it as most children would do. I often think about that part of my life and what it would have been like to actually know my parents." I paused for another sip. I continued, "But my friends and I were lucky. We consider ourselves brothers now, Dario and George, we were kind of adopted."
Rose said, "Ah, that is nice, you will tell me more about them. And when did your uncle from New York adopt you?"
I replied, "I should tell you, actually, he did not adopt us, we were kind of adopted from a couple in Italy."
Rose Marie looked at me, shook her head and said, "Now Marco, I am getting confused, you will tell me more later. For now, I need to take a walk as this meal and drink has made me sleepy. I think we are done here, let's take a walk."
She got up and opened her purse. I quickly interrupted and said, "No Rose, dinner is on me, remember?"
She looked at me with a smirk, "Thank you Marco, but I will put this on my business expense list."

I was kind of surprised to hear that and replied, "Really? Rose, I'm not really used to being treated to good company and food. Thank you. Next time I hope you will allow me to reciprocate."

Rose smiled and said, "Let's go Marco."

We waved off to Anselmo and quickly we proceeded outside.

As we walked about and explored around town, I wanted to ask her if we could spend some time together and maybe go tour the city.

Rose said "Well Marco, I think now we should get back to the port. I will need to take the bus home as it has gotten late. Tomorrow we both have work."

I replied, "Yes, I think you are right, perhaps this weekend we can spend some time together? Maybe we can visit Sugarloaf?"

Rose Marie replied, "Yes, I would be happy to go with you."

I smiled and said, "Great!" We made our way back to the port bus station, I could see the ship in the distance. Rose needed to wait for her shuttle bus to the ferry to get home. I didn't want to leave her there, so I started to talk. I said, "How long does it take you to get home from here Rose Marie?"

She replied, "I Take the ferry boat to Niteroi and then it's a short walk, but it goes by quickly, maybe 30 minutes. Niteroi is a nice quiet community with beautiful beaches, very clean. I live there with my mother since I am a little girl."

Her shuttle arrived and she quickly said, "I will tell you more tomorrow."

She grabbed my shoulder and reached over and kissed me on the cheek.

She said, "Boa Noite Marco."

I was in a trance as she quickly got on the shuttle and I watched her depart. I stood there and stared at the shuttle as it drove off. Once they were out of sight, I turned towards the ship and started to walk. I felt something and I attempted to understand as I was confused. Wow, I said to myself. I already felt I wanted to see her again. This was more than a pretty face, I felt I knew her, as if I had known her all my life. It's not logical I thought to myself. I continued to walk and think about her and to see her again.

Chapter 12

My senses revived to the invigorating scent of freshly ground coffee. I observed the horizon as the sun lit the morning clouds and outlined them with pink hues as they swiftly moved across the sky guided by the will of the wind. My ship would depart late this afternoon and I would not sail out to sea with her. I planned to get my duties accomplished early so I could say goodbye to my crewmates. And hopefully go visit Rose before she left the office. I had my bag packed and ready so I would not have to rush last minute to gather my belongings.

We managed to unload yesterday and I wanted to make sure that everything checked out on the manifest. Today we expected a late delivery and also some supplies for the voyage. The lunch whistle sounded and quickly the loading dock was left lifeless. I decided to bring my bag over to the office and leave it with Rose Marie. I walked into the office and asked the receptionist if I could go up and see Rose.

The receptionist pointed her finger up and said in Portuguese "Espere un minutino, por favor."

The receptionist went upstairs. I put my bag down. I thought to myself, I guess Rose Marie is busy this morning. Soon after I heard someone as they walked downstairs, it was Rose Marie. She waved me over to follow her.

She said, "Come up Marco."

I followed without hesitation.

As we walked upstairs she said, "We have a visitor this morning."

I replied, "Oh, am I interrupting? I can come back later, I just wanted..."

She interrupted and said, "No Marco, actually it is good that you are here."

"Really?" I said with surprise.

She replied, "Come to my office, we will explain."

We walked in the office and there was a gentleman that stood by her desk. Rose introduced me to the gentlemen.

Rose Marie placed her hand on my shoulder and said, "Señor Hoelck, I would like you to meet Marco, the shipmate that first spotted the..."

She removed her hand from my shoulder and then continued. "Refugees."

I was taken a minute and thought to myself 'refugees?', what could this be about.

Then she turned to me and said, "Marco, this is Mr. Hoelck, he is from the German Consulate here in Rio."

Mr. Hoelck and I shook hands. I said, "Nice to meet you Sir."

"It's nice to meet you as well Marco." Mr. Hoelck replied.

Mr. Hoelck walked over to the door and closed it. Then he pointed to a chair. "Sit down Marco, please."

I complied with his wishes. Rose took my bag over to her closet.

Mr. Hoelck said, "Marco, the German government is grateful to you and we would like to express our gratitude."

I looked at him with a confused look and said, "Forgive me Sir, gratitude for what?"

He smiled and replied, "Marco, the doomed vessel you spotted, and the people aboard. They were not refugees."

I looked at him incredulously and said, "They weren't?"

He shook his head and said, "No Sir. They were thieves."

I became more confused by the minute. Then I said, "Why were they in the middle of the ocean?" He walked over to Rose's desk and sat down. Rose sat next to me.

Mr. Hoelck replied, "It's a little complicated, but that small boat was not the vessel they had sailed out in. That was their life boat."

I listened attentively now.

Mr Hoelck said, "They had left Brazil in a larger vessel with intentions to arrive to Puerto Rico we believe."

I nodded.

Mr. Hoelck continued, "Their vessel was old and took on water very quickly after a storm, they had no choice but to get on that life boat."

I replied, "Well, it's a good thing they had a life boat."

Mr. Hoelck replied, "Yes Marco, and it was a good thing you were there that day to see them, as they only had a few hours left before they would go into the sea without a boat."

I sat in silence as I attempted to make sense of this discussion.

Mr Hoelck said, "You see Marco, the men you saved, they carried stolen German passports with them."

My mouth dropped open. I do remember one of them that would not leave the boat without his sack. Joe had to board the boat to assist the last man on the boat with his sack. That bag must have held the stolen passports.

I responded. "I had no idea."

Mr. Hoelck stood up and said, "Oh no, we know you were not aware, actually, we know who the men were and they are now under arrest."

I started to wonder why I was given this information.

Mr. Hoelck continued, "You see Marco, they stole the passports from my office."

I speculated the reason he would have so many passports at his office in Brazil in the first place.

Mr. Hoelck continued, "There are not too many people that know about this, and frankly, I need to keep it that way."

I contemplated why he was telling me this information.

I replied, "Sir, you don't need to worry about me, I won't tell anyone."

"Thank you Marco for your confidentiality. But, I have confided in you this information because I need your help. I need to get these passports to Germany and I need someone to carry them there without going through Customs." He said earnestly.

I think I started to understand why I was here now. Mr. Hoelck walked over to me and he put his hand on my shoulder.

"Would you carry these passports to Germany for me Marco? You are the perfect candidate. You will be assigned to a vessel destined for Bremen, you will have high clearance and I will make sure you are not to be subjected to Customs inspection." He said assertively.

I was silent as Mr. Hoelck walked back to his desk and sat down.

Mr. Hoelck continued, "Marco, as a token of appreciation for this service, the German government will award you a gift of One Thousand Dollars."

I almost fell off the chair.

Mr Hoelck walked over to the closet and put his jacket on, picked up his bag and walked back over to me. I stood up and he gave me his hand to shake, and I reciprocated.

Mr. Hoelck said, "Marco, I will leave now as I have given you all the information you need to know at this stage. I know you will stay in Rio a few weeks and will not sail out this evening as you had intended. I will be in touch with you through Rose for further instructions. If you should think of any questions or if you would like to speak to me of any particulars during your encounter on the vessel, please contact me. You are a bright young man. I know you will do the right thing."

He opened the door and left.

There were many thoughts that went through my mind as he left. I reflected upon the events of the rescue in my mind. Rose Marie sat with her hands on her lap as she watched me in silence.

Rose Marie stood up and said, "What is wrong?"

With an inquisitive look, I replied, "When did you find out about this?" She seemed puzzled as to my question and perhaps a little annoyed.

Rose Marie replied, "Mr. Hoelck arrived this morning to my office and asked me if I knew about the refugees, and then he told me what he just told you. I didn't know you were responsible for their rescue."

She lifted her arms and ran her fingers through her long brown hair as if to comfort herself while she looked out the window. I cherished her figure as she stood there. Then she turned her head towards me as the sunlight dimmed and her facial features left me speechless.

Smiling. I looked at her as I waved my head back and forth. And I said, "I'm confused."

She got up and walked over to me, placed her hand on my shoulder.

Rose Marie said, "He told me everything except of the $1,000 reward."

She seemed more excited about the reward than I did.

Rose Marie said, "Marco, what is the matter, why do you look worried?"

I got off the chair and said, "I don't know Rose Marie, I guess I need to reflect. Will you come out with me after work, perhaps we can take a walk somewhere?"

With a comforting look, she said. "Yes, of course I will, I just need to finish up, give me an hour or so."

"Okay, in the meantime, I will bring my bag to Santa Teresa and check into my room. I will be back soon." I replied as I prepared to leave.

"Good idea Marco, you go ahead, I will meet you there later. Um beijo", Rose Marie replied as she caressed my shoulder with her hand and blew me a kiss.

As in a trance, I raised my hand and said, "Bye". I walked out the door.

I arrived at the Santa Teresa hostel. I entered and Paulo was not at the front desk, so I walked on up. I entered the room and placed my bag down, went over to the balcony and looked out at the view. It was a pretty view, however, there was something else on my mind. I was trying to go over the passport story in my head. Should I get involved? I thought of the reward, it was a lot of money. It would take me years to save that kind of money. And then I started to think about Rose. I had only known her a few days, however it felt as if I had known her since childhood. Soon I would leave here, and I think that troubled me. I didn't want to leave her behind. Suddenly the ring the man gave me on the way to the infirmary came to my mind. I took it out from my bag and looked at it closer. It was an awkward ring with many strange markings and letters. I just could not understand what was written on it, or maybe it was a design of some kind. The phone rang. It was Rose.

"Hi Marco, I am so sorry, but I won't be able to come and see you this evening. My mother needs me to accompany her to see the doctor.", She said with affection.

I was disappointed and I replied, "Oh, I'm sorry, I hope she is okay."

Rose Marie replied, "Yes, she is okay. But she needs me to accompany her as the doctor is far away from our home."

I replied, "I understand Rose Marie. Is there anything I can do to help?"

With appreciation she replied, "Thank you Marco, you are kind. We will be fine. I will see you at the office in the morning, okay? You should take a walk around town and have a nice evening, the weather is nice."

Disappointedly I replied, "Okay, you too Rose, have a nice evening."

"Have a nice night dear.", She sweetly replied.

So here I was now, I had hoped to see Rose tonight. I had a lot on my mind and I needed some company. I decided to go for a walk and clear my head, perhaps I would go over to see the beach.

I took the trolley and then the bus and then another bus. I found myself near the ocean and I went for a walk in the sand. I found a bench and took a load off my feet as I had walked a long way. I Stretched my arms and looked out to sea. Darkness came quickly and many stars appeared in the clear sky that night. I dreamed about Rose and I wish she had come here with me. I decided to walk down to the shoreline, where the sea meets the sand. It was so tranquil, the only sound was that of the gentle waves as they rolled up on the shore, and then washed away. I walked in the wet sand and left my foot prints, for the waves to wash them away as if they were never there. Comparable to a soul as it inhabits the flesh momentarily, and then washed away in passing. This was a place of interaction and transition, or perhaps an illusion.

My evening with the stars passed quickly and I found my way back to the hostel after I satisfied my belly with some cheese bread and empanadas. Paulo was at the front desk as I entered.

Paulo said, "Good evening Mr. Marcos."

I replied, "Hello."

Paulo replied, "Is there anything I can assist you with?"

I replied, "No Paulo, not at the moment. Thank you."

I went on up to the room. I sat in silence for a while as I pondered my thoughts. I was infatuated with thoughts of Rose Marie and I decided to try and write something to clear my mind.

The Sea and Sand

Here by the sea and sand,
is a point where two worlds band.
It's an enchanted place,
as if created by grace.

The sea being smooth and creamy,
and the sand being coarse and stony.
One complements the other,
as if designed by Natures Mother.

It is a place where one feels elated,
and burdens seem abated.
A place where waves of the sea,
gently caress you and me.

And the beauty of this creation,
both elements essential in its formation.
sea needing sand to hold its domain,
sand needing sea to smooth it's coarse grain

Like a man needs a woman,
and a woman needs a man.
Only a divine Creator,
can forge such a nature.

And so I added it to my box of poems and went off to bed.

Chapter 13

I received a phone call from Rose early the next morning. Rose said, "Good Morning Marco, did I wake you?"
It was 6 AM and I was not quite awake yet. I replied, "Rose Marie? Good Morning. How are you? Are you downstairs?"

Rose laughed and replied, "No Marco, I am not downstairs. Sorry to wake you but I wanted to let you know that you will need to see Mr. Hoelck today."

Now I awoke quite quickly. I said, "You mean the man from the Consulate? Is he coming to the office again?"

She replied, "No Marco, he phoned me and asked that I ask you to meet him at the Consulate this morning."

I thought about it a bit and replied, "At the Consulate? where is it? Do you know what he wants?"

Rose Marie replied, "I am not sure Marco. He said to meet him at Rua Presidente Carlos de Campos, number 417 around 9 AM."

I replied, "Let me write that down, will you be there?"

She replied, "I'm sorry, but I cannot Marco. Besides he asked for you to be there. I have to report to work at 8 AM today."

I replied, "Oh, okay, I thought maybe..,"

She interrupted and said, "Come to the office afterwards and you can tell me all about it, okay dear, don't worry, he is a nice man. Remember, Rua Presidente Carlos de Campos, number 417."

I replied, "Okay Rose Marie, so I will see you later."

Rose Marie replied, "Ciao, ciao Marco. Um abracao."

I made my way to Rio de Janeiro city center and speculated what Mr. Hoelck would tell me. He had mentioned he wanted me to go to Germany. I arrived and rang the bell. A man opened the door and guided me to his private office. I found Mr Hoelck as he sat at his desk, the man announced my arrival. Mr Hoelck got up and walked over to me.

Mr Hoelck said, "Good morning Marco, come in. Please sit down here next to my desk."

I obliged and took my seat.

"Have you enjoyed your stay in Rio?", said Mr. Hoelck.

I replied. "Yes, I haven't explored much yet, but it does seem a place of enchantment."

"Yes Marco, Rio is one of those special places that one never seems to forget. It does have a magical or perhaps mystical aspect, and people become fascinated." Mr. Hoelck replied with a smile.

He walked over to his safe, it was open and he reached inside.

"These are the passports that were recovered, thanks to your keen eyesight." Hoelck said with passports in hand.

He brought the large bag and placed it on the desk, he looked at me in the eye."

Hoelck said with assurance, "I would like you to bring them to Bremen. Let me reiterate and expand on our previous meeting. I will appoint you as a Diplomatic clerk and you will not be subjected to Customs checking. You will meet with my representative in Germany and deliver the bag only to him." .

He sat down in front of me.

Hoelck continued, "I will have the bag placed in your quarters on the vessel. You will be assigned as assistant in the navigation room."

When he mentioned navigation, the offer began to sound appealing, I looked to him and said, "How soon would I be required to depart?"

Mr. Hoelck stood up and walked back over to his side of the desk.

Hoelck replied showing confidence. "The vessel leaves in 5 days. Marco, I need to ask you, did any of the men give or say anything to you during the rescue?"

Without hesitation I instinctively decided to keep this to myself. I replied, "No Sir, anything in particular?"

Hoelck replied as he sat down, "No, I only want to make sure there is nothing more that perhaps they tried to hide. In any case, I will have your Diplomatic ID with contact information for my contact in Germany included with the bag in your room. You will receive your payment once you have completed the mission."

I was silent and in deep thought.

Mr. Hoelck looked at me and said, "Are you on board Marco?"

I pouted my lips and nodded "Yes."

Instantly he replied, "That's a very good decision Marco, I knew you would accept my offer. You won't regret this. I wish I had such an opportunity when I was your age. I can see the winner of a horse race right at the start off the gate. Your life is about to change, don't look back and be loyal to the people that help you. Ahh, to be young again, and Rose, now that is an opportunity. Don't lose your opportunities young man, we are only young once in this life."

I got up and replied, "Thank you, Sir, I'll wait your further instructions." And I waved goodbye.

Once I arrived back to the office, I found Rose as she was at work on the typewriter. I entered and said, "Hi Rose Marie."

She looked at me and replied, "Hi Marco, I am working on the manifest for your uncle's shipment, the first lot has arrived this morning."

I replied, "Oh, already, that's very good."

Rose Marie replied as she pulled the paper out of the typewriter, "Yes, actually, this is good so you can start to check the markings."

Rose Marie gave me the manifest and said. "You will need to check that all the bags from this lot have these shipment marks. Look on the manifest, I have circled them here for you. If they are not shown on each bag, then you will need to write the shipment marks on each crate."

I looked at the document and replied, "Okay, I will get to work on this right away."

Rose Marie asked with curiosity, "How was the meeting?"

"He wants me to leave for Germany in 5 days.", I replied.

"That is very soon, how do you feel about it?" she replied inquisitively.

I replied with a puzzled look, "To be honest, this entire trip has been bizarre, almost daily my life changes. I'm kind of overwhelmed."

She smiled and replied, "Oh Marco, you think too much. You need to relax."

I picked up the manifest and said, "Okay Rose Marie, I will get out to the warehouse and check the markings."

Compassionately she replied, "Good idea, I'll see you at lunch time. Tonight, I want to take you around town so you can relax."

Rose suggested to go for a walk after work and we made our way to Avenida Atlantica. It had been a hot day and now there was a nice breeze from the ocean. It was a nice evening to take a walk by the beach. There were some people that sold trinkets and called us to have a look, so we decided to go closer to shore and get away from them. The view on this shoreline was magnificent with the giant rocks positioned upright over the sea. They were so spectacular that to me it was difficult to comprehend how nature could create this landscape on its own. There were some boys that played soccer, and a young man walked over to us with some coconuts, he asked if we wanted a drink, and we agreed to the offer as we were both thirsty. He took out a large knife and stared to chop a hole in the coconut, then he placed a straw in it and handed it to us. It was very delicious, and I felt instantly refreshed. I said to Rose Marie, "This drink is wonderful."

She smiled and replied, "This is one of my favorite places, the people here are always friendly and the sound of the ocean waves places my mind to tranquility."

I had to agree, this seemed truly a magical place. We walked in silence as we watched the sun set over the ocean, it was God's way to express good night to his children. I became a little tired and I saw a tall chair that looked like a good place to rest for a moment, so I turned to Rose Marie and said, "Would you like to sit a few minutes?" She agreed and so we walked over and climbed onto the chair. We relaxed our legs and looked out to sea, the sun made its final wink of the day and the colors were fading briskly leaving a lighted path for one's eye to follow over the dark sea. And then I thought, a unique path could be seen from all points on the beach, for anyone to see. As if they all led to the same place.

Darkness faded in and it became a little chilly, Rose leaned into me and placed her hand on my belly while resting her head on my shoulder.

Rose Marie said softly, "What are you thinking Marco."

I was very relaxed and I replied, "It is lovely to share this sunset with you."

And then she looked at me with her smile and said, "And what else are you thinking."

I looked in her eyes as I attempted to read her thoughts. Before I could reply, she leaned close to me.

Rose Marie said, "Is this what you want?"

And she kissed me. And then I could not see anything else but her beautiful face and I became captivated by her eyes. I kissed her as well. And it was lovely as we continued to kiss and keep each other warm as the breezy ocean winds attempted to cool the heated sands that the sun left behind. The sense of time became insignificant as we comforted each other into the darkness. And then I noticed a light. It was the moon now that appeared over the horizon. And it was a full moon, as it led a path of light over the darkness of the sea. We were both without words, as we held each other warmly and looked to the moonlight as it continued to rise over the sea. At first it rose quickly, and then it seemed to pause over the ocean and lit the entire beach, provided by its reflection of the sun.

And then Rose said to me, "Marco, I think it's time to go home."

And I agreed.

We climbed off the lifeguard chair onto the sand, grabbed our shoes and walked our way back, hand in hand. I said to Rose. "It's late, would you like me to accompany you home tonight?"

Rose Marie looked at me, smiled and said, "Oh Marco, you are so thoughtful."

And then she pointed to the bus and we ran off to catch it. We were both quiet on the bus ride, we held hands much of the way. The bus stopped at Santa Teresa and we both got off. Rose seemed concerned.

Rose Marie said, "Oh my, it has gotten late and I think the last bus has already left for my home."

We started to walk, so I said to her. "You are welcome to stay in my room tonight, I can sleep in the lobby."

Rose Marie looked at me and said, "My mom will be worried."

She thought a moment and then continued. "I will call her and tell her I will stay overnight with a friend."

We stopped at a phone booth and she called. I waited nearby and she spoke Portuguese with her Mom. Everything seemed okay and she finished off her conversation with 'Um beijo Mama, boa noite'. She walked over to me smiling and grabbed my arm.

Rose Marie said, "It's okay, let's go."

And we started to walk. She seemed happy, and I was happy to see her happy.

We arrived at the hostel and entered, Paulo was not at his desk, so we went upstairs. Once in the room, I said to Rose, "You take the bed, I will go downstairs." Rose came over to me and put her arms around my shoulders and smiled.

Rose Marie said, "Marco, do you really mean that?"

And she kissed me on the cheek. Then she walked over to the window and gazed outside.

Rose Marie said, "I would like you to stay here with me Marco, it's your room and I wouldn't feel right if you didn't have a comfortable place to sleep. Besides, it would be very lonely for me to stay alone in here."

She dimmed the lights and got ready for bed. Then she climbed in.

Rose Marie said, "We need to get some sleep, tomorrow is a work day."

I didn't know what to do, there was only one bed in the room, it was a big bed, but only one bed. I sat in the chair by the bed and started to get comfortable. I sat quietly and rested my head back on the chair. Soon after I realized I was not going to get any sleep unless I got into the bed. Rose was silent and seemed already asleep, so I climbed in next to her. I was not used to sleeping in the same bed with a girl, well.., a woman. As I lied silently next to her, I noticed the scent of her hair, and then she turned and placed her hand on my belly. She kissed my chest and held me tight. And soon after, I felt like a man. That night I realized, God created woman so she could tame the beast in men. I felt peaceful next to her and quickly, I faded off to a peaceful sleep.

I awoke as the sunlight peeked through the large windows, I slept solidly as I must have been very tired. I rolled myself out of bed and rubbed my eyes. Then I remembered and looked over to the bed, Rose was not there. I walked around and realized she was gone, she must have left early this morning I thought, why? I hurriedly got myself ready and made my way downstairs, she was not there, although Paulo was at his desk. I said, "Good morning."

Paulo replied, "Good morning Sir, may I help you with anything?"

I looked at him with a doubtful face and replied, "No." There was no mention of Rose and I left as usual and made my way to the bus stop. I arrived at the office and Rose was at her desk.

Rose Marie looked at me and said, "Bom Dia."

I replied swiftly, "Why did you leave early?"

Rose Marie replied, " Well Marco, I did not want Paulo to see me as I walked out of your apartment for one thing, he would talk all over town."

I looked at her and humbly replied, "Oh. Sorry, I didn't realize. You could have told me Rose, I was little worried."

Rose Marie stood up and replied raising her arms in the air, "Oh Marco."

Then we went to the lunch room for some coffee.

No one was in the lunch room except us and we sat down facing each other. Rose reached for my hands over the table.

Rose Marie said excitedly, "Marco, you will be leaving on a long trip in a few days, are you ready?"

I replied, "To be honest Rose Marie, part of me doesn't want to go. I think I have more things to do here, and, well..."

Rose Marie interrupted and said, " Marco, you need to go, this is an opportunity for you, there is not much more you need to do here for your uncle's business."

And I replied, "I wanted to stay here longer so I could be with you."

She let go of my hands, stood up and sternly replied, "Marco, you are very sweet, but I am not the girl for you. You must take this trip, those people you saved at sea were placed in your path for a reason, and you should not ignore this chance that is offered to you. I will always be here if you want to see me again, someday, but right now we are not ready for each other. Not in that way. We are friends, Marco."

I replied, "But Rose, I feel, you are so special, from the moment I first saw you." Rose raised her hand and stopped me.

Rose Marie replied showing frustration, "Stop Marco, please. It's not you, it's just I don't want a serious relationship. I remember what happened with my Father and my Mother, and I just don't want a serious relationship in my life, I want to be friends."

I stood up, Rose Marie looked into my confused and misty eyes, and I had no words. I walked out the door and quickly out of the building, she did not come after me.

That evening I stayed in my room at the hostel and thought about my new travels to be. I tried to understand Rose Marie, but I could not. I took out my frustration on paper.

With open eyes I see,
a soul full of grace.
Your eyes wide open,
Curious with beneficence.

Our words are spoken,
A part of me does hear.
Yet a stronger articulation,
Is spoken by our hearts.

Our paths newly met,
our hearts feel desire.
I can see it in your eyes,
As you sense by intuition.

Firmly desiring to embrace,
passionately absorbed in a kiss.
My conscience knows to refrain,
As this time is not our own.

And so here I remain,
In this skin I reside.
Knowing you exist,
anticipating we persist.

I named my poem 'Through our eyes', I had thought I understood what my heart felt, however, the perception was only through my own eyes. I was not prepared to give up on Rose, so I decided I would remain her friend. But I knew I needed to move on.

Chapter 14

I decided not to go to the office the next day, I had already accomplished the necessary work for my uncle's outbound shipment and I needed to prepare for my departure. I finished to pack my bags and I decided to go out and get some lunch. Paulo stopped me in the Lobby.

Paulo said, "Marco, you have a message from Rose to call her."

I looked at him, I was kind of surprised and replied, "Oh, thank you." And I continued to make my exit. He picked up the phone off the receiver and raised it with an inquisitive look in his eyes.

"Don't you want to call her?" , he asked.

I stopped for a moment and replied, "It's okay, I will call her later, thank you Paulo." He smirked and placed the phone back on the receiver.

Paulo replied with a confused look on his face, "Have a good afternoon Marco."

I made my way down the front steps, I looked to the left, I looked to the right, I decided to cross the street with no insinuation of where I was destined. I placed my hands in my pockets, it was a sunny day and I started off to the right. I walked and I walked absorbed in my own thoughts, I started to wonder how George was doing back in New York. I wanted to call him, however, it was kind of expensive to try that from the hostel. I thought to myself that I would try to call him from Europe once I would arrive there, and I would also attempt to contact Dario at the University. I decided to sit down later today and write them both a letter so I could send it out before I departed.

I walked my way around all morning long, eventually I made it to the beach. I was tired and took a seat. I looked out to the ocean, I remembered that I had a message from Rose. But I really was not up to talk to her today. I decided to admire the scenery instead, there were some people that flew their colorful kites, others played futbol in the sand and some just enjoyed the scenery, just like I was. I spent a couple hours as I meditated in my thoughts. I was upset about Rose Marie and I did not want to give up on her. I knew I was to depart shortly on this trip, but deep down I did not want to. Eventually, I got the urge to change this scenery. I explored around town and became restless and bored. I started to realize perhaps it was a good idea I leave this city as there was nothing for me here. I got on a trolley and just went around town to look at the sights. I kind of got lost and spent the afternoon as I attempted to find my way back to Santa Teresa. Eventually I found the correct bus. I got off at the usual stop and started to walk towards the hostel. Suddenly I heard someone shout my name. I turned around and it was Rose.

"Where have you been all day, I've been looking for you." Rose Marie called out excitedly.

I responded calmly, "Oh, nothing much, I just took a walk."

Rose Marie replied, "Mr. Hoelck came to the office this morning, he wanted to speak with you before you leave as he will leave for Argentina this afternoon."

I replied with surprise, "Argentina? Hmm, why is he going there?"

Rose Marie responded in annoyed tone, "I don't know, it doesn't matter, he is with the consulate, they always travel. He gave me this letter for you with instructions and contacts in case you should need assistance."

I raised my eyebrows and said, "Assistance? with what?"

She put her hands on her hips and said. "Marco, you should have been there to see him. He wants to help you with a future career. But he has to know he can trust you."

I took a deep breath and sighed.

We started to make our way towards the hostel.
Rose relaxed herself and spoke to me in a softer tone, "Marco, I don't understand why you did not come to the office today, I know Paulo gave you my message because I asked him about it."

With an annoyed voice, I answered. "Well Rose', I just was not in the mood to see you this morning, that's why."

She looked at me incredulously and said, "Marco, I really do not understand you. I like you, you are a nice person, but you are too serious."

I stopped a minute as she paused and looked at me.

Rose Marie continued, "You are young, we are young. Why are you so serious about our friendship?"

I looked at her sternly. "Because I feel that I love you, that's why. And I don't want to lose you. Why can't you understand that?"

Rose Marie looked at me with a blank stare.

She replied softly, "Marco, that is very sweet, but you don't love me."

We continued to walk.

Rose Marie continued, "I think on this upcoming trip you will reflect and realize I am right."

We arrived at the hostel, I was annoyed at Rose, myself and this entire city.

Rose Marie looked at me and said, "Are you okay Marco, what will you do this evening?"

I did my best not to show my emotions and I replied , "I am okay, I plan to get ready for my departure."

She looked at me with the eyes of a mother as she would speak to her child.

She replied with compassion, "Would you like me to help you, would you like some company?"

I looked to the hostel door, and then at Rose. I said,

"Rose, actually, I need to write some letters to send out before I set sail, so I prefer to be alone."

Rose Marie pouted her lips incredulously and said, "Okay, if that is what you prefer, then that is fine."

I said "Goodnight."

Rose Marie asked, "Will I see you tomorrow?"

I thought about it a bit and replied, "Is there anything I need to do at the office?"

She replied, "I'm not sure, I guess we can speak later if you like. I thought maybe you wanted some company."

I replied, "Okay, that's fine, have a good night."

Rose Marie said, "Goodnight."

And she walked away. I walked up the stairs and I looked back at her, she had a certain walk about her that captured me since I met her. I felt as if I would not ever see her again.

That night I felt sadness in my heart, I did not know what to do with myself. I remembered the letter that Rose Marie handed to me and I decided to open it. Inside I found a list of phone numbers and instructions. Also, there was a note that I was to hand over when I would arrive to Germany. I looked it over and it was a very strange language. At first I thought it was perhaps German, but upon further observation, it appeared not to be German nor any language I had ever seen before. There were some strange symbols on it. I didn't think of it anymore and I spent the evening as I wrote to George and to Dario. I explained to them what had transpired without much detail, and that I would sail for Germany and I would call them once I had the possibility. I wondered what they had been up to and I looked forward to perhaps going to visit them soon. Especially Dario as I had not seen him in a long time. I also wanted to go and see Domenico and Elisetta. I wanted to see what condition he was in after the stroke he had suffered. I was tired and I laid back on the bed, I started to think back to the times we spent together in the fields. We worked hard and had a good time. It was a wonderful experience to share that family bond. One that I would keep with me forever.

I didn't sleep much that night, I was restless as I thought of the events that surrounded me recently. My subconscious felt that this situation I found myself involved in did not completely make sense. Next morning, I found the note that Joe had given me during our voyage that held his contact information. I decided to give him a call. I found a public phone booth and made the call. The phone rang several times with no answer and I was about to hang up. Just as I almost hung up the phone, someone picked up the line and said "Alo?" I replied. "Hello, I would like to speak with Joe."

Joe replied, "This is Joe, who is this?"

I replied, "Hi Joe, this is Marco, do you remember me?" Joe paused a second.

Joe said, "Ooh, Marco Polo, the Hawk!"

I smiled and replied, "Yes, that is me. How are you doing."

Joe replied, "I am okay. I took some time off from being a seaman. I actually took a job on land for a freight company, it's a little dull, but my life is a little better, I think."

I replied, "That sounds nice, hey I'm in town few more days before I set sail again, do you have time to see me?"

Joe replied, "Sure, how about today after work around 6 o'clock."

I agreed.

I met Joe at a restaurant that he suggested. It was a Churrascaria and they served all kinds of fire braised meats. It was something I had not tried before and very good. They would cook the meat over the fire pits on skewers, the servers slice the meat as they serve you on your plate. Joe told me to eat as much as I wanted to. The server continues to fill your plate until you tell them to stop.

"Marco, have you enjoyed your time in Rio?", asked Joe as we ate.

I replied. "Yes, you were right, I have enjoyed it here. But I am ready to move on now." He smiled as he took another bite of steak. Then I said, "You know, I wanted to ask you something."

He replied with curiosity, "Yes."

I replied, "Do you remember those guys we rescued off that boat?"

Joe replied with a smirk, "How can I forget that one, I almost drowned for that last idiot with the sack."

I replied, "Apparently, they were not refugees."

He looked at me incredulously and said, "They weren't?"

I shook my head and said. "Nope. They originally departed from Brazil with some stolen passports, and their vessel sank. The boat they were on when we took them on board was their life boat. They did not leave from Venezuela as we had thought." Joe sat back in his chair a moment, took a sip of his Caipirinha.

Joe asked, "And how do you know this?"

I folded my hands and placed them over the table as I leaned closer to him and said, "This is between you and I and you cannot tell anyone."

Joe nodded and replied with assurance, "Okay, go ahead."

I looked around me and then back at him, and said, "A couple days after we arrived at Rio, I was approached by a gentleman from the German consulate here in Rio. He explained to me what I just told you." Joe thought about it a bit.

Joe dubiously replied, "So they carried passports?"

I replied, "Yes, actually, German passports."

Joe opened his eyes wide and replied, "German passports?

Joe scratched his head and continued, "Now why did they have German passports out of Brazil?"

I looked down at the table a moment with my hands folded together, and then back to Joe. I said, "That's why I'm here, I need someone to talk this over to help me understand."

Joe replied. "Understand what Marco, why do you care? You did not carry the stolen passports, just let it be."

He took another sip of his drink and continued, "Wait, why did the man from the consulate come to see you and tell you this?"

Now I paused and asked myself the same question, Why me? I replied. "I'm not sure Joe, however, he has asked me to carry the stolen passports back to Germany."

Joe placed his Caipirinha back on the table.

Joe said, "Oh, my."

Joe sat back in his chair and folded his arms. Then he said, "I have seen some strange things happen on my voyages at sea, this one does not really make much sense."

He paused and then continued. "Are you sure this person who came to you is with the consulate?"

I replied, "Well, I met him at the Consulate here in downtown Rio."

Joe replied, "I suppose he found out that you were the crew member that spotted the doomed vessel from the ships log which was likely provided to him by the vessel owner. But really, what is the reason that they want you to deliver these passports to Germany?"

I thought about it a bit and responded. "I don't really know, except he said he needed to keep this as secretive as possible and that since I already knew about it that I would be a good candidate to carry these passports through German Customs."

Joe leaned over the table and said, "Marco, you must have missed some kind of detail from this story, that's all I can tell you, from what you've told me that is. Do you feel comfortable to transport the passports to Germany?"

When he mentioned 'something missing' and the mystery of why did they pick me to divulge this secret to, the strange ring popped into my head. I responded in a distracted tone, "Frankly Joe, I realize this as well. I suppose I am a little unsure about it".

Joe asked, "How soon are you to leave on this journey?"

I sat up and placed my hands on the table and replied,

"The day after tomorrow."

Joe finished off his Caipirinha.

We split the bill and left a nice tip, it was a good meal. We decided to take a walk around town to burn off some of the dinner. It is difficult to pass up the meat that the waiters seem to constantly serve to the table at a Churrasco dinner. Joe seemed relaxed now and he started to talk.

"I never would have thought those guys carried stolen passports. I remember when I first came up to the boat, they were quite scared and seemed to be in shock. Although, there was that one guy that seemed more in control." Joe said.

I knew exactly which man he spoke of and I replied,

"I agree, when they came on board they shivered from the cold and were not able to speak. I do remember the sack as it was pulled on board. I wonder if the crew master found the passports?"

Joe replied, "More than likely he did not go through their belongings. I'm quite sure they handed their bags over to the authorities when we arrived at port."

We continued to walk and I said. "It's quite possible you and I are the only people from the ship's crew that are aware of these passports."

Joe replied. "It could be, perhaps the man from the consulate heard about the rescue and spoke directly with one of the detained 'refugees', or criminals I should say. My instinct tells me that they came to you for a reason, was there anything one of the men said to you? I mean, they already have the passports. Why did they come to you? They need something they did not find with the passports."

And then I thought to myself {But I am the only one to know about the ring}. I stopped and looked Joe in the eyes and said, "Joe, I am sorry to bring you into this. I just wanted someone to know before I leave, just in case."

Joe replied. "Just in case, what?"

I replied, "I don't know Joe, but like you, I feel there are other links to this story."

Joe replied, "Marco, if you are worried, you are still in time to change your mind and tell them you don't want to participate in this venture."

I started to walk again and said, "Well, Joe. I have thought about it, but my intuition tells me it won't be that easy."

Joe replied, "Marco, I feel I am also involved in this now and I feel obligated to help you. What do you need me to do?"

I replied, "Joe, I just wanted someone else to know about this. I think you have helped me already."

Joe put his hand on my shoulder and said, "You can count on me Marco, if you need anything, I am here for you."

On my way back to the hostel, I pondered about that note Hoelck gave me and the ring, somehow, there was a connection. I arrived at the room and I took out my bag to have a look at the ring and the note together. The written note had some strange symbols included in its body and I remembered the ring also had some strange symbols. I looked for the ring and I could not seem to locate it. I thought I had it in my bag, but it just was not there. Could I have forgotten where I placed it? I looked in my shoes and my clothes and all my belongings. It just was not there. Who would come in here and take it, only that ring and nothing else. I doubt Paulo would come in here and search all my things to take only that ring. I sat down and thought about it, who could have gotten in here without breaking in besides Paulo and gone through my things without being noticed. There was only one person that came into my mind. And it had to be Rose.

The following morning I awoke and glimpsed out the window as I had done on the previous mornings here in Rio de Janeiro. The view no longer had me mesmerized as I had adored at first sight adored so much. I realized first impressions are not always what they seem to be. Now I felt betrayed and I looked at a world of deceivers. I thought to myself, why would Rose take that ring? It wasn't pretty or valuable. Perhaps Mr. Hoelck would like to have that ring and maybe he was the one to break in and take it, but how without a key.

I decided to go to Rose's office and confront her. On my way to the harbor terminal, I realized how Rose had seemed to change after that night we spent together. I was sure it was her that took the ring. I arrived at the office and I noticed there was a new crew. I asked if Rose was in and the attendant looked at me strangely.

The attendant said, "Eu não sei."

She didn't know? How is that possible I thought to myself. I proceeded and made my way to the third floor office. The attendant didn't seem to care either way. The door was closed, but unlocked, I opened it and walked in. Mr Hoelck sat at the desk. His presence took me by surprise.

"Hello Marco, welcome, I thought I would see you hear today." Hoelck said with a grin on his face.

I replied, "Hello Sir, where is Rose?" As I walked in I heard the door close behind me and there were two men behind me by the door wearing suits.

Hoelck continued, "Rose is no longer here Marco, she has been reassigned to another position."

I was shocked and replied, "what? why?" Mr. Hoelck stood up and walked in front of the desk towards me. Pointing to the chair.

He calmly demanded, "Marco, Please, have a seat. We have a few things left to discuss."

And then he reached in his pocket and took the ring out and placed it on the desk. I decided to comply and I sat down as I looked at the ring.

"Do you recognize this object?" , Hoelck asked as he looked into my eyes.

I replied, "Yes."

He was pleased and replied with a smile, "Good."

He picked up the ring again and held it between his thumb and forefinger, he observed it with curiosity and then he sat on the desk next to me and looked at me in the eyes again.

"Who gave it to you Marco." He demanded.

I replied, "It was the man we rescued, he gave it to me."

"Did he tell you anything else, or explain why he gave you this ring." He sternly asked.

I took a deep breath and exhaled. I said, "To be honest, I didn't really want it, I was instructed to deliver him to the medical office and I didn't pay attention to this ring. He tried to give it to me at first as a gift, then I refused and he placed it in my pocket as we had arrived at the medic's office. From there the medic took over and I was relieved of duty and proceeded to my next instruction which was to report to crew master's office."

Mr. Hoelck interrupted and asked, "So why did you not mention this to me when I first asked you if you had been given any objects when we first met."

I rolled my eyes down and then up. I replied, "I had forgotten."

Hoelck chuckled and replied, "Marco, really, you forgot!"

We stared at each other without much expression.

Mr. Hoelck said, "Look, Marco. Now, you are already too much involved, and so I will give you some more information so you understand what you are involved in. Those passports were to be delivered to the German Ministry of Security, or Stasi for short. The note I had included in your documents is a coded message with instructions on how to or better yet whom to provide the passports to. The trick is that the note cannot be read without this ring, it is a decoder ring."

I was stunned. I started to think about Rose, how was she involved in this. I demandingly asked, "Where is Rose?" Mr Hoelck walked back behind the desk and sat down.

"Marco, Rose is an agent. You will never see her again as she has been reassigned to another duty.", Hoelck bluntly replied.

I didn't know how to feel, so much was going on here, I was angry, sad, heartbroken and excited all at the same time. I got up and walked towards the door, the 2 men stood to attention and I backed off."

Hoelck, sat at his chair and calmly said, "Marco, don't get excited, I realize this is a lot of information to take in at once. Sit down and relax a minute."

I asked, "How did you get the ring?"

Hoelck placed his hand on his desk, "Marco, you already know the answer. Don't torment yourself. There are many other Roses you will meet while you work for the agency. You like travel and to experience adventure, well, now you are with us and that is what we do best, travel and experience adventure! Your first assignment will be to carry the passports and this note to your instructed party. The ring, I will keep with me and I will deliver it by other means."

I thought about it a bit and a part of me wanted to stay involved. I think I liked the adventure of it all. The thought to leave Rio as soon as possible sounded good to me, I had enough. My consolation was that at least now I knew the truth. And then I asked, "And what if I decide I want to resign from the agency once I am done with this mission."

Hoelck smirked and replied "Well Marco, that would truly disappoint me. Let's just say, I don't think you will make that choice. Most people decide to stay along with us, the pay is excellent and the work is very rewarding."

And I absorbed his reply and I interpreted the reward was for me to stay alive.

Chapter 15

Once again I was at sea, my heart was content by my own accord as I danced with the rocking of the ship. No plans except my duties, no distractions barring my own thoughts. With the exclusion of what I carried in my cabin. I felt as I did on my first voyage at sea, like Columbus or Marco Polo as they sought adventure. We chartered a course to cross the Atlantic, first stop would be Porto, Portugal, then Bilbao, Spain and then Le Havre, France to deliver predominantly coffee beans and sugar. Afterwards we would be stop at Ostend, Belgium and then the final leg to Bremen.

That evening after my shift in the Navigation room, I went back to my cabin. I decided to relax and ponder my thoughts for a while before going for dinner. First I thought about Rose, how could she be so phony, it felt so real. I was so confused. Then I looked at my bag. I took a deep breath and exhaled. Inside were the tickets to freedom for former Nazi officers to receive refuge in Brazil. I didn't really know the people that these documents were to be gifted to, nor the reasons they did what they did. I remember not long ago as a child I would hear the adults speak of the Germans and the bombings. And I also remember the destruction of families due to this war. So many people died and suffered. Why? Land, Power, Greed.

It seemed to me the problem begins when people lose respect for one another, for whatever reasons. Life is full of hardships that many people cannot endure or accept. And ultimately, we always find someone to blame. And then we start to fight, like children, or worst, like mobs of evil spirits as we seek our own justice. And we move from one war to another war, only the name is changed. But the reason stays the same, the inability to treat others as you would like them to treat you in return. Being human is a flawed existence. The universe is perfect, we are not. We are here to make our mistakes and learn by our imperfections. Our salvation is only found when we help others before ourselves. Once the cycle of evil starts, the only thing that will stop it is forgiveness and kindness. Too many of us forget until the damage has already been done. It is important for all of us to maintain integrity within ourselves and respect for others. Clearly, the war was evil, however, can we blame only a select few? Can one truly state what induced the Lords children to create and establish the atrocities this blessed earth confronted during the World Wars. Is it right when a child steals another's toy? If it is not corrected, the child will continue to behave unjustly. And ultimately friction and bad behavior will arise and develop. The saying 'Two wrongs don't make a right', is correct. To turn one's cheek may be considered just by some. However, to turn one's cheek is too easy and not enough, one must teach and communicate by one's actions to prove their personal valor. And most importantly, that the force of good will always outshine evil. My opinion is that the cause of the War was instigated by economic hardships, political instability and unemployment. This brought the opportunity for the forces of evil to gain strength, and specifically the perspective for some of being superior. The only superior beings are the ones that will sacrifice themselves for others. There were some good people amongst the German soldiers. I remember Patrik very well. He followed orders from his superiors and he was just as much a prisoner of evil as I was a prisoner. And he chose to risk his safety to save the lives of 3 young boys. There is good and evil in all of us. It is up to us to choose which to follow. And at that moment in time, the combined forces of evil overtook that of the forces of good. We should all learn and remember to not allow that again. Finding Domenico and Elisetta in my life has taught me that their goodness will stay with me forever, and I intend to keep it with me and share it. And most importantly, when a person is in need, teach them to stand on their own feet. God helps those who help themselves.

I felt appeased on my first days on this new voyage, I spent my days as I plotted and changed course as per the Captains requests. I really enjoyed to follow the Captains orders and to assist with Navigation, I felt like a real seaman. However, I had difficulty to sleep at night. I had the constant thought of the passports on my conscience and as a result I kept mostly to myself. That night at 3 AM I was wide awake and I could not sleep. I was confused and I tried to listen to my conscience, was it right to carry these passports? Was Rose truly in my life only to lead my life into disarray? What would Domenico and Elisetta say to advise me. So I decided to write in order to justify my mind.

The Angry Young Man

He opens his eyes,
the sun is high in the sky.
He is burdened with thoughts from last eve
that have kept him from dreaming.

Why is it we are captivated,
when classmates are wicked.
Do you like what you see,
are you inclined to the powers that be.

Your heart is Good,
but your friends are all deceivers,
and your eyes see nothing but cheaters.

Feel who you are!
hold on to your heart,
grab hold and be Bold!

The seeds you plant today
will take you far away.
Be true to yourself and find your own destiny.
For once you have arrived, you will realize,
the greatest gift is the one you create and appreciate.

I was content with the poem and I added it to my box. I went to bed and this time I fell asleep.

At breakfast the next morning, I decided to sit close to the crew master. He spoke of the new cargo container technology where cargo would first be loaded into steel containers and then loaded and stacked onto the cargo ships by crane. The idea did intrigue me. It seemed that it would make cargo transport much more efficient.

The Captain walked in and said, "Good Morning men."

We all stood up, greeted him and replied, "Good morning Sir."
The Captain said with a concerned look, "I'm sorry to cut short your breakfast, however, we have a weather front on the way and we need to prepare. Emmanuel, Hans and Marco, please report to the bridge. My first mate is not well this morning and I would like to have some breakfast before the seas start to get choppy. Crew master, please appoint your men to batten down the ship as we are to have gale force winds from the northeast to start around 1400 hours. Make sure the cargo is secured."

Emmanuel, Hans and I reported to the bridge as instructed. The communication officer Victor was at the helm.

Victor looked at us and said, "I hope you boys have strong stomachs, have a look at the weather chart."

I sat at the navigation table and noticed the concern, the Low pressure was very strong and the pressure gradient lines were very close together, I had not seen them this close before.

Victor said, "Marco, plot a westerly course so we can try and go around the back of this storm."

I immediately got to work.

Victor said, "Hans, I've already set our course to west, await Marco's coordinates and adjust accordingly. I need to go to the radio room and send our position and course back to Hamburg Sud headquarters."

Victor started towards the door and said, "Emmanuel, come with me I will need your assistance to update the weather charts."

My preliminary calculations had us charted pretty much directly west as fast as we could make possible. I said to Hans "Hans, set us at 285 degrees and full speed while we can. We need to try and get away from the strength of this Low Pressure. I see winds of 55 knots and upwards possible, that would make for some pretty big waves, the likes I've never seen." We all worked swiftly the next few hours. The waves intensified and the strong wind had made its appearance as the Captain came back to the bridge around 13:00 hours.

The Captain entered and announced his arrival, "Good Afternoon gentlemen."

Hans and I replied, "Good afternoon Sir."

The Captain walked over to the helm and said, "I see we are still heading west."

Then looking at me the Captain continued, "Marco, Has the storm made any significant shifts since this morning?"

I replied, "The storm has held the same northeasterly direction. However, it seems to have gained strength. Currently winds at the center are around 75 knots."

The Captain replied with concern, "Marco, let me see the latest weather chart."

I brought it to his desk and he placed it down. He examined the chart intensely.

The Captain looked to me and said. "Marco, you plotted correctly, this is an intense Storm and could gain even more strength. We are going to lose a lot of time. However, this vessel would not be able to handle the 50 foot waves close to the center of this low pressure."

The Captain looked at Hans. "Hans, maintain course, however, you will need to slow us down once the waves get stronger. Actually, I think that may already be upon us so bring us down to 12 knots."

The Captain looked to me again and said, "Marco, let Victor know we have reduced speed to 12 knots and to notify Hamburg Sud.

The Captain studied his chart with a look of disbelief.

The Captain said as I exited, "From the looks of the intensity of this storm, I intend to get out of its way."

It was 16:00 hours as the ship climbed massive waves. We appeared to fly over each crest, only to fall back down with our bow submerged into the immense existence of blue. Even during its tempestuous state, the sea continued to allure me. As if I were there to tame its enraged wrath. Unexpectedly, updated weather data was received and I quickly proceeded to plot a new chart. It appeared the Low had now shifted course directly from the south. I suddenly felt a knot in my stomach, I knew our vessel could not outrun the storm. I alerted the Captain and said, "Captain, I have the updated weather charts ready."

The Captain replied, "Bring them over."

He looked over the chart and pouted his lips.

The Captain looked to me and asked, "Marco, are you sure this is correct?"

With a serious face I nodded and replied, "Yes Sir, I checked the coordinates twice."

The Captain stood up and said, "Men I need your attention please. We are going to be in for a rough 12 hours. Hans, change course to west south west and maintain 12 knots."

Hans followed the Captains orders and we were all were quite tense as Hans steered the ship around in the intensely agitated sea. The waves started to slam hard onto our starboard side and the ship shuddered at each blow. We maintained course for about an hour until the ships bow was being submerged with each wave. I realized we must have been very close to the eye of this storm. It seemed to me that the storm took control of the ship and we could no longer attempt to out run it. It was as if the storm chased us. I noticed we had lost all communications.

The Captain shouted, "Hans, we can no longer climb these waves, try and turn us quickly as possible and point the vessel at a high angle into the waves as they approach." Soon the waves were crashing portside right over the bow. With each blow the ship seemed to list portside, and then lean into the next wave starboard. The ship was being thrusted in all directions and we did not have much control. The Captain was standing right up to the glass as he attempted to see into the oncoming waves. Visibility was zero with the constant rush of water making the wipers useless. The ship was

174

clearly now governed by the sea. We viewed a large wave approaching from starboard window. It overwhelmed us and went right over the ship. The wave nearly lied us down on our portside. We all fell over and a lot of water had entered the bridge. This time the ship did not snap back into place. Hans had hit his head on a metal pole and was bleeding. The Captain pulled himself over to the controls.

The Captain managed to grab the wheel and said, "We need to turn into the waves, another wave like that on our side and we will turn over."

Quickly he turned the rudder and did his best to point the ship into the oncoming waves.

The Captain shouted, "Marco, get a hold of the engine room, I need to know how much water we have taken on. Tell them to pump out the portside chambers first!"

I attempted to make my way down to lower deck, the ship swayed and jolted in all directions. An unexpected jolt caught me off guard and I fell and hit my head on the stairway rail. I sat there in pain and held my head, I looked at my hand and I realized I cut myself. I got up and continued. I had not seen anyone and it was quite eerie. Once I got close to lower deck I could see the water. It was very high. I yelled out and said, " anyone down there!" , I heard a shout back from a crewman.

"Yes, who is there?" , shouted the crewman.

I continued into the cold water and found myself waist deep. I noticed the portside chamber doors were locked and closed. I shouted to the crewman, "The Captain said to put all pumps on the portside Chamber."

The crewman replied, "We locked all chambers once we saw the water coming in."

The crewman waved me on and said, "Come with me, we need to close some valves to redirect the pump flow."

I followed him to the ships aft control room on this level. We diverted all the pumps to portside. I said to the crewman. "Stay on post and alert us if there are any changes in the water level."

He replied, "Okay, but will you let us know if we are going to abandon ship?"

That caught me by surprise. However, by the looks of all the water down here, that could be a distinct possibility. I looked to him and the others and said, "Keep pumping, we will make it. The eye of the storm has passed south of us, the wind will be abating soon, but we need to get the water out of the portside chamber." I wasn't quite sure of what I just announced, but I attempted to calm the crew.

The crewman replied, "There are another two pumps in the engine room, we can shift them to portside chamber, but there is risk to flood the engine room."

I thought about it and quickly replied, "Switch them over to portside, we need to do get this water out quickly, we will have to take the chance." He nodded and ran off to the engine room. I yelled out, "I'm going up to notify the Captain. I will be back soon."

Once up at the bridge, the Captain could see I was out of breath and my clothes all wet, as well as I bled on my forehead. Hans sat on a table holding a bandage to his head.

The Captain looked to me and said, "What are the conditions down there?"

I took a deep breath and replied, "Captain, portside is completely flooded and all doors are locked and sealed. We have diverted all pumps including engine room pumps to portside."

The Captain looked to me and replied, "Marco, we will need to monitor the engine room, we can't afford to flood the engines. But that was a good call, if we don't pump out the portside we won't be able to sustain this much longer and likely we will capsize."

I replied, "Captain, shall I go back down below and monitor it?"

The Captain looked at my forehead, and pointed to the first aid kit.

The Captain replied, "Go get the first aid kit on the wall and put a bandage on your cut first."

We seemed to have a good approach on the turbulent sea, either the storm shifted or the Captain succeeded in turning the ship in the right direction. I think the Captain may have underestimated those last swells as they nearly turned us over.

The Captain asked, "Marco, how deep was the water when you arrived."

I replied as I was placing a bandage on my forehead, "They had already sealed off the portside forward chambers and we were about waist deep. The engine room had about a foot of water."

The Captain was worried and replied, "Marco, there are a few portable pumps down in the cargo hold. We need to get them to the engine room."

Then he looked over to Hans. "Hans, you go with Marco, I will man the helm."

We both leaped into action with bandages on our heads. and made our way the cargo hold. I said to Hans, "Do you know where these pumps are?"

He replied, "Yes, there are three of them and they are quite heavy, we will to need to find some kind of dolly or cart."

I replied. "Okay, let's go have a look around down there."

It was difficult to walk as the ship listed severely. We put our arms out and balanced ourselves as best as possible while the ship bounced about. Once we arrived at the cargo hold, we opened the hatch door and we carefully climbed down. We found the cargo hold to be mostly dry. This was due to all the entrances being sealed, however, the cargo was thrown all about and there was much damage incurred. We didn't waste any time to survey the damages and focused on the location of the pumps. I followed Hans as he seemed to know where they were located.

Hans pointed and said, "There, behind these crates, do you see the door?"

I looked and I could see some steel doors, however, the crates were placed directly in front of them. We both tried to push and they did not budge.

Hans looked at the crates with frustration and said, "How are we going to move these things?"

We both looked around for a tool we could use for leverage. Hans found a winch with a cable, we tied one end onto the first crate and secured the winch with a steel cable to a post. And we started to crank on it. It was a slow process, but we managed to move the crate. One by one we continued as the ship swayed. Eventually we reached the doors and opened them up. Inside were the pumps, and as Hans had said, they were heavy. We looked around and found a wooden pole that was used as a prying bar. Also, we found a couple of steel dolly carts. As I lifted one end of the pump with the bar, Hans slid the dolly underneath. First one side, then the other, now we could push the pump around. We got as close as we could to the engine room with the pump and then placed the hoses. One into the water and the other out of the ship. The crew saw us in action and quickly we told them to take the dollies from us and to go get the other pumps. We were exhausted. Once we got the first pump set up in the engine room, I said to Hans. "Hans, you continue with the crew, I'm going upstairs to update the Captain." He nodded yes and I went off.

As I climbed the stairs I could feel the ship was still listing severely. Perhaps more than previously noticed. I struggled my way back up and I fell more than once in my effort. I eventually arrived at the helm and the Captain was still at the wheel.

He turned his head to me in distress and said, "Marco, are all the pumps working?"

I replied as I caught my breath, "Sir, one of the portable pumps are set up and running in the engine room. I instructed the crew to set up the others and they are working on it as we speak Sir."

The Captain turned back to the sea view and said, "The ship is listing severely, we need to maintain the ship portside into the waves. Otherwise, if we catch a big swell it could flip us over entirely. The only good thing is that the center of the storm has passed south of us."

The Captain paused to wipe his brow.

The Captain said, "Marco, go to the communications room, Emmanuel and Victor were in contact with a cargo ship to the northwest of us. I asked them to signal for help. Ask them if they have any update from them. Report right back to me."

I replied to the Captain "Yes, Sir."

It became clear to me that we were in danger, yet I somehow kept myself under control. I arrived at the communication room, Victor and Emmanuel looked quite intensely into the radio.

Victor said, "Marco, what's going on down below, are the pumps on?"

I replied, "The pumps are on, however, there is a lot of water portside. I'm not sure we will be able to get enough water out to revert the ship upright. The Captain asked me if there is an update from the ship you had contacted."

Victor replied, "Marco, tell the Captain they responded to the last communication I sent. They said that they diverted their course to come and meet us, I gave them our position and our course. However, they have not responded since."

"Seems we are in a predicament.", I replied.

Emmanuel looked at me with a despaired look.

Victor replied as we took another large wave, "Marco, Tell the Captain I will continue to send out our position and course."

"Very well, I'm on my way." I answered as I held on to the railing.

I could hear the wind howl as I approached the helm, I was under the realization that if this ship did not find us, we might find ourselves using the lifeboats as this vessel could very well sink. The passports entered my mind, this would be the second time that I know of that these documents are threatened by a vicious sea. What are the chances of that?

I arrived at the helm and the Captain was still in the same position.

The Captain turned to me and said, "Marco, what did you find out?"

I grabbed onto the navigation table and replied, "Captain, Victor has had a reply from the vessel earlier that they had changed their course towards our position. However, Victor has not been able to hear from them since. He continues to send out our position and course over the radio repeatedly."

The Captain gained control of himself and replied, "The storm has dissipated some and the seas have abated somewhat, I need you to take the helm."

My eyes opened wide. I had never taken the helm, nevertheless the helm of a doomed ship. I replied doing my best not to show my fear, "Very well Captain." And I walked over to him. The Captain grabbed my left arm and brought my hand to the wheel.

The Captain said, "Pay attention to the angle I approach the waves, it's important you keep the ship pointed into the waves at this angle so we don't flip over."

I put both hands on the wheel and looked out to the waves as they approached. The Captain put his hand on my shoulder and pointed out to sea.

The Captain said, "That is good, keep us in this position, I won't be long. I need to go assess the damages."

With my eyes squinting out into the darkness, I replied, "Very well Captain, I understand." The Captain jolted out the door and I was alone at the helm. The ship listed into the waves and the forward section of the ship seemed very low in the water. I doubted if the pumps were strong enough to pump all this water out. And then I wondered, how did all the water enter the hull. Deep down within myself I felt everything would be alright. However, the reality that this ship would likely falter emerged quite vividly as I stood at the helm.

I held the wheel intensely as each wave collided with our bow, sometimes submerging the forward deck. The silence of the bridge was more ominous than the howl of the wind. Every minute intensified the angst of our fate. The passports entered my thoughts, I remember to have placed them on the top bunk of my cabin. Would I have enough time to go and get them if I needed to abandon this vessel. Should I attempt to save them as the previous couriers had. I thought about it as I held the wheel into the waves like the Captain ordered. It was in my instinct to never give up on your commitments. I think I was just born that way. Suddenly, the door blasted open, it was Hans. I looked towards him while I held the wheel and he looked to me. We both had questions in our eyes.

Hans yelled out in panic, "Where is the Captain!"

I quickly replied with a dumbfounded glance, "He went down below to assess the damages, you must have missed each other."

Hans looked at me. "This ship is sinking. The water below has risen even with all the pumps working."

I looked to Hans. "You need to go find the Captain."

He looked to me and replied, "Marco, there is not much time, we should alert the crew to abandon ship."

I replied. "That is the Captain's call. Go find him now, I will hold the wheel."

The wind continued to howl and my time became evanescent. I wanted to leave this helm and at the same time I wanted to hear from the Captain, and he was nowhere to be seen. I stayed and contemplated my course angle with each wave. The darkness had masked the face of this vicious sea. My preoccupation of our lost Captain and now Hans in despair told me what my subconscious already knew. I had deluded myself and overlooked that the darkness was now fading. Unexpectedly I could see out to the horizon as the light of dawn gave its first glimpse. And almost instantaneously, the engines lost power and with that the ships lights flickered and all went dark. I could now clearly see the new dawn as the sky went from black to deep blue. And consequently, also the ships bow was submerged completely. I continued to look out and I observed in the distance what appeared to be a small boat, I looked more intensely, and then I saw another. I ran out to have a better look and I could see our life boats were all off the ship. In a state of panic, I ran and abandoned the helm. First I ran to see if Victor or Emmanuel were in the communications room. The room was empty. My next thought was to get to a life boat, and then the passports came into my head. I had to go below to my cabin and try to get them, and more importantly, my box of poems. I found a flash light in one of the drawers and then ran towards the stern, as not only was the ship above water level in the rear end, but my cabin also was located aft in lower deck. As I got closer towards aft, I could not find any available life boats left on board. My instinct was to attend to that issue after I retrieved my bag. I entered the ship by starboard aft entrance and made my way down to the cabins. It was very eerie as I ran down each level as I could not see or hear anyone. I heard the water as I approached my cabin level. The flood level was at least three feet, and it was cold. Luckily my cabin was far aft close to the stern and I did not need to wade through the water very far. My door was open and the bag with my belongings was where I left it, on the top bunk. Luckily the safety net held it in place. Quickly I grabbed my precious belongings and put them on my back. With the flash light in one hand, and the bag straps in the other. I waded through the hallway as fast as I could. Suddenly, there was a loud blast. The floor beneath me shook and I fell to one knee. As I continued towards the stairs I could see some water movement, the ship had shifted and the stern had risen. As I proceeded to climb the stairs and get out of the water, I heard a deep sound, it was the stress on the ships metal as it bent. I knew I had to get myself off this ship quickly.

Once I arrived at Aft deck, my instinct was to see if there were any life boats left. I first looked portside and then checked starboard. I noticed the bow was now further under water. There was not much time left. I grabbed a life ring that was strapped to the ship railing and I ran to the stern of the ship. I looked out to sea and I could not see anyone. As far as I could see, all life boats were gone. I had never felt so helpless in all my life. Suddenly I remembered the storage bin on the top deck marked 'Inflatable Raft'. I had previously passed by there without any thought to depend upon its assistance. I grabbed my bag and made my way up the stairs to top deck. There was the cabinet, it was still closed and locked. Where was the key? Probably back at the bridge I had thought. There was no time and I remembered the axe mounted on the wall near the stair well. Quickly I went to get it. I had to break open the cabinet. There was also a rope ladder enclosed and I grabbed that as well. As soon as I got back to the storage bin. I gave a solid look to the pad lock, took the back side of the axe and slammed the lock bracket with all my might. The latch did bend, so I took a deep breath and gave it another blow, and then another. After the fourth blow, it broke open. I opened the cabinet and inside was a green bag zippered up marked 'Life Raft' and another bag marked 'Survival Pack'. There was also an air tank with a hose. I brought everything down to the main deck as fast as I could and I proceeded to inflate the raft with the air tank. It only took a short time to inflate the raft and I gave it a quick look over. It wasn't large but it would have to do. I took the rope ladder and tied it to the side of the ships rail. I then grabbed a rope and tied it onto the raft. I lowered the raft into to the ocean, hand over hand until the raft was in the water and rolled with the waves.

Well, this was it, I needed to leave the ship before the ships descent would accelerate. I grabbed everything and strapped it on my back. I tied the rope that held the raft around my waist, and over the railing I went. I climbed down the ladder, very carefully I made my way down. Once I got close to sea level I put my arm around the rope ladder so I could pull the raft as close as I could. The sea moved the raft forward and back, and I lingered in the crashing sea for the right moment to make the transfer. It was not an easy task as my instincts told me not to leave the large ship which had carried me safely thus far. It seemed as a long moment in time, however, my subconscious grabbed a hold of me as the raft approached again. I let go of my instincts and I jumped. I landed and by miracle made it into the life raft with all my belongings. I sat up and gathered all my things and secured them as best as I could. The raft moved quickly away and down the ship line. I was overcome by the sight of the large vessel with its forward section submerged. One does not fathom the possibility that such a large object can submerge where it once floated on water. It appears to float as naturally as the birds that fly over the sea. However, I now see that we should not believe everything we see.

I sat up in the raft for a while pondering my current situation. I looked around. There was nothing but turbulent water around me. It was difficult to lookout as the waves would lift the raft and then drop me down and block my view. All I could see were waves of water as I held onto the raft. Each time I could look toward the vessel, it appeared smaller. Eventually, I was no longer able to see the ship over the horizon as I drifted with the swift current. Soon I was alone at sea with my new best friend, the raft. I lied down and looked up to the sky as I was exhausted. For the time being my goal was to keep this raft upright. From the last calculations, we were a little over 600 miles west-south-west of the Canary Islands. I pondered if that cargo vessel would appear in my view, I did have some flares in the emergency survival kit. As I looked up at the Clouds, I speculated how I got into this position, my life in danger, but I was too tired to be afraid. I focused on survival. I closed my eyes and I prayed.

I must have fallen asleep since my next moment of awareness, I felt the warmth of the sun on my face. I opened my eyes and I could see the sky appeared behind the now dissipated clouds. The waves finally abated and the raft and I now drifted a bit more peacefully. The perilous storm had passed, and now I could concentrate on my troubles. I had enough water to drink for maybe 3 or 4 days. There was a life raft food ration can in the emergency survival kit as well. I had no idea what else was in there and I hoped I would not need to know. The sky was now clear and I could see far into the horizon. It was difficult to believe that a storm of such magnitude which had the strength to sink a vessel had passed by here not long ago. And now the sea was calm and serene. I looked and I looked, there must be a vessel out there somewhere. I remember all the ships I would see while I worked on the vessels. I remembered the time I spotted the refugees. And now I truly understand how they had felt. It had become a possibility that I may not survive this ordeal, and my very short life could end abruptly. My only consolation was that I followed my own desire, to travel the oceans and see the world.

Dusk approached and the face of the ocean had changed as the sky darkened. Luckily the moon was out and it provided ample light. However, the reality was, I could hardly see my hands in front of my face. I hoped to see some lights in the distance, but there were none. I had become a little thirsty, and I thought to drink some water. I looked at the bottle, and then I held off. I decided to wait till morning. I was tired but I did not want to sleep. I continued to look out for any glimpse of a light over the horizon. I laid back a little and leaned my head on the raft, still I looked out. My eyes wanted to close, and I sat up again, I peered and squinted as I looked for a reflection. And none appeared, just pitch black. My only consolation was to see the trail on the sea from the moons reflection, and then I thought of the night I had spent with Rose when we were on the lifeguard chair.

184

My next moment of consciousness occurred as the sun showed its morning glow. At first I was relaxed and then as I became alert I realized I had slept the entire night, here in this raft all night long without a glance out to sea. I hoped I did not miss my chance to find my salvation, but I would never know. I could not let that happen again. I sat up and started to search the survival kit. There was canned water, a knife, a whistle, some flares, blankets, hats, a compass, a fishing kit, a bucket, a hand pump, a mirror, a small tarp, a first aid kit and a battery powered signal beacon. That was a good find I thought to myself. And then I looked at the food rations in the cans. Well, I was indeed hungry now. I opened one. There were some dried food bars and I took a bite out of one and started to chew. Well, it was better than nothing. Soon the sun rose overhead and its rays became quite strong, I had to cover myself up to avoid a sunburn and dehydration. I looked out towards the horizon and observed the open sea. The compass showed which direction was north. It did not do me any good as I had no power to move this raft in any direction. I drifted with the current, and likely on the way back towards South America where I came from. Which was a long way. My only hope was to find another vessel to rescue me. I wrapped myself with my blanket and squinted my eyes out to sea.

The day moved slowly, I had lots of time to my own thoughts and found myself back at the orphanage. I remember to have played with my friends as we pretended to be pirates. I recalled one time I fell in mud in the midst of playtime with my friends and I ruined my clothes. The sisters were so angry with me when I returned to the dormitory. They made me take my clothes off and told me to wash them outdoors in the fountain that was used by the farm animals. My friends all went inside and I was left alone in my underwear. I felt so alone. But I did what I had to do and hung my clothes out to dry. Now, as I look back, I wonder what it would have been like if I had my mother to take care of me at that time. She probably would have scolded me and sent me to my room, and then she would have washed my clothes and given me some new clean clothes and maybe a good dinner too. Perhaps that night she would have tucked me into bed and kissed me on the cheek. It was my fate that I was to

185

quickly learn that life on this planet was hard, and that I had to take care of myself to survive. And here I was now, alone on this raft in the middle of the ocean, going who knows where. Hopefully not the bottom of the sea. They say the Lord loves all his children, and I had faith that I was here for a reason, so I was determined to do what I had to do to survive.

Dusk appeared again, I decided I would try out the beacon light tonight and I tested it. It flashed a bright light and seemed to work well, I was confident that if anyone was nearby, they would see this light. I felt I now had a chance to be seen and found. I continued to observe the vast sea, soon to be darkness. That night I found a chocolate bar in one of the survival food cans, and that was my treat. I sat in the darkness, as I listened to the water as it caressed my raft. The beacon light kept me company as it flashed, slowly in the vast darkness.

As I drifted into the night, I looked up to the stars, and there were so many. I found the big dipper, and then the north star. I thought of how many people would see the north star tonight, if only they could find me in its reflection. I rubbed my eyes with my fingers as I tired through the dark night. There were no lights over the sea and I was starting to lose hope for the night. I did not want to go to sleep. I decided to write to keep myself awake.

Look at your hands,
what do you see.
Ten fingers free,
as creative as thee.

I touch and I feel,
my eyes fathom.
All fed by blood,
produced by my entity.

Reach into your heart,
go deep inside,
goose bumps appear,

186

embracing perseverance.

I feel I'm alive,
in this world I can see.
Perceiving here and now,
this soul reaching presence.

My thoughts create,
the world I envision.
The Creator provides,
myself comprehends.

Lord I am grateful,
for I can perceive.
Your love is accomplished,
and I will deliver.

Chapter 16

Another night passed, and again I was alone at sea with my good friend, the raft. I had become complacent with my morning food bar and afternoon blanket wrap. The salt of the sea had dried my skin, and I could feel the beard on my face as it filled in well. Now I was a real sailor I thought to myself. If only I had a sail. The clouds were different today with very high tops, and the wind started to blow a few white caps. I wondered where I was and determined that I had no idea. The winds calmed that night, and again I lighted my beacon of hope. I had lost count of my days at sea and to be honest I'm not sure I cared. I only wanted to see an existence beyond this endless blue sea.

Morning arrived and I looked at the usual food bar, my body craved some meat. I thought about the fishing kit, however, how could I cook a fish if I did indeed catch one. I suppose I should eat it raw? What a thought. Rather than sit and watch another day of myself lost at sea, I decided to play fisherman. I was very careful with the hook and lure and gently I placed them in the water and let out the line. I wrapped the other end of the line around my hand and I sat back under my blanket. I really did not expect to catch any fish. I continued to squint against the suns glare out to sea. Unexpectedly, I saw a gull. Swiftly I sat up and removed my blanket. The gull circled the boat. I lost attention of the line that drifted maybe 50 feet away until the gull dove into the water, and forthwith came out of the water with a fish in his beak. So much was going on in my mind and with much excitement I started to bring in my line. Much to my surprise, I felt a tug. And then a pull, and so I pulled back and started to pull in the line, hand over hand. I lost track of the gull in the excitement as I pulled the fish into the raft, it bounced around vigorously and I decided to put him into the bucket that came with the survival kit. I held the fish by its gills and gently removed the hook with pliers from the kit. There was a small cutting board that came with the fishing kit and I placed it over the bucket. I carefully put the hook away into its holder. The fish continued to bounce in the bucket a little while, and eventually went limp. The gull was no longer in sight. I looked as far as I could see and there was no trace of him. Either there was a vessel around or I was near land, my hunch was another vessel had to be in the area. My only hope was that they would move closer to me.

I sat back the rest of the day and contemplated my water rations, I was so thirsty and I had to have a little more than I should have. Dusk was soon to arrive and I had no sight of any vessel. I had hoped to see my friend the gull, and neither occurred. I was quite hungry after all the excitement and my thoughts were on the fish I had caught. I uncovered the bucket and there he was. I carefully took him out and washed him with sea water. Placed him on the cutting board and carefully handled the knife that came with the kit. I sliced his belly and removing the inners. I then removed his head and tail and fins, and finally his skin. The flesh was white and fresh, I separated the flesh from his spine and then washed it. I looked at it and refreshingly appeared appetizing to my stomach. Without any thought about it, I sliced it and put a piece in my mouth and chewed. It tasted good and I swallowed with contentment. I was indeed hungry and followed my instinct until I ate the whole fish. I slept well that night with my beacon light on and one eye open. I dreamed of the gull and thanked him for the fish I ate. I hoped to share another fish with my new friend soon. I completed the night with a new poem in honor of my new friend. Yearning to see him soon.

Steadfasting forward,
wind thrusting aft.
I've pondered this vast sea,
an old man I've come to be.

I've learned many things,

189

on my course of destined fate.
Our best friends have wings,
once realized, it's too late.

This voyage without meaning,
each day holding course.
A gull streaming starboard,
catching breezes, without remorse.

So far from land,
the gull followed in flight.
This sea so grand,
diving swiftly, catching delight.

Day after day the gull followed,
jointly we provide companionship.
Creating time as sun and clouds meld,
gliding starboard, as one with my ship.

The next day there was light rain. I was concerned that water had accumulated in the raft, until my lips tasted the fresh water. There was a small tarp in the survival kit and now I understood what it was for. I stretched it out and funneled the water from the tarp into the bucket, and that was a great sight to see. I sat there in delight with my arm stretched as I harvested as much fresh water as I could. Once the rain stopped I carefully took the empty water jugs and filled them with the water I had harvested. I could now rest assured, provided there were clouds to grant rain, there would be water to drink. And with the Lord's consideration to provide fish, I would have food. I had reached an inspirational sentiment. However, what I really wanted was to have a vessel of any kind find my path.

The days and nights passed, I'm not sure how many weeks or months as I had drifted at sea. My beard was long and my skin dark, wrinkled and dried. My original rations were gone and I now was accustomed to rain water and raw fish from the sea. I was eager to stay alive and very determined to survive. Every morning I prayed, and every evening as well. I knew the Lord was with me and this was not the end of what he intended of me. My spirit was strong. However, my body grew weak. Each day that passed I felt older and feeble. My soul held my faith, however, my body sensed its fate. One morning, I lied back with my fishing line in hand and my eyes closed, I listened to the waves ripple along the raft as we glided this perpetually diverse glass ingress curtain between water and air. This raft was my savior, how much longer would it hold my fate. Unexpectedly, I heard something move and instinctively I squinted my eyes open. An object stood on the rafts edge. My vision was blurred and I tried to focus, it was the Gull! At first I thought it was a hallucination. I opened my eyes wider and placed my hand over my forehead to cover the sun's glare. I stayed still for as long as I could and the bird just stood there, as he occasionally turned his head. I wondered if it was the same gull I had seen previously. It was a long time since I had seen him last and he had never landed on my raft. Why did he return? he must be a long way from home I thought. Did he want me to give him a fish? I supposed he was too tired to fly and perhaps he was lost as well. I was exhausted and I really didn't care. I wanted to sit up, but I didn't want to scare him away. I relaxed as he stayed longer than I had expected and I enjoyed his company as we both rested on the raft. And then an intrusion into my quiet reality sounded, a loud horn blasted. At first I was shocked and didn't recognize the sound for what it was. Was it a strange howling wind? a whale? A ghost perhaps. I pulled myself up and I watched the gull fly off. And there it was, a fishing boat. My salvation.

Although my body could barely sit up, I felt young again, as if I were reborn. I was gifted a chance to live again. I felt a happiness in my heart that only my blessed Lord could understand. And the horn blasted again, and I could see at least 3 men waving at me. And I waved back, with all my might and heart. The vessel came closer and I could hear one man as he yelled out, "Salve, adesso ti tiro questa corda. C'e la fai a prenderla?" It was an Italian fishing boat, and he threw me a rope. I grabbed on with both hands, and I would not let go until they pulled me to the ship's hull. Two men climbed down to assist me. One grabbed my bag and the other tied a rope under my arm and then pulled my arm over his shoulder, and all together, we climbed as the others on the vessel simultaneously pulled me on board. And then I passed out.

The next thing I remember was when I opened my eyes. I was in a small cabin. At first I was disoriented and I had difficulty to recall my whereabouts. I attempted to sit up, and quickly I lied back down as I was very weak. I looked around the cabin and I noticed my bag on the floor against the wall, it remained closed. It seemed they had not searched my belongings. I placed my hand on my face and felt my long beard. It reminded me of how long I was at sea. I wondered why the Lord allowed me to survive. And then I thought, perhaps because I refused to die. And then I looked to my bag, and those passports hidden within.

There was a knock at the door, I looked over and the door slowly opened. A man walked in quietly.
    The man said, "I see you are awake?"
    He came over close to me and took my wrist with one hand and placed his other hand on my forehead
    The man said, "I am Captain Salvatore, what is your name?"
    I replied, "Marco."
    Captain Salvatore looked to me and said, "You are Italian?"
    I replied, "Yes."
    He let go of my wrist and forehead and walked to the door.
    Captain Salvatore said, "You must be thirsty and hungry, you have slept for 2 days since you boarded the vessel. I will call for some food and water."
    He opened the cabin door and looked down the hall and shouted, "Carlo, portaci una minestra calda dalla cucina per favore, e una brocca d'aqua."
    He closed the door and he sat down at the desk next to my bed.
    Captain Salvatore asked, "How did you get stranded at sea?"
    I struggled as I tried to sit up and the Captain came over to help me lean up on the bed. With a weak voice I replied, "Our ship went down."
    "How?" asked Salvatore.

I took a deep breath and replied. "The crew abandoned the ship and I was unaware."

"Were you asleep?" he asked.

"I stood at the helm as per Captain's orders. I was waiting for his order to abandon ship. He never returned to the bridge. I was able to get on board the raft as our vessel sank." I laid back down exhausted.

"That is unusual, are you sure you remember well ? Was it a cargo vessel?" asked Salvatore with a puzzled look.

I replied, "Yes, we were in route from Rio de Janeiro, heading to Bremen. We encountered a strong storm. (I coughed) We attempted to move out of the storm's path, however, we were not able."

Captain Salvatore looked to me and said, "I remember of a cargo vessel going down about, maybe just over 3 months ago.

You were west of Capo Verde heading north going towards the Canaries. There were no known survivors."

Captain Salvatore put his hand on his chin and paced the cabin floor.

"Marco, we found you just as we had left the Cape of Good Hope." He said with an astonished look

Captain Salvatore stopped and looked at me in disbelief.

Captain Salvatore said, "Young man, you are very lucky to be alive. That Captain did you an injustice. Unless, he could have been injured and not able to advise you to abandon your position."

There was a knock at the door and Captain Salvatore opened the door. The crewman placed my food on the desk.

Captain Salvatore asked, "Are you able to walk over to the desk?"

The crewman came over to assist and I slowly made my way to the chair with his help. I took one sip of the soup and I felt as if I had never tasted anything so good, I immediately began to devour it.

Captain Salvatore said, "Slowly Marco, Slowly. Have some bread and chew slowly."

Then the Captain paced the room and watched me eat.

The Captain said. "Marco, you have not had a good meal in over 3 months, how did you survive?"

I took a break between mouthfuls and cleared my throat. "I ate raw fish and drank the rainwater that I collected."

The Captain looked to me and said, "You are a real Robinson Crusoe. I will leave you finish your meal, I will check on you soon. Eat slowly."

The next morning, the same crewman came to my room, only this time with a barber's kit. He gave me a proper haircut and removed my beard with scissors and a razor. I started to feel human again. I had a good breakfast of eggs and potatoes and later in the day I had my first real shower with soap. I was in my cabin later in the afternoon when I heard a knock, the door opened. It was Captain Salvatore.

Captain Salvatore looked at me with a smile and said, "Is it you Marco?"

I smiled back at him and said, "I feel like a new person, how can I repay you?" And then with a serious face, I continued. "For saving my life."

Captain Salvatore looked down for a moment, and then looked at me.

Captain Salvatore said, "Marco, as much as I would like to accept your gratitude, really, this miracle you have been granted was purely up to fate. And your ability to think clearly and persevere. My gift has already been granted to me by the Lord that has allowed me to offer my assistance in his work. There is no other explanation needed."

Then I said, "Sir, I thank you anyway. And yes, I am also convinced I received a gift from the Lord above."

Captain Salvatore nodded his head and said with a smile, "Well, Marco, you have further luck. Since our fishing trip departed from Sicily, we will also return to the same origin point, specifically Palermo."

I smiled and said, "Thank you Captain, momentarily, I am still captivated by the miracle of being on board your vessel. I cannot explain to you how grateful I am."

Captain Salvatore replied, "Do you have family in Sicily?"

I replied. "Not that I know of Sir. I was originally from up north, but I have since emigrated to America and have been at sea as a crewman for some time now."

Captain Salvatore replied, "Now you have a story to tell people for years to come, in any case, from Palermo you can take a ferry to the mainland, and from there, you will decide."

I replied, "Thank you Sir."

The Captain exclaimed with his hand raised, "Stop thanking me Marco, I did what needed to be done. You would have done the same as any seaman would. At first I thought I had found some debris from another ship, however, as we came closer, I could see a person."

A tear came to my eye.

Captain Salvatore continued, "Well, perhaps tomorrow if you are up to it you can come up the main deck, perhaps assist at the helm."

I replied excitedly, "Absolutely Captain."

The Captain opened the door and said, "Have a good evening Marco, enjoy your rest. We shall be at Palermo in about 3 days. I have to get this fish to market so we are moving at full speed."

We arrived at Palermo 5 days later, although the Captain had hoped 3 days, it was not possible. It was a good thing they had plenty ice for the fish. I said my goodbyes to Captain Salvatore whom I shall never forget, and the crew as well. I had contemplated my next action during the last few days and I just could not make up my mind. Although I had just been perhaps traumatized by a life changing experience, I still had the burden to carry these passports. I wondered if they had anything to do with my still being alive after I drifted in a canvas raft for 2 or 3 thousand miles in shark infested waters.

I walked a bit with my bag and I quickly became fatigued and sat down. As I stood on firm ground, I looked out past the port of Palermo, I could see the vast ocean, of which I had just floated and drifted upon for several thousand miles. I wondered why I wanted to go back again, with this bag in hand. I knew I needed to do something with these passports, somehow God or fate brought them into my life, I almost lost my life with them by my side. I resolved to put it back into God's hands. I decided to tender the passports to the Vatican and leave them there for fate to decide their destiny. My

195

mind was made up. I got up and walked over to the terminal office to search for a vessel destined to the mainland. There was a ferry that would depart to Naples which would leave in a few hours, so I bought my ticket.

I took my bunk early that night and slept solidly till morning. This was my second time to Naples. This time I wanted to see how the cities profile appeared from the sea. The ships horn sounded, and I made my way to the lounge. I could see Naples in the distance as the sun made its first peek. The view was colorfully picturesque. Crystal blue waters overlapped by mountains and green cliffs. Antiquated buildings and serpentine roads carved into the mountainsides. The character here was truly unique and deserved to be explored. I remember stopping here with George on our first stop after we had left Genoa. I recall Giulio very well, and the scuffle that brought us some trouble. However, it also brought us our first jobs on board the vessel and we learned some good things as a result. Sometimes things that appear to be bad, can be good things in disguise.

We docked, and I quickly debarked the ferry. I grabbed a coffee and sfogliatella at a local bar, oh my, this was very good. They seemed to have improved the recipe since the last time I had one. I asked the Barista, "How do I find the train station?"

The Barista replied, "Where are you going Sir?"

I replied, "Rome."

The Barista pointed to the left, "Go to the bus stop two streets down. Tell the driver you want to go to Naples Central train station."

Naples was a very active place, people seemed very loud and emotional. I got off the bus at the Train Station and a little boy approached me immediately.

The little boy said, "Signore, may I shine your shoes?"

I was on a mission to get these passports out of my life and I expressed a very blunt, "No." The little shoeshine boy continued to follow me and eventually I thought I had to give him a coin to get him to stop. He then tried to grab my bag as I took it off my shoulder to take the coin out of my pocket. It was a good thing I was bigger and I held on to the bag strap firmly. He eventually ran off. I just shook my head while I cursed under my breath. Here I was with this bag that almost sank to the bottom of the sea twice. And now a little boy tries to steal it from me. I wonder what he would have done with it once he found those passports. Oh well, next stop would be the Termini train station at Rome.

I arrived at Rome late that night, Termini station was very large, and I was tired and felt lost. At first I walked aimlessly as I did not know where to go. I needed a room for the night as I was very tired after my trip. I noticed a middle-aged man as he stared at me, and I walked over.

The middle-aged man asked, "Are you looking for a room Sir?" At first I hesitated as I already experienced an attempted robbery. However, I cautiously replied, "Yes."

The middle-aged man replied, "Very good, I know a good hostel, not too far from here, it is clean."

I nodded and asked, "How much does it cost for the night."

The middle-aged man answered, "Ten dollars, US. I can take you there now, included."

He smiled. I was tired, I asked, "How far is it from here?"

The middle-aged man replied with a sympathetic face, "With my car it's 5 minuti."

He pointed to the door and said, "Con mia machina, andiamo." I started to walk with him. He had a Fiat 1100. Compared to the American cars I remember, this car seemed truly a bit small. However, when in Rome, do as the Romans. He put his hand out as he opened the car passenger door for me.

The middle-aged man said, "Do you have the ten dollars please?"

I quickly thought about the little boy experience. I replied, "How do I know you will bring me to the room?"

The middle-aged man frowned and said in an upset tone, "Va bene. Give me $5 dollars now and $5 after I bring you there."

I agreed and gave him the 5 bucks. Getting in the car was tricky with my large bag as I refused to put it in the 'cofano' as the man insisted I should put my bag in the rear for storage. I refused. Anyway, after a short drive, we arrived at Via Pannonia. I admired the old structures and the street-side water fountains everywhere. I gave the man the $5 bucks and he introduced me to the owner of the hostel at the entrance of the building.

The middle-aged man said, "Buona sera Tonino, questo ragazzo cerca un posto per dormire."

Tonino held his palm out open towards the middle-aged man and replied, "Va bene."

The middle-aged man handed three dollars to Tonino and immediately exited the scene.

Somehow I felt as if I had been robbed. Tonino quickly waved me on and guided me up the staircase. I was too tired to chase the middle-aged man and I followed Tonino. It was a dark building, almost creepy. The sound as I walked on the marble steps echoed throughout, luckily, the room was on the 3rd floor as I was too tired to carry my bag up any more of these steps.

Tonino said, "Sir, over here in this door is the bathroom."

Then he pointed across the hall.

Tonino said, "You sleep in this room."

He walked over and opened the door. There were several beds inside, he handed me some sheets and a pillow. There was an empty one by the window.

Tonino pointed to it and said, "Buona notte."

And he left.

I was so tired after my journey, I had trouble to fall asleep. My body was tired but my mind would not shut itself off. I think my adventures at sea finally had caught up with me. My mind was obsessed with the struggles I had transpired during my course of survival at sea. If I had to do it again, I don't think I would survive. There I was, as I glanced at almost certain death, and I felt so alone. There really was no one else in my life but God. I wanted someone to love, my Mother, my Father. But I never knew them. Domenico and Elisetta were very good people, however, we did not share a parental bond. We did not struggle a lifetime of hardships together, from birth till death. When a child is born, they are comforted by their parents love. When that child matures, they yearn to carry that love within their soul, and eventually it becomes their only gift of significance. I realized that when I was stranded at sea. I would lie at night in my blanket as the waves rocked me about in the darkness. Constantly I controlled the fear that haunted me day and night of the distinct possibility that my raft could fail and I would submerge into the cold sea. It was as if my mind evaded reality and engaged only by mortal instinct. And in that raft, I realized, although I was truly alone in this world, God my Father created me and I would hold him in my heart dearly. My earthly parent's circumstances I could not control. It was up to me to be true to myself and the Lord's intentions.

Chapter 17

It was difficult to open my eyes in the morning, however, there was a lot of movement in the room from other guests. I found a paper bag and I packed all the passports neatly in the bag while I was in the bathroom in private. Once I left the building, there were many shops and the first one of interest was the coffee bar. I got myself un cornetto and a cappuccino. I was getting used to this breakfast menu. Much better than raw fish and rainwater. Although, I'm not sure which was healthier. I asked a passerby for directions to the Vatican. I was told it was about 2 or 3 miles away, so I decided to walk. From the moment I arrived here to this city I was intrigued. I stopped for water at the nearest water fountain, and it tasted so good and cold. What a wonderful idea, and to think they were placed here hundreds of years ago and fed by the same aqueducts the ancient Romans had built long ago. To think of all the people that had walked, lived and died along these streets and buildings over the centuries, boggled one's mind to say the least. I continued my walk and finally I reached the Via del San Gregorio. In the distance, I could see the Colosseum. I wanted to go visit it, but I had more important issues to attend to. I continued along the 'Via dei Cerchi' and raced may way passed the 'Circo Massimo'. I envisioned the ancient gladiators as they raced in their chariots. It must have been a true spectacle. I arrived to the river Tevere. I noticed an interesting structure along the way surrounded by columns, it was the 'Temple of Hercules'. The roof appeared to me as if it did not belong to the original structure as it was very old and likely added on sometime in centuries past. There was a bench and I sat to rest a little. I looked over and noticed a fountain, there were two strong men that supported clamshell on their backs. I walked over and as I got closer, I noticed they were half men, half creature. Perhaps Merman, instead of Mermaids. The clamshell held a coat of arms. It held an eight-pointed star and what appeared as a Papal Crown. On top of the clamshell there was a mountain with water that trickled out of the top of it and into the shell and overflowed into the bottom basin. To me it seemed the Mermen held up the weight of the world. A symbol of strength. The Catholic Church clearly has a strong influence in this city. I walked a little further and found the remains of a statue. It was a piece of a giant hand. I wondered what happened to the rest of the hand or statue. It must have been tremendous in size. I continued my trek towards my mission and I walked along the 'Lungo-Tevere' and I was surprised to see a Jewish settlement this close to the Vatican. I realized there was a lot of History here to learn. And a lot of it likely repeated itself throughout the centuries. I continued my swift pace as I carried my bag and I became tired. I sat down on a bench to rest. As I sat down, I noticed out in the distance, I could see a castle. I asked someone if that was the Vatican.

The passerby replied, "No signore, quello e 'Castel Sant' Angelo'. Il Vaticano sta dal altra parte."

The passerby pointed to the left, and I could see the Cupola, a very large Cupola.

I found some energy and ambled myself along the 'Via della Conciliazione'. I was in awe of the broad width of the street and the pillars that led the way to the majestic cupola. As I drew myself closer, it became evident that the Vatican was colossal in size. I entered the St. Peters Square and absorbed the vast space where one could clearly view the Vatican. Then I noticed the Egyptian Obelisk in the center of the square. I wondered how an Egyptian Obelisk made it all the way to Rome. Clearly, this two thousand years old city had many tales to tell. I decided to walk along the colonnade which surrounded the piazza. A Saint stood atop each of the columns. The columns stood in rows of four in depth, and they surrounded the entire piazza. To me this brought about an impression of being protected by the arms of a majestic entity. It was a marriage of engineering and art at its perfection. I sensed an atmosphere of Peace and benevolence within my presence.

Thoughtlessly, I became conscious in regards of the weight I had carried all day. I looked to the front doors of the Vatican, and I felt it was time to enter. I started towards the Basilica and followed a group of people as they entered. They were all in awe of the massive doors and I attempted to resemble their same appearance as I looked up to the ceiling as I walked in. It is an incredible masterpiece of construction. I walked slowly as I admired the magnitude of this majestic creation, there was so much to observe and absorb. I was attracted by the altar which sat under the Cupola. There were beams of light that radiated from above and provided a heavenly appearance. My curiosity drew me closer to the altar. I felt a need to kneel and pray to the Lord. I found the nearest pew to the main altar and knelt. I asked the Lord for his forgiveness and for his strength and guidance so that I could live my life in the way he intended. I prayed for the children of the world as they should not suffer for they are innocent. I thanked him for his protection that he provided while I stranded at sea. I asked for his divine intervention so that I may assist him while I remain here under his heavenly power. I raised my head and noticed a priest as he approached the altar. He knelt and made the sign of the cross and then walked up the steps and placed a chalice on the altar, I suppose he prepared for the next service. I stood up and walked slowly as I admired all my eyes could absorb. I came upon a bronze statue, there was a red and gold mosaic in the background. I realized the man was St. Peter as he sat in a marble chair. He seemed very pensive as if he prayed or meditated. I noticed he clutched some keys in his right hand. They were marked with a cross and I realized they were the keys to the gates of Heaven. I bowed my head in a moment of silence. I raised my head and slowly I walked over to a table on the side of the statue. I placed my package on it. I knelt one more time and made my sign of the cross. I rose to my feet and slowly walked away, I abandoned my burden behind.

I casually continued towards my point of entry. This time I looked only to my exit and not to the artworks and ceilings and adornments which are everywhere. As I approached the doors I noticed the motionless Swiss Guards as they guarded the massive doors. As I approached the exit, they appeared to not pay attention to my existence. As I walked by them and exited the Basilica, I progressed in the same fashion out of the Basilica and slowly towards the colonnade. I felt in a sense as if I had done an injustice to myself. I had carried these passports, it seemed almost an eternity. Virtually endangered my life as the result of their penetration into my path. And now after all this adventure, I was left without a closure to this predicament I arduously endured. In one sense I felt free, and in another sense, I felt it was all meaningless and a waste of my time.

I was startled by some shouts behind me. I could not hear at first. Then again, this time it was clear.

I heard, "Fermatevi, Ferma!" And then I knew I was being called. Or perhaps chased. I pretended not to hear and walked deeper into the colonnade. I tried to walk briskly and attempted to disappear behind the columns. And then the Swiss Guards appeared, maybe 20 meters in front of me, they placed their staffs forward without a word as they stood still. They did not need to make a sound, I knew what they meant and I had nowhere to go. I stopped. From behind I heard footsteps as they clacked towards me.

I heard, "Scusatemi." And I turned around. It was a Priest, and he carried the package I left by the statue. He slowed his pace as he approached me.

The priest said, "Sir, you left this bag inside by the Statue of St. Peter."

I looked at the bag and I did not say a word.

The priest continued, "Do you speak English?"

I replied, "Yes."

The Swiss Guards came closer and stood by my sides now. The Priest looked to the guards sternly and then he said to me. "Follow me." The guards grabbed me by my upper arms and pulled me towards some closed gates.

Alarmed I said, "Where are you taking me?"

The priest did not answer and they rushed me towards the gates more aggressively. Two more guards arrived from the interior of the gates and opened them swiftly. As we entered they closed and locked them again.

I struggled and shouted, "Help, Help."

The priest stopped, grabbed my upper arm and said. "Sir, you carried stolen passports inside the Vatican City. I suggest you be quiet and cooperate with us as you are safer in our hands than if you were caught outside of our authority a short distance from here.

I decided perhaps I should listen.

There was a doorway to the left and one of the guards opened it with his key. As they opened the door I could see some stairs that led down into a tunnel like entrance. It was very dark and became darker as we proceeded going down. The further we entered, the more I felt we were in an ancient catacomb. We went down at least three long flights of steps. The steps were very long and everything was of stone and bricks and mortar. I noticed ancient frescos and carvings on the walls. We arrived into a grotto and passed by some ancient crypts with Latin markings everywhere. Indeed, this was a catacomb. I think I was more frightened now than when I was stranded at sea. I did not know where they led me or what they had in mind. We arrived at another door. As they opened the door, it appeared to be more of a jail cell than a room. There were no windows nor decorations. The room was musty and cold, entirely made of stone and mortar. There was a desk with some chairs.

The priest pointed to a chair and said, "Please sit down."

I sat as he requested.

The priest said, "What is your name"

I replied, "Marco."

He paced around me and said, "Marco, where did you get these passports?"

I replied. "I found them at the train station."

The priest looked at my eyes incredulously with a smirk.

The priest said, "Marco, please let's not play games. If you had found these Passports, why did you take them with you and carry them to Vatican City? Why did you pick them up? most people would have just left them there where they found them or notified the local police."

The priest started to pace slowly and said, "Marco, I will ask again, how did you get with these passports, who gave them to you?"

I replied quickly. "I told you, I found them."

The priest stopped in his tracks, looked to my eyes and said, "Marco, do you realize the penalty for possession of stolen passports? I can turn you over to the Carabinieri and they will put you away for life. I suggest you cooperate with me while I still wish to help you."

I took a deep breath and released some stress. I said to the priest, "They were given to me in Brazil and I was told to deliver them to Germany."

The priest smiled and said, "That's better."

The priest now sat down in front of me across the table.

The priest said, "And why did you carry them to Rome instead of Germany?"

I folded my arms and said, "I was on a ship that sank at sea and I was stranded on a raft by myself with these passports for months, I don't remember exactly how long." Then I continued in a frenzy, "The passports were given to me due to my participation in a rescue at sea of some other men that were stranded at sea while in possession of these passports. I have shared a good part of my recent life with spies and agents of spies and I don't really know who or how, but somehow these passports have brought me from one state of despair to another. And now I find myself here, being questioned in a catacomb under the Vatican." I Paused. Then I continued, "May I ask you Sir, whom are these passports for?"

The priest paced slowly and handheld his chin while he absorbed my outburst.

The priest said, "Marco, now that is a story, I don't even think you could make this up if you wanted to."

He looked to the guards and said, "Show him to one of the Camerlengo's empty servants chambers. He needs a bath and some food and rest. Guard his door as he is not to leave the city."

The priest looked to me and said, "Marco, you need some rest, follow the guards and I will see you tomorrow morning. My name is Giuseppe."

I was led by the guards through a labyrinth of tunnel like hallways, eventually up some long staircase and into a building. They showed me my quarters and there was already a plate of food on a small table ready for me as I arrived. I was so hungry, I had forgotten of my present troubles. I sat down and devoured my meal while looking at the stone cell like room. I felt almost like a caged animal. After I satisfied my hunger, I walked to the door, I tried to open the door, it was locked. I then looked around the room, it was very simple, with high ceiling and a fixed window up high. It was too high for one to be able to see out of it, nor could I reach it if I had wanted to. One could easily meditate in prayer in this ambiance. I did not have any of my belongings. I sighed and walked over to the bed and sat. I sat and pondered what my future could entail. Would they send me to jail? What will they do with the passports? How would they ensure that I would not reveal any of this to the authorities? Then I came to the realization that perhaps they could kill me to keep the matter quiet. I laid back on my bed and tried to remain calm. I recalled being in the raft, not knowing what would be of me without water or food. And somehow God showed me the way. I did my sign of the cross and prayed for protection and guidance so that I could assist the Lord with his intentions. I then dozed off to sleep. I dreamed of being back at the orphanage. Dario and Isabel and George and all the kids, we were playing. Except, we were older. We were all aboard a pirate ship as we searched for treasure, from one island to another we travelled. Once we found the treasure, we brought it back to the orphanage, and we buried it. George made a map with the treasure location and offered Dario a copy. Dario did not want it and asked Isabelle to follow him over to a tree where they sat down. George gave me the copy and I stuffed it in my shirt pocket. Then the wind stared to blow and I noticed the maple seedlings as they spiraled around. I picked one up and placed it on my nose, I started to run around the trees with my arms open wide as if I had wings and pretended to fly in the wind. My treasure map flew away in the wind and I did not care.

There was a knock at the door, and I awoke. The door opened and there was a Swiss Guard. He brought me some clothes. It seemed I slept the entire night as I could see only by the light of the sunrise through the high window. The guard informed me that Giuseppe would be here to see me shortly. I put my clothes on while the guard remained in the room. He asked me to place my old clothes in a bag he was carrying, he said they would wash them and return them to me. The door knocked again and it was Giuseppe, the Guard left and closed the door behind him."

Giuseppe said, "Good Morning Marco. Did you sleep well?"
I replied, "Yes, thank you."
Giuseppe paced around the small room and then looked at me.

Giuseppe said, "Marco, I reflected upon your story last evening after my time of prayer and meditation. I also did some research on your past, you are an orphan and you were accommodated at the Monastery of San Benedetto as a child."
I replied, "Yes, that was long ago."

Giuseppe continued, "It's curious as I found a record of your entry into the facility. however, there is none of your release. Do you have any explanation for that?"

I replied, "My friends and I escaped and we made our way to America."

Giuseppe replied, "All the way to America? On your own? That is impressive."

Then I continued, "Does it mention in the record who my parents are or were?"

Giuseppe looked down and pondered my reply a bit.

Giuseppe said, "The record shows that your Mother died during childbirth. Whomever brought you to the orphanage chose to not supply any information regarding your parents. Your father was not mentioned and I don't believe he was there when you entered the orphanage. In any case, you certainly were brave young boys to take on such a challenge."

There was a moment of silence. I was hoping to have some information regarding my parents, and as usual, I found myself alone with God. Giuseppe sat down and faced me.

Giuseppe said, "Marco, as I am getting older, my duties here at the Vatican have become more difficult for me to handle on my own. I presently seek, well, an apprentice."

The idea did intrigue me. And I thought perhaps this was meant to be my new home.

I asked, "Father Giuseppe, what would be required of me?"

Giuseppe smiled, stood up and said, "Well, I need assistance with the management of investments. You see, the Vatican has to produce income, this allows us to provide aid for charities and children that need food and shelter."

There were a lot of thoughts that entered my mind. I pondered my present choices and situation and I decided my best choice.

I replied, "I would love to assist, sir."

Chapter 18

The next few days I spent at Giuseppe's office. I assisted with long distance calls and being introduced to several members of the clergy. My first assignment was to travel to Switzerland and exchange the passports for a large sum. I was instructed to deposit the funds into a bank account under an alternate identity using false identification which I was provided with. In my mind, I served the Lord's will as the Vatican investments were used for the cause of goodness and mercy for deprived souls.

Plane travel was much less romantic than sea travel, however, I quickly became accustomed to its convenience. It was a small plane and I sat next to the pilot since Giuseppe had arranged for a private aircraft. I quickly became accustomed to the luxuries that came with my new position in life. Upon my return, I could see Rome in the distance from high above. I imagined the city as it was when it was in its prime a couple millennia in the past. And I wondered what the Romans would have thought if they saw our aircraft in the sky. We would have been treated as Gods when we landed. We touched down at Ciampino airport and glided down the runway. I saw a Mercedes parked at the side of the air strip. As we approached I could see Giuseppe as he stood by his car. He waved as I exited the aircraft, we walked towards each other."

Giuseppe said, "How was your flight Marco?"

I replied, "It was a new experience for me, the world looks a lot different from up there."

Giuseppe chuckled and replied, "Yes Marco, I understand what you mean. As we travel through life, our world seems to change. Although it is only our discernment that changes due to our mature insight."

I remained silent as we walked to his car, the driver opened the door for us and we entered.

Giuseppe said, "Marco, you performed an excellent transaction, I spoke with our banker this morning and the mission went smoothly and was successful."

I replied, "Thank you."

Giuseppe said, "Marco, I know a member of an organization called 'Uomini di Fiducia', he wants to meet you."

I replied, "Uomini di Fiducia, that means men of trust."

Giuseppe replied, "Yes, exactly. I can see right away that you are a prime candidate."

I was soon meeting with high profile people on a regular basis. Giuseppe consulted with me every day. My next trip by plane was to Sicily to meet a business man and exchange some business permits for cash. I was met at the airport and driven to an office located in a secluded lemon grove where we exchanged documents for cash. I was swiftly returned to the airport and our next destination was Switzerland again to make the deposit. I travelled to Spain, Germany and even France to make similar transactions. In time, I became a mediator amidst highly influential people always for the interests of the Vatican investments.

I always envisioned myself as to perform the works that the Lord had intended for me. I knew that some of the people I traded with did not entirely acknowledge government laws. However, I enjoyed what I did and I felt it was all for the benefit of good interests overall. In the years that followed, in consideration that I had become one of the men of trust. I was privy to much information. Not only that which regarded the Vatican bank, but of the power within, that was concealed. And, unfortunately how it was being abused. I learned of people I had participated with going to jail. Others disappeared or had been found murdered. I wondered if I would share the same destiny. When I first arrived at the house of God, with all its majestic presence. My perception was to be welcomed and embraced. I remember as I entrusted my gift. And in return I was captured and captivated into a world of greed and corruption. And yet I continued to wear my mask and silently held my troubles within. I always prayed for the Lord's forgiveness and that one day I may have the chance to change my life of deceptions. I lived a life engulfed by material wealth, gold, majestic arts, illustrious people, luxurious travel and life in magnificent accommodations. And yet I was miserable. I felt inadequate as a participant in an illusion of dignity. It became evident to me I was part of a hypocrisy. And the most significant revelation to me, the deceptions were omnipresent. This was not the message Christianity intended. The message of Christ was a benevolent message of salvation. Not about control and greed. And I pondered much, day after day, week after week, month after month.

I sat in the Chapel one evening prior to an honorary dinner for a guest from Spain. I did not wish to attend and I had expressed my lack of interest to attend earlier to Giuseppe. However, Giuseppe insisted for me to be there. I prayed in silence. I realized I was at a loss for words. I did not feel worthy of prayer as I had no genuineness of contribution in the Lord's intentions. I realized I lost touch with my soul. I asked for guidance and I prayed to St. Joseph. As I prayed, the chapel door opened and someone walked in. I looked over and it was Giuseppe. He made his cross and walked over quietly. I sat up as he sat next to me.

Giuseppe placed his hand on my shoulder and said, "Marco, I need to talk to you."

Giuseppe discretely pointed to the door and I followed him outside.

Giuseppe said, "Marco, I need you to go to Germany, tonight."

I was surprised of the sudden request, and I asked. "What is the reason?"

He replied, "We need you to collect some funds and deliver them to our bankers in Switzerland."

I asked, "What is the urgency that I should leave tonight.

He looked to me and said, "Your bags are packed. Our car will take you to the airport at Ciampino."

I asked, "Do you have any instructions for me, whom will I meet with?"

Giuseppe walked away and said, "It will be provided to you once you are on the plane."

Giuseppe turned his back and waved.

Giuseppe said, "Your plane leaves around 1 AM so please be ready for the driver around midnight at the gate."

I sensed a change in Giuseppe's tone. He had always discussed particulars with me prior to leaving on a business trip. There was a different look in his eyes and I felt his sincerity was not true. I had an ominous impression and my senses told me I was in danger. I stood up and walked out of the chapel. As I traversed via the catacomb tunnel to my room, I decided to save myself and leave Vatican City immediately. I packed only my essentials. Swiftly and quietly I exited and made my way out of the gates. I hailed the first taxi that came about.

The driver asked. "Where are you going?"

I thought about it a little, and replied, "Germany."

The driver smiled and said, "You want me to drive to Germany?"

I replied, "Bring me to the Termini station."

Once in the station, I quickly walked about and studied all the first available destinations. And then it struck me, L'Aquila. I did not even think about it, I quickly went and purchased my ticket. The train would depart in 15 minutes so there was not much time to contemplate. Once on board the train I felt a slight relief that I made it out of Rome unnoticed. I felt like a fugitive, but I was happy to have regained my spirit. I decided to do something I had not done in a long time, write. I remember it would always make me feel good.

Twas not long ago,
I presumed to know.
My soul was tender,
yet wearing great armor.

I carved many masks,
and lifted my tasks.
Unaware of my yearning,
nor where I was going.

At times I was challenged,
my courage prevailed.
And always I seeked,
a latent part unveiled.

And now I've arrived,
a self forged unknowing.
And often I ponder,
Who was it I knew.

Early morning before sunrise the train arrived at L'Aquila, it seemed like yesterday we would come and visit here with Domenico. I was so worried that Giuseppe would send someone to chase behind me, but I didn't think they would look for me here as I never mentioned that I had lived here as a child. In any case, I decided to move by foot and I walked. I remembered the trail Domenico would hike with us and I decided to take that route. I would take advantage of the time on the trail in isolation to clear my mind of the pressure I was under. I bought some bread and sausage and wine from a local vendor and packed my lunch. Off I was with my backpack like in the old days when we lived here. I could hear the river in the distance through the forest and followed towards the sound of the water as it rushed down river. I reached a break in the forest and I could now see the river as its sound grew intense. I stopped to look. This is the spot Domenico first saw us and we spotted him from the river below. As if it were yesterday in my mind, although many years had since past. I was tired, and I sat down by a tree to have my lunch break. It was a real treat to be here again. I had some food and a sip of wine and then I closed my eyes. I reflected upon my present reality and all that transpired from the time I met Giuseppe. I was certain that if I had gone on the plane trip to Germany, I would not have returned. I wondered if it would be safe to live here anymore. And I already knew the answer. I kind of wished I could just stay where I was. Where did I indeed belong, I thought. and thought about my travels, and then out of frustration I began to write again.

We are placed in foreign places,
and we must interact and learn from our own choice.
We think we are clever, although our imperfections abound,
and sometimes beyond our control, our choices are called.

I find myself in a place not of myself,
the chosen path was stronger than I,
and now my mind has awoken.

Day after night, Dusk after Dawn,
I spill my soul and try to make this place rejoice the love I have in my heart.
Why has my path led me wrong … can it be my choices were so mistaken
or perhaps , I have forgotten the reasons for the path I have taken.

I find myself on this road, my fate carved in stone,
The only choice is to remember and be strong,
The love in my heart will not surrender,
For my Creator has placed this gift in me,
And I shall hold it till we meet.

I put my paper down and rested to the sound of the river and fell asleep. It was a very sound sleep. I only remember when I awoke it had become cold, as the sunset soon approached. I realized I would need to find my way to town in the dark and I quickly gathered my things. I had recalled the treks we would accomplish with Domenico as we followed the river up hill, and it seemed to have gotten steeper. I arrived at the town a couple of hours later. Even in the darkness, I remember this hike as if it were yesterday. I came upon the vineyard, and it was no longer there. I was stunned as now there were some new houses built there. Domenico must have sold the land I said to myself, and I moved on. Next I came upon the Cantina. I noticed a Mercedes parked outside. It was similar as the one that used to transport me to the airport. That vehicle did not belong here in this town. I quickly turned and walked back towards the old vineyard and into a road through what used to be Domenico's vineyard. I realized this town had changed and I feared Domenico was no longer. I knew I should flee quickly, however, I wanted to go see the home I considered my home. The place I remember to have been cared for by the two best people I had ever known. I hiked another mountain path that used to be behind the vineyard and then walked my way back down to the backside of the old homestead we used to live on. The home was still there and I saw no cars around, so I cautiously approached. A dog started to bark and I hid in the grass, I could see a figure in the window, it had to be Elisetta. I stood up and walked closer and she came to the back door. At first, she did not recognize me and was reluctant to let me in, then she told the dog to sit and opened the door. She had tears in her eyes and gave me a big hug without any words. She was old now, she moved slowly with a cane and took my hand as we walked to the kitchen table. She sat down and put her hand on the chair.

Elisetta said, "Marco, Sit."

She sat as well and we faced each other in disbelief.

She looked to my eyes and said, "Marco I didn't think I would ever see you again. I know you are in trouble. Some

215

men were here earlier today and they asked for you. I told them I hadn't seen you in many years. I'm not sure they believed me. I don't think you can stay here. She got up and gave me a bag with some bread and food. My heart bleeds, but I will have to ask you to leave here."

I had tears in my eyes and I responded as best as I could through my agonized emotions. "I understand Elisetta. I didn't want us to meet under unhappy conditions, I just needed to see you again and thank you and Domenico."

She stopped me and said, "Domenico, non c'e piu. He passed away some years ago. He loved you boys so much and always spoke about you. We were alone and we always had you boys in our hearts and thoughts. I am so sorry you are in trouble now, you should leave the country Marco, as soon as you can. They will kill you if they find you."

I could see fear in her eyes.

Elisetta continued, "They pretend to be good, but their eyes always tell the truth."

I asked Elisetta, "How are you Elisetta, are you able to take care of yourself without Domenico?"

Elisetta replied, "Marco, you don't need to worry about me. It was not easy to get used to being alone after Domenico passed away. It took me time to get used to that fact. Fortunately, I have a few good friends here in this town. I've lived here all my life. And some good memories help too. Carlo still comes around and takes care of the fields with his workers. He sells the crops and in return he takes care of me. He has a lovely wife now and a daughter. You should get married Marco, have children. There is nothing else in life."

She paused and looked out the window. I sensed her fear that the men would return.

Elisetta placed her hands on her lap and said, "Dario lives in Rome, he married a lovely girl named Isabelle. And they have a daughter, Giuliana. Sometimes they visit me. George, I know he is in America, but he is busy with his work. I don't hear from him much, only by other people."

Then we heard a car as it approached in the distance. Elisetta, panicked and grabbed her cane, walked over and turned out the light.

Elisetta said, "Marco, you have to go, now! Get out the back door and run out to the woods, hurry!"

I stood up and grabbed my bag, I gave Elisetta a big hug and said, "I love you Elisetta, I will always remember you and the goodness you placed in my heart, I learned so much from you. You will always be in my heart."

She pushed me away in tears, "Go now, leave the country as soon as you are able."

I went out the back side of the house and I could hear the vehicle pull up into the property. I bent my body close to the ground as I crawled myself swiftly through the field, behind the barn and over the old stone wall. I feared for her safety, however, I knew if I went back there it would not be good for either of us. I hid behind the stone wall in the dark and peered over the edge of a rock. The house lights turned on dimly. I could not hear a thing from where I was. I waited for the lights to go off again. And then I made my way back to the river and camped myself for the night. I knew it would not be a good idea to go to L'Aquila as they already knew I could be in the area. I would need to hike the trails. I camped out in an old barn for the night.

In the morning I decided I would follow the river. I would follow until I felt I was far enough away from the area to safely enter public places. I had enough food to last me at least a few days. Water I could take from the river. I picked up a strong stick and made it into a walking stick. It was nice and sturdy. And I walked, and walked, and pondered the past, the present and the future. Day into night and night into day. Eventually, I could see in the distance that the river flowed into a reservoir or lake of some kind. I found a path in the forest and eventually I came upon a mountain road. I decided to walk it and take my chances. I was very tired, my legs and feet hurt and I struggled to move on. Once every few minutes a car would pass by, and finally I had the nerve to raise my thumb. The cars passed by, one after another. I continued and found a cleared field off the road. I decided to sit down on a rock close to the edge of a bluff. I had to rest and catch my breath. It was a beautiful spot to view the mountains as we were high up. This place appeared to be a place where cars could pull over to rest. I was mesmerized by the high peaks and the valley down below. I could see the river I followed for the past few days. The clouds moved swiftly as the rays of the sun passed through their breach. The view was lovely. However, the reality I lived was arduous. I thought of all my travels about the world and all the disappointments I found. And I wondered why such a mesmerizing planet, with all its natural beauty and perfect symmetry, offered so much grief to humanity. I concluded that our human existence is only temporary and flawed. Only God's love is eternal.

I wrote on this rock.

For each passage,
a path is lit.
As a ray of sun, bursting,
through breaks of clouds.

Gliding over the mountainside,
bringing life to the darkness.

Our Time Created

As our ray of light shows passage,
we persevere to maintain life.

Moving toward the light,
ray's angle increases.
Intimating our moment,
advancing expeditiously.

Time is gifted,
one light per existence.
Once it has passed,
one cannot go back.

Afterwards, I closed my eyes, I felt so alone and I needed God's love. Enchanted, I felt as if my spirit became autonomous of my body. For an instance, I had forgotten my troubles and I felt at ease. I identified my body as a separate entity, a skeleton bound by flesh and blood that I resided in. Liberated of my burdens, I envisioned my first memories of being a boy at the orphanage. We all played in the yard under the maple tree, and we were all so happy. We did not think about being abandoned in this world. We were simply happy to play and run with our arms open wide, and we laughed at the maple seedlings on our noses. We lived for today, and cared not for tomorrow or yesterday. And now as I sat on this rock, I was alone and lost, not aware where or with whom I belonged. I felt forsaken.

My journey has taught me that the reality of human existence on earth is imperfect. We are here to make mistakes and wrong choices. And sometimes, we arrive to lost places. Holding the virtue of God close to our hearts is the only path that will provide the strength to reach our salvation. To accept and follow our chosen fate by the virtue of one's spirit.

We are born into this world and divinely granted immaculate innocence and life by the grace of God. Our gifted souls provide us the guidance to love others, without fear or intention. Once our innocence is lost alongside our earthly interactions and human egotistical needs, one will never be content, only mortal and lifeless.

Holding God's will in our heart is the only true fulfillment we can find in this human existence. As life on earth is temporary and God's love is everlasting. To boast one's superiority and to demand obedience by the force of one's wealth or fortunate position, is only to strengthen one's weakness. To be kind to others and teach by example, prior to consideration for ourselves is how one's Fulfilment is achieved. Unveil your heart, teach by your faith.

We are not here to judge one another, as we are all imperfect here on earth. We all walk an individual path with a cross to carry to our fate, to be accomplished by our faith. Respect those that walk their walk, those are the true heroes.

Once you hold and cherish the spirit of God in your heart, your soul's salvation is fulfilled, alive and timeless. I believe this was the true message of Jesus Christ. A message of benevolence and guidance, not one of obedience and punishment.

And now on this rock I seek the innocent heart I once held as a boy who played under the maple tree. I want to hold it and protect it and teach with it and carry it with me. Together we will be strong and alive with God, and follow the Lord's intentions for the rest of my journey and fate.

I heard a large vehicle as it approached, and so I opened my eyes. As it got closer I could see it was a bus full of people as they arrived for a stop. And soon people walked about and stretched their legs. I noticed a young woman as she walked towards the bluff. She held the hand of a young girl. The woman had dark red hair and the girl was brunette. They stopped at the overlook and took in the view for a short time. And then they continued to walk. The woman looked over to me as I sat on the rock. Shortly after they walked over close to me.

The young woman asked, "What are you doing here all alone?"

I smiled, and then I replied. "I'm not sure."

She gave an incredulous look and replied, "How did you get here? Where are you going?"

I replied with the same look and tone. "I walked, and I am traveling by foot."

She replied, "This seems a remote place to walk alone. You don't know where you are going?"

I shrugged my shoulders.

The young woman said, "My name is Maureen, I am a missionary from Scotland."

Then she looked at the girl and said, " I am here to bring Carolina with me back to Scotland."

Carolina looked to me and smiled. I looked at them and said. "I am Marco" and then I stood up. And I asked, "Are all these people destined for Scotland travelling with you?"

Maureen replied. "Oh no, it's just me and Carolina."

And I looked to the bus and said, "Well, that's nice that you have each other's companionship for the journey." And then I looked out to the vista. I asked. "Carolina, what will you do once you arrive to Scotland?"

Carolina replied, "We will live together and make a home."

And I smiled to Carolina and replied, "That's a wonderful thing Carolina, it's the best thing you can have is a home." And with those words, I realized, I had no home. And I looked out and I noticed a maple tree close by and I walked over. There were some seedlings on the ground and I picked one up and placed it on my nose as I did as a child with my friends. Carolina followed me and laughed, she picked one up as well and placed it on her nose. Then I opened my arms and started to pretend I could fly, and she followed with me in the wind.

Maureen laughed at us and said, "You two seem to get along well I see."

Carolina and I continued to play. The bus sounded its horn and Maureen looked over as the driver waved.

Maureen looked to Carolina and said, "It's time to go Carolina."

Then Maureen looked to me and said, "Marco, please, come with us. Carolina and I would love your company."

And Carolina took my hand and looked in my eyes deeply.

And I said, "I would love to."

The End

CPSIA information can be obtained
at www.ICGtesting.com
Printed in the USA
BVHW080955191221
624255BV00001B/47